# The Houlton Saga

## Book 1: Iron Horse

### Nathan L. Cole

The Houlton Saga: Book 1 – Iron Horse

© Copyright 1999, 2025. Nathan L. Cole.

TaTa Books Publishing

Paperback: ISBN 979-8-218-70650-0

Hardcover: ISBN 979-8-294-05953-8

Illustrations by: Nathan L. Cole

Edited by: Sarah Marie Burnett

Copyeditor: Laura I. Cole

Digital Illustrator: Octavio Rodríguez

Cover design by: 100Covers.com

Printed in the United States

www.NLCole.com

# CONTENTS

For Laura:

My wife, my love, and my best friend, who has encouraged me every step of the way. Love you forever.

- Nathan

# PROLOGUE

The planet Teraqueos, features a variety of distinct environments that contribute to its richness and diversity. In the central regions, is an arid savanna, which transforms into a lush, dark green landscape once a year during the rainy season. This area is home to the clans and families of the Equiantus people.

To the North, there are expansive grassy plains, to the West lies mysterious and thriving swamplands. Southwestern Teraqueos is marked by a high and long mountain range, which serves as a natural boundary separating the vast desert from the boggy marshes and deep oceans. The oceans are home to some of the most incredible creatures and communities. Finally, along the Eastern borders, there is a vibrant tropical rainforest with a thick canopy teeming with life, and captivating beauty.

The wild animals here are called behemoth, dinosaur-like lizards of different breeds and species. Several of them have been domesticated and trained over the last thousand years, such as the *rock-behemoth*, the *quantum* and a few species of *tyriancia-col.*

The inhabitants of Teraqueos live according to their corresponding domain or realm, which has led them to carve out their very own existence within the breathtaking landscapes, weaving their unique cultures and traditions into the very essence of this awe-inspiring world.

Yet it was not always this way, but it is the only way peace could be found.

### After the War of Realms – (AWOR)

Each realm is now separated and organized by each one's phylum or humanoid race, which are governed by The Council of Kingmen, each forming part of one of the seven realms. The realms are as follows:

1. **The Equiantus Realm** (a horse-like race): Established in the great and famous Houlton City. A metropolis with ancient Asian-styled architecture, is found amid a dry, shrub dotted savannah landscape, which has become the unofficial center of realms. The realm extends further than the city itself including several open territories where specific clans can be found.

2. **The Bisonteus Realm** (a buffalo-like race): A plains people found in the grasslands and prairies to the North, who live in mudbrick huts. Those dwelling in

this realm are fond of family traditions and have a close connection to the planet's flora and fauna.

3. **The Amphibtius Realm** (a toad-like race): Who live in a marsh swamp city to the West. Extraordinarily little is known of their infrastructure, as they keep to themselves.

4. **The Terratius Realm** (a reptile-like race): They are a very sophisticated, elegant, and technologically savvy race. A people who live in the upper part of the mountains of the Southwest, which run through the edge of the plains and separate the oceans from the savannah and marshlands.

5. **The Mareviteaus Realm** (an underwater, oceanic realm): Through their adaptation and knowledge, they have created a complete ecosystem of their own. They are a people who cannot only live, breathe, and thrive underwater, but can train others to do so as well. The only downfall of this realm is that they are plagued continually by the candariain, small and medium sized invertebrate creatures, pests really, that come up from the deep waters.

6. **The Aprosmarteus Realm** (a society made up of all the unwanted misfits from other realms): Found in the

hot tropical lands of the East. Some live in treetops, others in freshwater ponds near the great waterfalls, and others in caves found in the rocky hills. They have established an *orderly–disorder* if you will. A community in which anyone and everyone can belong.

7. **The "Unspoken Realm"** – its actual location is unknown to the common person, all we know is that it is guarded by the wise and elegant Cornua Cerviteaus race (a deer/elk-like race) who take the secrets guarded there very, very seriously.

These are the seven realms of Teraqueos, all of which were established "After the War of Realms." Two years following (2 AWOR) the Council of Kingmen was established to govern society after the leaders realized they could not succeed or survive without one another as the Creator intended.

Our saga begins some four centuries AWOR where we find General Santos Houlton, of The Equiantus Realm, in the middle of a great conflict known as the Epic War, fighting and standing his ground against the mighty, and fierce Dark Prince and his great army of soldiers, collected from all over Teraqueos...

Equiantus Realm

# CHAPTER 1

The war rages on, and the armies of the Dark Prince are advancing against the outer borders of the Equiantus Realm. Many provinces remain loyal to the Houlton Dynasty despite the deafening sound of explosions now being a common sound throughout the provinces. The once peaceful roads and joyous city are now barren, and the inhabitants hide in fear of losing their lands, homes, and sons to the will of the terrible Dark Prince, who promises power to all who follow him. Smoke rises from the horizon as an outer province collapses under the unrelenting might of all those loyal to The Betrayal and the unseen forces of the Unspoken Realm.

As the wind blows over the dusty plains, shadows of stealth fighter ships, in perfect attack formation, move quickly about on the sandy terrain.

The Dark Prince's ship cruises through the sky like a flying fortress. It bears a striking resemblance to the silhouette of a dark knight chess piece, commanding a strong feeling of power, due to the sleek and formidable design. The ship's angular contours and profile create an imposing aura as it unleashes a devastating onslaught of torpedoes and lasers, effortlessly dominating the skies with lethal precision. Those who witness its awe-inspiring display are captivated by the ship's menacing yet elegant appearance, marveling at its unparalleled strength and agility.

Shouts of battle-worn generals leading their soldiers head-on into war against the strong forces of the Dark Prince and his vast array of warrior troops from all realms, can be heard in the distance as they quickly approach the Houlton Dynasty's base. The base was once a palace of peace and beauty, is now unrecognizable, battle-worn structure on the verge of collapse from the laser blasts of the veloci-pods. These robotic creatures closely resemble sombru dragons, and can be sent to destroy any targeted area. They are fired like missiles from the torpedo launchers of the Dark Prince's ship and once the sharp tip penetrates the ground, the hooked tip is now seen as its velociraptor toe claw and the rest of the head and legs emerge from the body of the missile forming the robotic veloci-pod. They are controlled by the captain's battleship, and used not only as weapons, but also as eyes, ears, and sensors within a five feet radius of it.

As the robotic war machines create a perimeter around the fortress, and their lasers fire upon the front gates, an Equiantian, horse-like humanoid, in his mid-40s, son of the late Grandmaster Houlton; now a war-hardened general with more than 20 years of experience, can be seen leading the Iron Horse army against the opposing forces.

"Stand your ground, do not let them breach our perimeter!" shouted General Santos.

Each soldier was armed with a laser blaster, a *corundum,* a katana-style ray sword, and enhanced armored suit. The armored suits are innovative, fully integrated combat system designed for elite soldiers in high-risk missions. The advanced exo-suit combines lightweight, ultra-durable alloys with artificial muscle fibers, providing extra strength, agility, and protection. General Santos and his loyal soldiers held their position as the veloci-pods continued to strike. As the laser blasts hit the sides of their base, splintering off small pieces of the building, hitting them in the face, chest, and arms.

"Stand firm team!" he yelled as he flinched again as the pebbles springing up from the ground, turning into small penetrating bullets as the blasts came closer to their position.

The strong odor of smoke from the blasts lingered in the air burning their eyes and nostrils. A whistling sound raced past them as a cluster of small, flat devices spun past them through the air. Santos looked down as he saw several of the discs hit the ground dangerously close to him and his team. As the high-pitched sound emerging from them grew louder, he realizes they were explosives! In an instant, there is a huge flash, followed by an ear-splitting crack. The Equiantian's elite team has been hit.

As the ringing in their ears ceased and the smoke drifted away, General Santos with blurred vision on the very soil, where not long ago, he practiced kata with his father.

**(30 years earlier; 396 AWOR)**

"Back straight, breathe slowly, concentrate," Santos heard whispered into his 10-year-old ear.

As he opened his eyes a single bead of sweat slowly ran down the side of his face and fell to the ground. Concentration, controlled breathing, and excellent self-control are demanded while practicing kata, which is a prevalent traditional martial arts form, one of his favorite pastimes he enjoyed every afternoon with his twin brother and the instruction of their father.

Looking to his right he was once again challenged to see, in almost perfect stance, his brother, seeming not even tired or tasked by the exercise. His skin was so dark that it seemed to shine in the sun, in direct contrast to his pale skin.

"Excellent form Dantias," his father said. "Head up, look forward, back straight, relax."

Dantias was gifted in every area. At times Santos felt his brother was much more capable than he was, though. Both boys were equally balanced both physically and mentally. Friends, companions, and even rivals at times, they did everything together.

As Kingmen Houlton stood on the worn patch of grass, surrounded by the beautiful palace garden, the cool air surrounding him was infused with the scent of history and a faint trace of lilacs. A quick wave of nostalgia surged in his heart as he watched his two young sons as they meticulously mirrored his every movement.

Together, they embarked on the journey of mastering the intricate movements, a series of graceful motions steeped in the rich heritage of Houlton leaders.

In this very place, where shadows danced and echoes lingered, his father had imparted the ancient wisdom of their dynasty.

Memories flooded his mind, transporting him back to his own boyhood days spent amid sweat and effort, striving to master the very same kata he was now instructing his sons. He could almost hear his father's firm, yet encouraging voice guiding him through each step, pushing him to surpass his limits. As both of his sons struggled, their brows scrunched in concentration, Lord Houlton felt a profound connection to his past, a bittersweet blend of pride and pain.

He recalled the spark of joy in his father's eyes as he successfully grasped a particularly challenging concept, making it his own.

Emotions grew within Lord Houlton's heart as he recognized that he was now the bearer of that same legacy, weaving the thread of tradition into the fabric of his children's lives.

As he watched them, a smile spread upon his face, knowing that the future of the Houlton Dynasty would one day be in good, worthy hands.

"Very good boys, that's enough for today, your mother awaits you," said their father.

Bowing in gratitude with a salute, they then ran off to the palace terrace where their mother awaited with a smile. As usual, she was dressed elegantly in afternoon attire. Her gown, crafted from the finest satin, was a deep sapphire color and trailed just above the floor. It featured a neckline that was slightly higher than most and sleeves that fitted her arms perfectly. A silver brooch of intricate design, showcasing the Houlton Dynasty crest, which had been worn by her husband's mother, grand-mother, and great-grandmother was pinned in the center of her gown, just below the neckline. Even on family days due to her position as the First Dutchess, their mother was required to be dressed in a presentable manner.

Their father has been the highest-ranking Kingmen and leader of this realm for more than three decades and being the wife of the Grandmaster of the Houlton Dynasty is no simple task and thus made her the strongest woman both politically and administratively in the realm. She must always be ready because, at a moment's notice, she could be summoned to a meeting at the high office or chambers.

"Come boys take this and go buy the daily portion of panú , and don't take long, you mustn't keep your father waiting," she stated.

"Yes Dutchess," the boys replied as they received the three coins.

For an unknown reason they had always been required to address their mother as Dutchess, and never as Mother, but they had long become accustomed to it.

So, running down the lower terrace steps, down the long entrance path and to the main palace gates, they then waited for the guards to open the gates to exit. The palace was a place of tranquil beauty with lush gardens,and ancient architecture which included the most elaborate artistry and statutes from generations past, which represent their great heritage, not only as a family but as a realm as well.

As the large wooden doors with iron frame opened, they ran out the gates into the busy streets of Houlton City. There was always something to see and do as Houlton City was the center of commerce and supply of all precious metals for the Equiantus Realm and the other five existing realms since the Council of Kingmen was established. All sorts of fine metalcrafts, arts, tools, and structures could be found here. Each made from of precious metals mined in the outer provinces.

The boys could not linger, as it takes a good while to make the trip on foot down to the panú bakery on Market Street.

While they quickly ran down the street the grunting sound of a medium-sized rock-behemoth could be heard as it pulls a wind carriage, which appeared as though it was floating behind him.

The behemoth are beasts of burden native to Teraqueos, though domesticated breeds are common around the dry savannahs where Houlton City is located, there are wild breeds. The rock-behemoths are slow and a bit clumsy, but ever so strong. As legend tells it they once were used to carry whole families of 10 or 15 people on their backs, using a rig of sorts. They are majestic-looking creatures with thick, strong legs and an even stronger neck. Their tails are like a small round cedar tree, yet short and curved up at the tip. Their skin is tough and warm like that of a rhinoceros, warm and ruff to the touch, but they are cold-blooded. Even though they are now bred to be docile, they still have an overwhelming silhouette, from their tail to the two small round horns that come up off their noses, the ground shakes slightly as they walk.

The carriage driver waved and greeted the boys as they trotted past. Many people were out today, and the streets were full of activity. Weaving in and out between the public, the boys arrive at Market Street. Everything and anything that one could imagine, or need could be found there. Anything from; new clothes, to daily food rations, to ancient coins from before the War of Realms. It was such a fun place to be.

Turning the corner the strong smell of panú, an Arabic-style flat bread made of rice and barley, fills the air. As they approach, calls from one of the nomad tribes down the street.

"Come one, come all, sugar beads for sale," could be heard in the distance.

"Hurry, buy the panú ," Dantias said, "We must get a few sugar beads!"

"Dutchess said we mustn't linger," said Santos. "I'm not getting the rod because of you."

"It will only take a moment. Besides, we can run back or catch a ride on the back of a wind carriage," Dantias replied eagerly.

Santos paid for the panú and though not in agreement, followed his brother down the street. Dantias was always fascinated by all the wonderful things found on Market Street.

Market Street was lined with booths and tables of the featuring a wide variety of wares.

The Clydesdale-clan, iron working blacksmiths, sold all sorts of knives, tools, and curious puzzles.

The Asno and the two-blood clans were always selling different varieties of rocks and stones, as well as an assortment of unique, and remarkably interesting artifacts they found deep in the mines.

There was always an abundance of fruits, vegetables, and grains laid out on display from the Pinto-clan, who work in the fields. They also sold a wide variety of hand-woven clothing.

Then there was the beautiful jewelry, blankets, and distinct spices from the Arabian light-foot clan, which his family descended from.

The Houlton's descendants came from the Arabian-clan, it is said that Grandmaster Houlton's great, great, great grandfather was from a faraway clan and had migrated from the deserts, crossing the mountains, alone, to the savanna plains and once there established what now is known as the Houlton Dynasty.

There are two large nomad clans that made up a great part of the population of the Equiantus Realm, the pale-foot clan and the light-foot clan. Both were very homely plain people, who mostly kept to themselves, but are incredibly open in sharing their crafts with others, especially on Market Street.

After a few minutes of trotting, they arrived at the pale-foot clan's makeshift tents,where all sorts of the handmade items are sold. Most importantly, they have sugar beads!

"You have returned once again my young friend," said the kind elder.

The elder was a kindly older man with a gentle and compassionate demeanor. His face reflected a life lived with integrity and kindness. His eyes were a warm and welcoming blue, shining with a spark of understanding and empathy. His hair, a soft and curly mane of blackish gray, is tied back in a loose braided ponytail that swayed gently in the breeze.

"Yes! I would like a bag of sugar beads, please," said Dantias, "Quickly pay him!" Dantias told Santos while he looked about the tent.

Santos paid the elder for the treats, they thanked him and quickly were on their way back to the palace. As they trotted away a young girl came out from behind a curtain.

"Who was that grandfather?" she asked.

"Oh, nobody in particular, just the boy and his brother, who always buys a bag of sugar beads each week," the elder, her grandfather, said with agrin.

The young girl smiled as she watched the twin brothers trotting away, weaving in between wind carriages on their way back home.

Arriving back at the palace the boys bathed, put on their finery, and joined The Dutchess and their father, the Grandmaster, for their family meal.

The table was laid with a wide offering of food. Every province was represented in each of their family meals, as established by the ancient writings and *scroll of laws*.

Before eating, a thanks was to be given to the non-created one, *"He who has always been and always will be."*

Every realm speaks of Him and holds true to these customs, honoring Him in all they do. It is said and openly taught that He gave the first scroll to their ancestors and brought the world into existence.

Once the family meal was finished the boys quickly cleaned their places, went off to their shared bedroom and prepared for sleep.

When they were ready, their father accompanied them at their bedside, as was tradition. Each night their father would recite the written laws of the ancient scrolls to them.

This was of utmost importance. The scrolls were received as the written word of *"He who has always been,"* and passed on from generation to generation.

One day they would both take their place in the Houlton Dynasty as Grandmasters fulfilling the ancient prophecy that, *"Two heads would reign as one."*

They must not only obey these words and have these laws written in their hearts, but they must also be able to lead others to do the same.

Listening to the soothing voice of their father repeating, the well-known laws, they drifted off to sleep.

# CHAPTER 2

With a jolt, General Santos was jarred back from his thoughts by a nearby explosion. It was hard to rest these days with so much tension and war. He looked about frantically to make sure his team was still with him.

"Report," he said over the com-link system.

"Here, on target," he heard in his earpiece as each member of the Iron Horse team reported in.

His team was made up of the best warriors, pilots, and tech-savvy members from each clan.

Each one, faithful to the Houlton Dynasty, was ready and willing to lay down their lives. As he looked at his positional scanner, he was relieved to see each team leader was leading their secondary teams and had moved into position. Even though it was late, they were always prepared.

From the Clydesdale-clan, there was, "Hammer," the heavy lifter, and artillery expert. He was also an expert craftsman who forged by hand each of their 'corundums,' the laser-ray broadswords used in battle.

Then there was also one of the Appointed Cavalry Equiantus riders, they just called him Ace for short, he was from the Pinto/Worker clan, and one of the best quantum riders and pilots in all the realms.

The quantum are behemoths that are mounted to ride. They are a bit smaller than the rock-behemoth but walk upright on two legs: with quick, fast movements. It takes a special skill to ride one, because they can be spooked easily, and they are smart and tricky, always trying to kick their riders off and try to get away in a hurry. However, Ace is patient with them, and quicker than they are, he learned to dominate them with sureness and love thus earning their trust. Once their trust has been earned, a quantum will stay with their rider until the end. Ace was that type of person too, loyal until the end. He was abit trigger-happy, but hardly ever misses.

Bliss, from the nomad pale-foot clan, was not to be trifled with. The only female on the team, she might have been the smallest in size but is a leader like no other. Bliss was motivated by a personal vendetta against the Dark Prince, which she never likes to speak about. She was the best sharp shooter on the entire team, even if Ace did not like to admit it, most times she didn't even use her targeting systems.

Last, but certainly not least, there was The Professor. The team wouldn't be what it is without him. He was very tech savvy, and helped develop everything and anything that General Santos required to advance in the war. The Professor had a father-like quality to him, especially when it came to Santos.

Just outside the door, the war raged on. Santos heard a noise coming from the southend of the building. Quickly, he and his secondary team rushed into position to find that they were now surrounded by veloci-pods, armed for complete destruction.

Santos closed his eyes, took a deep breath, and prepared to charge. An eternity went by, but then in an instant, he jumped to his feet and commanded his troops to charge.

The secondary teams rise to the challenge with him. Hammer and his team flanked in from the east, Ace, and his team of quantúm riders from the west, while Bliss provided cover fire from above on the second-level terrace of the fortress. Santos rushed head-on with his team blasting and cutting as they fought their way forward.

The veloci-pods were frustrating and annoying things to fight. Robotic and raptor-like, they move quickly, slashing and biting with their razor-sharp claws and teeth, all the while shooting with the laser blasters mounted on their shoulders. Their armor easily bested by a blaster or by a corundum ray-sword, they were more of a nuisance than anything else.

Their eyes had infrared, sensor cameras, which had a direct visual imaging that feeds inside the Dark Prince's flying fortress. Thus, revealing the Iron Horse team's position and status.

In addition, these robotic beasts had the ability to transform into a mountable hover speeder, which can be driven by a foot soldier.

Santos and his team had been trying for some time to hack their memory chips, so the beasts could be reprogrammed and could be turned back upon the advancing troops, but Santos and his team have not yet been able to crack the code.

Falling to the left and right, veloci-pods exploded, and laser fire is everywhere. With a great shout, Hammer launches off some 30, 40, then 50 laser blast rounds with a blaster in each hand.

"Come on veloci-scum! I got what'ch ya lookin' for!"

General Santos crashed through the enemy lines with his arm shield, a retractable shield that infantry soldiers wear on their forearms, like a personal forcefield. As he moved, he took a good four or five down in a single motion. One after another, the hundreds of veloci-pods, now numbered fifty or sixty.

It was looking like a quick victory as Bliss took precise shots, freeing up the area around the General and his infantry team. Then all at once, out of nowhere, all the veloci-pods' eyes turned red, as they crouched to the ground. Simultaneously they triggered their self-destruct function, which was a new and previously unknown feature to Santos and team.

As Santos glanced down, seeing the red eyes blinking at him, he knew what was coming next. He closed his eyes and said to himself.

"Well, that's new."

The ground rumbled as all the pods exploded in an instant.

His ears rung, dust flew everywhere, and Santos couldn't even tell which was up. Santos struggled to open his eyes as he drifted in and out of consciousness.

**(404 AWOR - 23 years prior)**

Once opening his eyes, he could but only see a blurry face standing above him, laughing.

"Ha ha, I thought you said you were the best with a han-bo staff?" Dantias said with a grin, "Here let me help you up."

Standing to his feet Santos realized that Dantias had gotten the best of him. The brothers, shortly before their 19th birthday, enjoyed sparring with each other, simulating different combat fighting styles. It seems that this time, in not an uncommon occurrence, Dantias had gotten the upper hand.

"You know, I often wonder why we train so much?" Dantias said.

"What do you mean?" Santos asked.

Dantias continued, "Yeah, why do we train so much if we will never even use our training? You and I both know as Father has told us repeatedly..."

"Oh, you mean the stories from the ancient scrolls?" Santos interrupted.

"Yes, that when the Council of Kingmen was established, all wars and fighting ceased, each Realm was separated by their phylum, which means their kind or species," said Dantias.

"Well, it brought peace and unity to the Realms. Why is that such a dreadful thing?" said Santos.

"I'm not saying that it's bad, I just don't know why we train and practice so much for something that will ultimately never happen," stated Santos.

"Well, we train to be prepared... and if we don't use our training, it's for the best. Hey, look at the bright side, we get a good workout, right?" Santos said with a smile.

"True, want to go again?" Dantias asked.

"Come on, we better go get ready for the family meal," Santos said with a smile, "But I will get you the next time," he said with a laugh as he patted his brother on the shoulder, and they headed toward the house together.

**(One month later)**

Early one morning as Santos awakened, he heard raised voices coming from the council chambers. He dressed quickly, left his bedroom, as each brother had their own room, and made his way down the stairs, then the long hallway.

The palace was an immaculate, and beautiful place full of splendor. The ceilings were unimaginably tall, and the main hall was vast in length. Tapestries were woven with scenes, which represented each of the provinces, hung from golden curtain dowels, fine linen runners draped wooden, hand-crafted, tables along the corridor. The entrance of each room was adorned with the most elegant hand-carved double doors, each engraved with a historical scene.

The downstairs always smelled of fresh pine, with the needles imported from the northern provinces, as the scent was not native to the area, and laid neatly on special aroma plates that allowed their smell to be blown throughout.

A slight breeze blew through the cracked open windows that ran down the full length of the main hallway. Allowing the sunlight to perfectly illuminate the main rooms of the palace.

As Santos came to the end of the hall and stood outside the council chambers' doors. It was the most exquisitely crafted and adorned doors in the palace, if depicting the carved images which told the story of the formation of the Kingmen council. The decalogue, the first laws, were translated from the ancient scrolls, and were engraved on each of the door posts from the top to the bottom in the original tongue. As translated, they would read:

> ### The left door post it read:
> *I. There is no other god but the Creator.*
> *II. Do not make or bow to idols.*
> *III. Do not misuse the name of the Ancient One.*
> *IV. You shall keep yourselves pure unto the Creator.*
> *V. Always honor your ancestors.*

> ### The right door post it read:
> *VI. Do not murder.*
> *VII. Be faithful in marriage.*
> *VIII. Do not steal.*
> *IX. Always speak and uphold the truth at all times.*
> *X. Do not desire what others have.*

As he peeked through the slight crack in the doors, he could see each Kingmen present at the council table.

At the head was his father, as he sat with rod straight posture, focused and thoughtful, Kingmen of the Equiantus Realm. To his right Lord Hyram the II, Kingmen of the Bisonteaus Realm, loomed over the council table with his great muscular buffalo-like presence.

The Bisonteaus were known for their great hunting skills, mudbrick architecture, and for being the greatest of warriors. Lord Hyram seemed to rise above the rest as he sat in his chair.

The Bisonteaus warriors were notable not only because of their size, but because the number of braids in their mohawk and mane denoted who was the wisest of all the warriors, with one braid for each year of service to the realm. The number of beads in their beards also held a significant meaning. Each golden bead symbolized the number of years they had served their realm, and because beads were passed on from one generation to the next, they showed how many years of legacy existed in the family bloodlines as well. Lord Hyram the II's beard held 12 of his own golden beads and another 25 from his ancestors making him one of the most respected members of the council.

Next to Lord Hyram the II, Kingmen Catodus, a toad-like humanoid from the Amphibtius Realm. The Amphibtius were known to be easily distracted. They are a curious people, ever so kind and welcoming. Though their kindness and compassion did not shine through initially, due to their almost grumpy, and unpleasant tone of expressions.

Thinking back Santos remembered one time when Kingmen Catodus spoke to him as he was entering the palace grounds, after Santos greeted the council at the main gates.

"You're looking quite pale boy," said Catodus abruptly, "You need to get out more, don't you ever go outside?" asked the short Kingmen. He poked at Santos with the bottom part of his spear that he used as a walking stick as he passed by. It was common for the Amphibtius men to use their spears as walking sticks.

Although he was a grown adult and a respected elder of his people, he was so short in stature he could just barely look young Santos in the eye. He then turned around quickly, revealing a small bag of candies, which were unique to his realm because the candies were made from the sweet nectar of the swamp lilies. He tossed one to Santos as he made a shhhing gesture with his long, chubby finger across his lips. A smile came to Santos' face as he remembered this.

Then there was Kingmen Aylo Kuang of the Terrartius Realm, a lizard-like reptilian race, who were sleek and elegant, and best known for their amazing technology.

The wind carriages that are extensively used by all, were first developed by them. They are an extremely resourceful people, who seem quite willing to share their technological advances with the other realms. However, they always kept their own best interest in mind. He sat, quiet, watching and pondering the situation.

Then next to him, wearing his strong, yet bulky robotic land suit, was Lord Systrico from the underwater Mareviteaus Realm. He was the most curious, as one could see what he was always thinking because of his transparent head. His physical brain seemed to move as he thought, giving off a purplish glow, and changed color ever so slightly when he spoke giving it more of an electric greenish-blue glow. The tentacle-like appendages flowing off the sides of his face were interesting to watch as they reacted to his emotions and expressions, mimicking his mood and ideas when he spoke.

Lastly, seated with his back turned to the door was Sir Cysilian of the Aprosmarteus Realm, a kind, yet strange society to which others who don't quite belong, end up migrating to.

The Aprosmarteus Realm was the youngest of the realms as is had been formed only 30 years ago. Sir Cysilian was a distinct-looking fellow, his arms like an eagle with sharp finger claws, his legs almost catlike with his claws turned in, and his body and face were like that of a hawk. He nestled back into his chair resting upon two wings on his back that draped around him like a cape. One bright yellow eye would seem to dance about as he continually looked around the room, the other covered with a mahogany brown leather eye patch. He never really likes to talk about how he lost it and always discreetly changed the story of how it happened when asked. He was so *elegantly dirty*, that the workers of the palace would always complain about the way he would lean on the table, placing his feet on the corner. There were always fuzz bunnies and feathers left over under and around his seat by the time these meetings were over. Even though he and is six brothers could run and fly most elegantly, they seemed to always like to travel by sitting back in their wind carriages leaving others to do the hefty work. He sat at the table representing the only realm with open and free borders.

These Kingmen have continued the respectful duty to read, interpret, and establish the laws as stated in the ancient scrolls. There were only a few hundred scrolls recovered after the great War of Realms. Found amongst the rubble, was a vault containing scrolls that spoke of each realm's history, culture, art, and architecture. A letter was found explaining the history of what took place on that grave, sad day when all good things ended. Written with hopes that those who would find this letter, could help rebuild what once was a wondrous, prosperous society.

"The Aprosmarteus Realm must respect our borders; they must not come further north!" exclaimed the Lord Hyram II from the Bisonteus Realm.

"No one has entered your realm, Lord Hyram! As you know we do not demand that each citizen be registered. All are welcome and free to come and go as they choose," stated Sir Cysilian of the Aprosmarteus Realm.

"Then why do your men carry arms if we are at peace? Why must your people enter other realms? There must be fair order and border integrity between all realms, including the Aprosmarteus Realm!" Lord Hyram, spoke with great frustration.

Each month, on the first day, all the Kingmen, one from each realm, met in the high chamber of the councilors. These meetings existed to promote unity, trade, and prosperity between the six known realms.

Grandmaster Houlton spoke, "Since the establishment of the Five Realms and the most recent Aprosmarteus Realm, we have had peace. Be at rest my dear friends, order and peace are our primary goals."

Turning now and addressing him directly Grandmaster Houlton continued.

"Sir Cysilian of the Aprosmarteaus Realm, will you bring order to the legitimate concern of the Bisonteaus Realm?"

"Of course," stated Kingmen Cysilian.

"But as you know, we have a history of defying orders, not out of spite, it's just who we are. Our people should be able to come and go as they please, and not be confined," he said with a smirk.

This sixth Realm was the most recently established. It was a Realm where those who were less likely to follow orders from each of the five realms came. They were sent to the jungle areas, where Sir Cysilian and his brothers lived carefree, to establish their realm. It became a 'misfits' realm of sorts. Sir Cysilian's family received all those who wanted to enter their jungles with open arms, making him the Kingmen of the realm. This was done in hopes of creating greater unity and not using or enforcing the 'law of banishment.'

The banishment law was used with great caution as it not only disgraces the individual and their family name, but there is no undoing of a banishment once it has been declared. The person who receives banishment is not allowed to move to other realms. The person is declared unfit for habitancy, honor, and are stripped of any title from them or their lineage. They are then forced to wander and search the wastelands or be forced into the unknown, unspoken realm forever.

There have only been two recorded banishment occurrences since the council was established, and no one ever speaks of these events. These instances were recorded in the new scrolls of time but, as is law, never mentioned again, and therefore forgotten.

"Lord Hyram, can you come to peace with Sir Cysilian? - Sir Cysilian, can we come to an understanding, that your realm was established to be free from orders, yet understand that the other realms do have regulations that must be followed and respected?" Grandmaster Houlton stated definitively.

"It is settled then, order of business is now concluded," said Lord Systirco. "All in favor, say yah'."

"Yah."

In unison, all Kingmen agreed, and the session adjourned. As each of the Kingmen left the council hall, and Santos saluted them with a slight bow as they left.

"Good to see you young Houlton. Are you keeping up with all your studies?" asked Kingmen Aylo Kuang.

"Of course, sir," replied Santos.

"Very good, you will need them to join the council one day," Aylo Kuang said with a smile and hand gesture towards the council chambers.

"It would be a great honor, sir, I pray I may fulfill my duty," responded Santos.

"Duty? Remember it is an honor for a Kingmen to serve his people and keep order in each province and village," said Aylo Kuang. "You will learn that one day, perhaps one day very soon."

He then dismissed himself with a nod of the head and went on his way. As Kingmen Aylo walked away, Santos reflected on those words.

"Santos my son, how are you this morning? Where is your brother?" his father asked.

"I'm not sure, I...," Santos couldn't quite finish his answer.

"Your mother buying in the market?" His father did not await his answer, "What are your plans for the day my son? – Well, I must be on my way, now I must meet with the province leaders. I hope to be back shortly," Grandmaster Houlton said quickly, once again not truly waiting for an answer, and went on his way.

Santos' answer was not entirely true, he did know where his brother was. However, he just did not want to be another burden on his overwhelmed father. Lately, he has had so many meetings with the province leaders. There was a bit more friction as of late between them and due to his weakening health, it was not important to tell his father where his brother was.

**(Nomad camp; an outer province)**

"No, stop," Namid said with a laugh. "You're going to break it."

"Oh, I will not break it, you know how good of a shot I am with these... these, uh..." Dantias was interrupted before he could remember the name of the crude, unsophisticated weapon.

"Bow and arrows," she snapped.

"Right, bow and arrows. Isn't a blaster so much easier to use? You just point and shoot," said Dantias.

"Not everyone has all the fancy equipment that you do. Besides, I can use my bow at anytime. You must charge capsules to use your blaster. What happens if you run out, and aren't those banned anyway?" she said sarcastically.

"Well yes, and you're probably right," he said as he let go and the arrow bounced off the ground as it fell short, not even closely hitting the bottle.

"Come on, I better get you back home," Dantias said not even looking at her, as he tried not to lose what little pride he had left.

Over the last several months, Dantias would sneak off early in the morning, just after breakfast and his morning duties to not attract attention and would visit the pale-foot tribe in one of the outer provinces.

Santos knew exactly where Dantias was because occasionally, without his brother's knowledge, he would follow him. Santos was not surprised he saw Dantias meeting with Namid, who was the very same girl whose grandfather would always sell them sugar beads when they were young. Now, she was older, smarter, and much prettier.

Namid had beautiful tan and cream skin, which gradually fading one color with the other, like coffee with milk. A few freckles dot her cheeks, giving her a unique and captivating appearance. She was from the pale-foot Mustang clan, and shorter in stature, but she had an inner strength that showed power and grace with her every move. Her gentle nature shone through her expressive eyes, which were a deep, soulful brown, reflecting intelligence and kindness. Her hair was long and full, falling down her neck in a beautiful mix of tan and chestnut brown, adding to her striking appearance. When she stood in the sun, her skin glistened and the muscles in her back rippled as she pulled on the bow string, creating a breathtaking sight as she shows great confidence and beauty in the warm light.

Arriving back to camp Namid's grandfather watched carefully as the two walked by, hand in hand. Even though they had his blessing, he was still cautious and watchful because the young man was a Houlton prince. A Lord over the provinces, as his ancestors before him. He was someone to be honored, but not fully trusted.

There were stories amongst the outer tribes, some of them myths, yet others true. The Houltons had served the Equiantus Realm, for generations, the twins would become the fourth.

Yet there was talk and questions around this. How did the Houlton family truly gain their place and fortune? The outer harvesting clans, the nomad clans, and the mining Asno-clan spoke amongst themselves. Many believed that the Houltons took from everyone else, taxed the poorer provinces, and fixed the numbers internally to show on the record that they had a fortune that truly was not their own.

It has been said, by some, that the great, great, great Grand-master Houlton; the first of his clan to become part of the council, back when it was first being formed, earned his place on the backs of his brothers who worked the fields and the mines, though that has never been proven.

If it had ever been recorded in the city's history scrolls, they no longer existed because they have never been found. Although there is no recorded history of these incidents, the stories, and rumors remained and still caused a slight tension in the hearts of the people, causing them to carry doubts and question, "How truly beneficial is the council of Kingmen for the common person?"

Dantias turned to Namid, "May I see you again the day after tomorrow as well?" Dantias asked with a big smile.

"Well, what would your parents say?" she asked flirtatiously.

"You know what The Dutchess thinks, we've already spoken about this," Dantias said with disappointment.

"And your father?" Namid inquired.

"He barely knows about me, let alone you," Dantias answered.

"He's always involved in his monthly Lord of the Realms council meetings or going over issues with the province leaders. Santos is the one who is more interested in politics anyways, it's just not for me," Dantias said sarcastically.

"That's true,but you are a prince, and you will have the opportunity to lead all our people, think of all the good you could do. You could create greater policies that would bring unity between the tribes, villages, and provinces," Namid encouraged him.

"Unity? Ha, we both know that is only an illusion," he rolled his eyes and then frowned. "Look at your people, they are not wanted in the provinces, and those who live in the village, work all day long, for little to nothing! Unity, what unity?" Dantias said with great frustration.

"That's why you should speak up and learn the policies of all our tribes and people. You could bring the unity that all of us are truly looking for," Namid said with a smile as she hugged Dantias and kissed his cheek.

"Well, maybe if you helped me, one day I could do all that you say," he responded with a deep breath, smiling, returning her hug, as they neighed to one another, pressing their foreheads together. Dantias said his goodbye and began home as the suns were setting.

The horizon was beautiful as the three moons rose over the far-off mountains, each aligning with the three tallest mountain crests. When the light hit exactly right, it was a site to embrace. With a cool breeze resting on your face and, the suns settling to its bed exactly right, one would admire the view, like someone painted a celestial painting each evening.

# CHAPTER 3

Looking out over the horizon, the new moons shined brightly. From within his flying fortress, the Dark Prince lifted his hand off the self-destruct button.

Smoke was rising from the area where General Santos and his team were fighting. The smoke was so thick that nothing else could be seen on the ground.

"As I said, we will end this war quickly, no mercy for any of them," the Dark Prince said in a short direct tone.

As he said this, his crew lowered their heads in shame, yet responded, "Yes, my Lord Prince."

"I have not brought us this far to turn back now, do not become soft," said the Dark Prince.

"If we destroy it all, what will we be lords of?" an Amphibtius tech-controller whispered under his breath.

"What did you say?! - Whoever speaks against the Dark Prince will find his place amongst the fallen and outcast! Do I make myself clear?!" shouted Captain Amin, the Dark Prince's second in command.

Captain Amin is an extraordinarily strong Terrartius soldier with a half mask made of titanium material, which looked as though it was created as one of the first models for the veloci-pods. He was missing a finger on his left hand, leaving only three long and scaly digits with hooked claws on the tip of each one. The metal countertop screeched just a little as he ran the claws of his right-hand over it as he walked towards the technician who spoke out of turn.

"Find them. Confirm it, and get it done," the Dark Prince said directly to Captain Amin as he turned and walked away. His flowing cape followed him like a shadow down the corridor to his quarters, the air-tight sliding doors closed with a silent swoosh behind him. Tension hung in the air.

### (Meanwhile in the Iron Horse Team's medical bay)

As General Santos breathed deeply, he regained consciousness. He coughed and turned onto his side. Blood slowly dripped from his ears, nose, and the side of his mouth. Even though several of his secondary teams were lost and he was hit hard, he seemed to have survived. He had a concussion, but was alive, nonetheless. Three medic troops came to his aid and helped pull off his chest armor and arm shield.

While they carefully removed his chest plate, they noticed something unusual about Santos' armor. It was lighter and had hinged pieces on the side of it, with a built-in infrastructure, which was quite different from the rest of the team's armor. Unknown to the rest of the team, The Professor, who was well-skilled in developing tech, armor, and weapons for the Iron Horse team, had been testing prototypes with General Santos several months past.

Santos breathed deep again, easier this time, as they continued to remove his armored suit. Santos extremely grateful now for The Professor's insistence on wearing it.

The Professor was not just one who helped develop new armor and tech or gave advice, he was a part of the family. He was there when Grandmaster Houlton took his last breaths. As Santos closed his eyes, it all came flooding back to him. The sound, the smell of the room, the stiffness and heaviness in the air.

**(403 AWOR) 3 years before Iron Horse was established.**

"Agh... uh...," a deep wheezing sound, heard coming from Santos as he clutched his stomach, now laying on the ground. Gasping for air, his ears began to ring slightly.

"Breath deep. The key is to breathe correctly. Receive a hit, 'ki-ushhh,' exhale. Give a punch, deep breath in, then, 'ki-ay,' out with power," Grandmaster Houlton spoke as he taught their ancient family battle techniques.

Rising now to his feet, Santos bowed with respect. "Yes, Father," he said.

Santos had been grateful for the teachings over the past few months. Lord Houlton had been spending less time with the council lately and had been investing more time with his sons. Or at least with Santos, Dantias has been quite indifferent as of late. He had been coming home late,not interested in the family meal, or much of anything for that matter. Santos even had difficulty connecting with him, he seemed like his mind was in another place. Santos had an idea as to where his brother's thoughts and presence were.

"Ahhgh, cough, cough, cough," Lord Houlton, tried to hide the pain in his side and difficulty breathing.

"I told you, you should not be out in the evening air, it's not good for your cough," said The Dutchess as she walked out onto the back porch,overlooking the family gardens.

"I must insist you come in and rest," she said firmly.

"Come my son, let's go in for some tea," Lord Houlton said with a forced smile.

"I shall help you Father," said Santos, with a concerned look.

"Nonsense, all is well, not to worry. Come now," but Lord Houlton spoke with half-truth.

They both turned towards the palace and walked up the path, past The Professor, who too looked on with great concern. As they found their way to the family room, there they received their evening tea.

It was a beautiful parlor. Three couches and two tall, backed chairs facing one another, each placed in such a way that they had their very own corner or place in the room. If you were seated in any one of them, you would never give your back to the others. As the evening approached it was most elegant because the western window was situated in such a way, that the last rays of the two sun's light, one reddish-orange and the other with its purple haze, would shine through. On the walls, glimmering rainbows projected from the hanging quartz crystals that decorated the windowpane.

The Dutchess was in complete control in these situations. Truth be told, the Grandmaster had been slowly getting worse and worse due to a medical condition. The doctors had given him months to live, yet this information was only known to the medics, The Dutchess, one or two members of the council, and the Professor, who has served the family for over three generations.

It was for this reason Lord Houlton had been spending more time with Santos. The council members strongly encouraged him not to resign, but to take a forced leave of absence from his monthly and weekly duties. The extra stress was unhelpful and unwanted at this time, and in his current condition he was unable to perform the needed tasks. His mind was occupied with other things.

**(Later that night)**

Under the light of the new moons, with candle torch in hand, Dantias came in through the side quarters entrance as had become custom now over the last few months. Quenching the small flame on the last torch just outside the door. He now found himself sneaking past the backgate guards once again, he made his way to the dining area to grab a snack before going to his quarters. Taking a few nuts and a piece of fruit from a basket on the center table, he turned to go up the back stairs that led up to his room. When out of the shadows The Dutchess appeared, standing firm, arms crossed, staring at him with nostrils flaring as she breathed deep. Startled Dantias took a step back cautiously.

"Where have you been? Why are you coming in at this hour of the night? Have you no decency? Your father is extremely ill," she asked curtly .

Unbeknownst to him she had been watching him and his late-night endeavors over the last few weeks.

"No—um, nothing, Dutchess," Dantias stuttered. "I was just out checking the security pylons, on the far border," he said with more confidence.

"Do not lie to me, boy. I know you're up to something. I have seen you now these past two weeks, coming in late, at the same hour, having no courtesy for your family, especially your father. Where have you been?" The Dutchess insisted on having an answer.

A quiet stare is all she received.

She waited... Still, no answer.

"I will not have any more of it. Am I understood?" she said firmly.

"Yes, my Dutchess," Dantias answered with a fixed look, not lowering his sight even an inch.

"Come here, my son," changing her tone completely, "I'm glad you're home now, that's the most important thing. Go on, get some rest, you must be tired," said The Dutchess as she hugged him close, kissed his cheek, and then sent him on his way.

As Dantias walked away, then up the stairs. He held so much frustration in his heart against her. He genuinely wanted to be rid of her, to be as far away as possible.

The Dutchess stood, leaning forward with both hands directly on the table, holding back her tears. They were not tears of pain or hurt, yet of frustration and anger. She was determined to find out what her son was up to and would put a stop to it, whatever the cost. Her family is just too important.

"What would the other council members say if they found out one of her promised sons was involved in unorthodox behavior," she thought. She would not stand for it.

She then went to the family room where she sat in her most elegant, high-backed chair. A small crackle from the dry sticks burning in the fire pit in front of her pierced the silence. She sat pondering, wondering, planning.

As a little girl, she relished the thrill of sneaking into the grand halls of the palace, her dark ponytail bouncing in rhythm with each happy skip; she knew full well that children of the palace guard were not to play about in such places.

The open corridors, adorned with intricate tapestries and glimmering candle lit chandeliers. It felt like a magical kingdom of wonder and fantasy to a young girl.

Her father, steadfast and proud, one of the most loyal of the Houlton Dynasty guard. He would often surprise her mid-adventure. Instead of reprimanding her, he would scoop her up into his strong arms and twirl her around, her delighted giggles ringing like a song in the air.

Being the sole girl among six rambunctious brothers, she held a cherished place in her father's heart, a shining gem amidst a treasure trove of boys.

While her five siblings were strongly instructed in lessons of responsibility and duty from an early age, she enjoyed the freedom to roam and play, feeling like a princess, basking in her father's unwavering affection.

While she sat, staring into the fire, The Dutchess recalled the countless moments spent racing through the lush gardens, where vibrant flowers danced along with her in the breeze. Her father often joined in her whimsical games. Even though he knew it was against the palace rules. The other guards failed to report him time and again, showing a grace that was not shown to others, due to the fact that his wife, The Dutchess's mother, died in childbirth, leaving him with six children to raise on his own, his daughter being the youngest, with no memory or recollection of her mother.

In those days it was not easy growing up the way she did, but it not only sculpted her into a strong and determined woman, but also instilled in her a strong, yet profound sense of duty, always striving for more, pushing her father forward, striving to see him content with her and life.

Although that took her father to his ultimate ruin, in her mind. Serving in the same position, same house, same everything her whole life. Not her, she had plowed out her destiny, now wife to the Kingmen of the Realm and leader of the Houlton Dynasty.

As she sat in her tall-backed chair, she was struck by the vivid contrast between her own carefree childhood and the stringent way she raised her sons. She had flourished under the warmth of exploration and play, her father's affection lighting her path.

Yet, now, as a mother, she found herself ensnared in the net of expectations, demanding nothing less than perfection from her sons.

Tears slowly ran down her face and, her hands trembled as she held her handkerchief close to her mouth. She stared out the window looking into the night as a slight glow from the fire shined upon her face. She was determined to unveil this mystery and be done with it.

As the fire dwindled and slowly burned out one could barely hear her as she whispered sternly to herself in the dark, "The prophecy will be fulfilled, my sons are the chosen ones."

# Cornua Cerviteaus Race

# CHAPTER 4

(APPROXIMATELY 500 YEARS EARLIER)

It was a most glorious time before the great War of the Realms. Teraqueos was full of life, and each realm was led by its respective King or Dynasty Elder. It was a time when The Scrolls governed the land and the Dynasty Elders interpreted its laws. A time of peace, unity, and a prosperous world economy.

Each realm was an open territory, and the citizens were not barred from passing or crossing from one place to the other because there were no borders. Every citizen was registered by their *kind* and free to build their home wherever they pleased.

Were it to be in the plains of the North, the jungle lands of the East, swamps to the West, on the coast of the vast oceans and rivers throughout, or the high mountain range that runs from the lower Southwest all the way upto the plains. They separated the Savannah lands of the Houlton Dynasty, making it a natural center of the planet's terrain. All areas were open for the building of homes, farms for production, or marketplaces for the buying and selling of goods.

At the furthermost edge of the Dynasty lands, there was a great white hall, which had become the unofficial center of all the realms. A glorious hall made of white, hand-cut, and hand-polished marble stone. Just one of these 12 pillars, which stood around the outskirts of the building, weighed more than one ton.

At the entrance of this magnificent building, there were enormous arched doors that stretched up to over 20 feet tall. Projecting a feeling of intimidation and greatness due to their sheer magnitude. Here, for centuries, the Dynasty Elders gathered to interpret the writings of the sacred scrolls, then create, and establish the laws that brought continued peace and order to all who lived there.

Laws for buying and selling, timings and rhythms of the sound music that were guaranteed to stimulate growth in every way, receipts for the most delicious dishes one could ever imagine, instructions for classes that taught ways to create some of the most extravagant pieces of art ever produced. Laws and instructions covered every imaginable way of life, from the cleanliness of oneself to the most beneficial ways of sowing and reaping the best crops for harvest, for every season and every type of soil that exists. There were even instructions on how to create, sustain, and establish a living underwater realm. Every area was to be under the law, nothing was left out or missed by the guidance and watchful eyes of the elders.

Scrolls upon scrolls, upon scrolls that had been translated, written, and passed down from generation to generation. The oldest of the writings were those that dated back to before any of the elders' grandfathers were even born, some of which were written in an ancient tongue that now only a few could read. The great white hall was a library of scrolls, rules, and laws that no one questioned, but embraced and practiced, a genuinely great society where everyone was accepted, appreciated, and considered a benefit for all those who lived here.

At the furthest most part of the hall was a long, solid, firm-standing wooden table, with 12 chairs equal in look and elegance. Cut from the thickest trees from the tropical jungles of the Eastern realm, they were a work of art in and of itself.

All 12 elders were seated in their high-back wooden chairs, at times discussing or questioning if their translation of older scrolls carried the most adequate wording and phrases. At other times there a great silence that would fill the hall, a heaviness that would hang in the air as each elder would read, write, and meditate on their work. They took their work, very seriously. Each one checking and rechecking the other's work. If one word or even just one syllable was considered misinterpreted, they would destroy their written document and begin again entirely from scratch. The scrolls must be written and interpreted correctly, everything depended upon this.

One given evening, an elder, which one we do not know, because that is not really of the most importance, was going over some scrolls from the deep vault. The deep vault is where the oldest and most treasured scrolls were kept. This vault contained air-preserving, water-resistant elements and was where all the original scrolls and documents were preserved until they could be interpreted, then to be used to establish or bring into law.

As the elder read and reread the scroll, he was puzzled by its content. After reading the scroll several times, he was eager to have one of his colleagues give their interpretation of this scroll as well.

It was now late in the day, a time when work would draw to a close and things were to be put back in their place and kept till the next day for further review. This was the time to go home, rest, and stop for the day. Yet, this evening it was not so. As the elder read the scroll once again, he began to write, and then read, and then write again. He was increasingly disturbed by what his eyes and mind were finding written in the ancient tongue of this old scroll that was now before him. He was one of four elders who could read and write the ancient tongue, yet none remain that knew how it sounded.

He quickly summoned Lord Estracks, who was one of the only other members of the elder council that could read such ancient tongues.

Lord Estracks was of the Cornua Cerviteaus race, an elegant, powerful, yet graceful people. When they entered a room, you could not help but feel small due to the way they carried themselves with such confidence, wisdom, grace, and authority.

They also had powerful leg muscles and the most beautifully adorned antlers with each tip revealing and representing five years of wisdom.

Lord Estracks was the eldest and wisest of them all, with his antlers revealing 25 antler tips. Without saying one word, one felt as if they should bow in his presence, as his presence demanded respect.

"Please come, I have something of great interest Lord Estracks," The elder spoke in a loud whisper.

Lord Estracks, the most respected of the elder's council, for more than 100 years he had interpreted and helped write the governing laws from the ancient scrolls. He turned and looked to the far end of the long wooden table, almost disturbed or even bothered by this demand of his time, as it was now time to go home, to have his usual evening meal, and then rest.

"Please, my great Sir, I beg you, it will not disappoint," The elder insisted.

A beautiful shadow of majestic antlers was cast upon the library's shelves while the lowering sun showed through the windows above. Lord Estracks carried himself with such grace as he walked the length of the room. His robe followed behind in such a perfect, quiet manner.

"What is it?" asked Lord Estracks.

"I have been reading over this scroll, translating, interpreting, and meditating on its meanings. I've come across something remarkably interesting, yet quite disturbing. For this purpose, I desire your council and opinion," The elder explained.

As Lord Estracks looked over the vexing document, his eyes widened, and a look of concern came upon his face while he read the scroll. The text translated, read as follows:

*"A day will come, in a time of great need, when two will be as one. Two heads will rule as one. One will be as two and they shall establish order and bring all under their authority."*

"What does this mean my Lord?" asked the elder.

"It is a prophecy. Giving hope of this... future event," said Lord Estracks.

"Or a warning?" The elder whispered, "We must bring this to the council at once, this information must be discussed immediately."

"I fear that not all things should be spoken of my friend. If this is brought to light now, in such times of peace and unity, I fear it will destroy centuries of order and bring out the worst in all of us," Lord Estracks stated nervously.

"I'm sorry my Lord, but we must not, cannot, keep this information from our counterparts. It is our duty to keep order by keeping our integrity," the elder stated firmly.

Lord Estracks looked deep into his eyes, with a warning in his gaze. He was not one to repeat himself or explain his reasoning. He always said what he meant and meant what he said. Seeing the elder's unwillingness to depart from his reasoning and this path of action, he spoke.

"Do as you must, but no good will come of this," Lord Estracks said as he gazed into the distance.

"I will bring it to the council, first thing tomorrow morning after our early reflection and meditations," the elder said determinedly.

Lord Estracks sighed, nodded, and was quiet. They both parted ways, each going to their homes. Lord Estracks did not, could not, dared not sleep that night; for the next day, the fate of everyone would be in the balance.

The next morning, as agreed, Lord Estracks, his equal companion, and the rest of the Dynasty Elders gathered in their respective places around the great wooden table.

It was a day of business as usual. They all stood and recited the morning pledge, quoted the 10 Ancient Laws.

As it was written in history, the first scrolls were handed down from the Creator himself, almost 3,000 years before.

The elders then proceeded with a praise unto The One above All, who is The Beginning and The End of all things, with their harmony of meditation, a most intriguing, harmonious low humming tone, which sounded wonderful as it echoed in the glorious hall.

Then they sat, each taking their places around the great table, as morning tea was served. The Cornua Cerviteaus elder stayed standing, as it was custom. This brought attention to himself as they all sat in their places establishing equality amongst them all. The elder stood there, holding the scroll in his right hand. As the other 10 elders turned and looked upon him, he began to speak. Lord Estracks kept quiet, looking forward, waiting for the now inevitable.

"My honorable, fellow elders. I have great, yet disturbing news to share with all of you. It is of the utmost importance, which is why I am bringing it to your attention immediately," The elder explained.

"Please continue," they said and nodded in agreement.

"Yesterday, as the day and activities were ending, I came upon something written in one of the oldest scrolls from the deep vault. As I translated, interpreted, and meditated on the scroll, that is before you now, I came across an interesting find."

"Well, what is it? State it," said one of his Amphibtius companions.

"Here written, is a prophecy which I believe is for our future. An uncertain future. It was written in a most ancient tongue; and it reads:

"*A day will come, in a time of great need, when two will be as one. Two heads will rule as one. One will be as two and they shall establish order and bring all under their authority.*"

"Has this translation been confirmed?" The Bisonteaus elder asked as they all turned to look to Lord Estracks.

Lord Estracks nodded in confirmation.

They sat in silence for a long while and pondered what they had just heard. As they looked at one another, without saying a word, it was as though each of them knew what the other thought, but no one wished to speak it aloud. Then after what seemed many hours, but was only 20 minutes, one elder stood, and cleared his voice he said with a firm tone.

"My dear elders, my equals, my friends. As many of us have pondered this great, meaningful word. I wish to bring, what we all are pondering, to the table. To which dynasty does this prophecy apply? From where will these great leaders come? Would it be from the Amphibtius Realm, the Mareviteaus Realm, the most honorable Equiantus Realm, or the mighty warriors of the Bisonteaus Realm. I assure you, and most respectably submit to you all, that my people of the Terrartius Dynasty will bring, not only authority and integrity but also balance. Honor, peace, and well-being. Our society will flourish and be known as the greatest to ever succeed!"

As he stated this declaration, all the rest of the elders stood quickly to their feet and declared the same for their people. This once peaceful, unified group now pointed fingers, accusing, and speaking harshly to one another with raised voices.

While the discussion gradually escalated, Lord Estracks sat and looked at his loyal friend and shook his head. The elder now understood why Lord Estracks made his recommendation to keep this information secret. There was now no more reason, no quest to find keep the peace. In a moment, centuries of peace were gone, destroyed by a few phrases. They were headed down a path of no return. Pride, the darkest of powers, had taken grip of their hearts and their egos had now taken control.

This dark power, like a quick, secret, slashing attack was tearing the elders and their realms apart. Reason, understanding, and their unified appreciation they once had for each other was now strangled. It was a swimmer in the deep sea, gasping the air or the sea for something that was not there, when there was no more strength in their body, feeling the undertow gently pulling you under. Lord Estracks looked to the ceiling as he took a long, desperate breath.

As they continued the debate turned further into uncontrolled chaos with fists slammed upon the table, chairs kicked over, and ungoverned yells.

Lord Estracks carefully and swiftly, unnoticed by the rest, swooped up the scroll and cautiously, calmly rolled it up while he tried not to bring attention to himself, put it in a protective cylinder, tucked it away under his cloak and proceeded to slip away. He and his colleague knew that there was no turning back, he planned to protect this prophecy for future generations to come. He planned to attempt to keep this dark power at bay. Until the time was right, he would hide the scroll and disappear.

It was not before the prophecy spread to each tribe and group. Quickly, this dark power took control of the hearts of every citizen. Unity turned into arrogance. Arrogance turned to discord, discord turned to frustration, and frustration turned into hatred. This hatred spread throughout the cities, provinces, fields, and schools. Outside the great hall people were bombarding its great majestic doors with stones. Each race, each person, declaring, even demanding that from their people would come the chosen ones.

As days passed, one early morning Lord Estracks inside the now dark great hall, quickly and steadily took as many of the scrolls as he could and moved the scrolls into the deep lower vault. He hoped his plan would protect the history of this once great society and preserve it to the best of his ability. In hopes that future generations would have the answer sand solutions to their difficult questions. One day, others, like himself would emerge and desire knowledge, truth, and peace. Knowing though that such a day was an exceedingly long time from then. He piled as many scrolls as possible, many of them translated, into the great vault. The door was massive and heavy, almost too heavy for one person to close. On the inside of the vault was a special lock, once turned, there was only one key that could unlock it, that he wore around his neck. He turned the lock, gave the door a final heavy push, and then the vault was sealed shut. A certain tranquil feeling washed over him, knowing that not even fire could open the door. He had done his best to preserve the truth.

After weeks of arguments around the once unified table, Lord Estracks, the once strong and decided elder, sat inside the great hall now alone. All he could hear now was the banging upon the great doors and the screams of those who demanded that the scrolls be given to them. People from all the known realms were now demanding and fighting for the same thing. Unified only in their fear and chaos. Peace no longer bringing them together, but fear tearing them apart. He sat in silence, knowing that he had been the cause this chaos. He knew now that the Great War of Realms had begun.

In the distance there was the vortex of smoke, circling and rising from the burning buildings and homes of the outer areas.

Months later all that was left was the rubble. Buildings lay in ruin and were all that remained of this once flourishing and great society that had lasted for more than a millennium.

# CHAPTER 5

(PRESENT DAY: EPIC WAR)

S taring at the computer monitor, General Santos was reflecting on the events of the day. He read the data output in front of him and was overwhelmed with anger and sadness while he evaluated the team's losses.

Many of the secondary teams had fallen in battle, leaving their numbers now even less than after the previous attack. He gritted his teeth and clenched his fists. Then, took a deep breath and once again controlled his emotions as he focused on his breathing sitting cross-legged on the floor. Clearing his mind, all he could hear was the whimper of a quantum in the distance.

The sounds of gunfire had ceased, for now. Soldiers were at rest in their quarters, some sleeping, others eating their daily ration of panú, yet others just still. Waiting. Waiting for the next wave of attack to come. Ace, Bliss, and Hammer were hunkered down in their positions. No radio chatter, no speech, just waiting.

As he breathed deeply, Santos' mind drifted to a similar time in his past, a time of hurt, sadness, and of loss.

**(403 AWOR) - 2 years before Iron Horse is established.**

"Aghh!" there was a loud shout and then a crashing sound of metal plates and a teacup shattering onto the floor.

The Dutchess ran into the main palace bedroom with an angry, frightened sternness in her voice.

"What have you done? You idiot!" she yelled at the weary Professor, as he knelt to help up Lord Houlton from the floor.

"Get away from him, you've done enough already!" she exclaimed.

"I'm very sorry my Dutchess, I served him afternoon tea and when he stood to receive it, tripped and fell onto me, knocking it all to the floor," explained The Professor.

"Nonsense! All you do is make him worse! You are of no help, no help at all! You are supposed to be making him better! But you, your medicine, and your science has not done anything, he is only worse off!" yelled The Dutchess.

"I am caring for him the best that I know how," The Professor assured The Dutchess almost begging for her tolerance and understanding, even though he knew he would not receive it.

"Just get out! Get out of here!" The Dutchess yelled once more as she knelt on the floor next to her fallen and frail husband.

"Forgive me Your Highness," The Professor said with much care as he bowed and left the room.

As he walked out the door, he crossed paths with, the now genuinely concerned twins. Santos and Dantias were now just outside the partially cracked bedroom door. The twins were now strong able-bodied young men, boys no longer, still they were cautious in this part of the palace.

This room was of immense importance, as to every Grandmaster had lived in this room. As far back as the family tree was recorded, 4 generations of Houlton Dynasty Grandmasters.

They quietly entered the room and knelt beside their mother, The Dutchess, without a word. They moved quickly and quietly to help their father up. Each brother took one side, and laid him down on the tall, comfortable mattress of the bedchamber.

The bed was carved by hand from walnut, a hardwood preserved from before the great war. It had beautifully ornate posts. The tops of the posts revealed the sculptures of the great wind-riders of ancient times before the War of Realms. They were elegant looking with their helmets, armor and most splendid wings extended out, simulating warriors in flight. Each sculpted warrior had a different pose, but all held their sword in one hand and shield in the other, pointing to towards the sky. They were the great elders of the Equantius Realm, none could match their wisdom and strength. On the headboard in a natural wood tone, painted with golden highlights that were slightly faded and worn now from decades of use, was a scene of breathtaking trees and a luminous sunrise which represented victory.

The walls of the room were lined with tapestries, and the most elegant vases sat on every surface. The room was illuminated with oil lamps that sat on round, heavy wooden bedside tables. A massive window overlooked the gardens, which boasted the best view in the palace. Though now the window was covered with heavy curtains, which blocked the view and prevented the sunlight from penetrating the room.

As Santos and Dantias lay their father up on the bed they noticed that their father was so light that the bones in his back and his ribs protruded through his robe. Their only communication was a silent glance of the eyes between one another.

"Thank you, my sons. How clumsy of me, I must have tripped again," said Lord Houlton in a weak and airy voice.

"Anything you need sir?" Santos asked before his brother could.

"Perhaps a cup of tea?" Lord Houlton replied.

"Enough tea for one day. Boys go. He needs his rest," The Dutchess replied harshly.

As they walked out of the room, the sound of faint wheezing could be heard as their father slowly caught his breath.

There was a time when the main quarters were one of the most extravagant and glorious rooms in the palace. Now, it was a gloomy place with a stale scent enveloping the room, a soon-to-be tomb. The Professor had said, he and the medical team had done everything possible to treat Lord Houlton. Despite their best efforts, Lord Houlton had been getting worse by the week for several months. It was now only a matter of time now it seemed. All they could do now was wait.

The brothers walked slowly down the great hall, then to the wide staircase leading to the main entrance. Both speechless and heavy hearted. Once outside they walked down the main walkway, then the side path around to the gardens on the west side of the palace. There they found themselves in a remarkably familiar place.

The garden here was very lush with bushes, flowers, and cherry trees. Even though the trees only bloomed once a year, there was an elegante beauty about them. Just under the largest of the trees, the grass had eroded to dirt and sand, as were most of the areas beyond the palace gates.

Houlton City was an arid, dry place to live. The palace workers watered the gardens daily, sometimes two or three times a day in the summer to keep it healthy and green.

This place, this area was extremely familiar to the twins. Here the ground was trampled from the continual practicing of kata, sparing, and the training exercises their father taught them for as long as they both could remember. There was a certain energy about it.

The suns were setting to the west, and the three moons just starting to emerge over the mountains. The brothers were burdened by their father's illness. Pain and worry etched on their faces made them seem lost as the shadows grew longer. Then, without a word and driven by shared instinct, they simultaneously removed their outer robes. They folded them with precision and laid them on the wooden bench with stone legs where their father had sat countless times before.

Dantias, turned as he looked over his left shoulder. He saw his brother's muscular back, his white skin glimmered slightly with the reflection of the setting sun. Santos, eyes closed, breathed deep, ears turned back. He listened for the very slightest of movement. With one solid, fluid motion Dantias turned and landed a perfect roundhouse kick to his brother's head. Santos, without even opening his eyes, ducked, turned, and countered with a punch; the kumite had begun.

They kicked, punched, and countered. Each with precision. One, two, strike, kick, breath, counter, repeat in a smooth consistent motion. They had done this more than 1,000 times before. Gracefully they moved, neither besting the other, equals in all they did.

All that could be heard was the swishing sound of their light gi and deep breathing as they moved. Their sparring training uniforms or gi were elegantly embroidered with the family crest over the left shoulder. The gi hung, loosely just below the waist, yet fitted enough that a slight snapping sound could be heard as they moved. The pants matched the light gray blue color of the jacket. Each brother was identical in so many ways, yet as they moved, it seemed almost like choreography, you could see slight distinctions in their art. Santos was a bit firmer and more precise, measuring each move in his mind just as it was executed. Whereas Dantias struck and hit first, then readjusting his technique as he went. A slight dust cloud arose now around them.

The power, and strength of each movement grew with intensity. Faster, harder, and more precise was each punch, every kick. Sweat ran down their brows as they continued for what seemed now like an eternity. Faster, harder, quicker, now with a warrior's scream, Dantias landed a strong blow to his brother's face, causing him to stumble back. Quickly catching his footing, Santos lunged forward with a counterattack punch, also with a warrior's scream. Their cries echoed across the courtyard.

The palace guards were drawn to the commotion, but hung back and observed from a distance, not wanting to interfere. As the sparring continued, it got became more intense.

Santos moved with a high kick, and Dantias crouched low and swept a kick as his brother landed him hard on his back. Without a thought, Dantias leapt upon him and with a strong punch to the face knocked Santos onto his back. A front punch to the face, elbow to the side of the head. One, two, three, as he repeatedly hits his opponent. Santos managed to gain a bit of clarity amidst this storm of hits, looked up through his arms covering his face. A small stream of blood dripped down into his eyes, and he managed to land one precise hit to Dantias's nose, setting his head up for a quick throat jab. While Dantias reacted, with a slight jerk back, it was just enough for a skilled fighter, like Santos, to move quickly. He pivoted his brother off him, and in an instant Santos swung around behind and wrapped his legs around his brother's waist, grabbed his head and neck around from the back, Santos now had the advantage. The brothers breathed heavily, Santos attempted to squeeze ever so slightly, however even the slightest of movements caused great pain. Dantias struggled to breathe. He could not manage to breathe deeply and discovered he could only manage short, shallow breaths. As the sun sets, Santos' sweat, and blood drip to the ground. A thin ray of sunlight lays upon his brow as he trembled with anger, holding his posture, and not allowing his brother to move, Dantias' eyes begin to close ever so slightly as his body relaxed and his breathing slows, to a stop.

The guards, now but about 100 feet away, watched, with worried faces and struggled to decide on how to react. Then all a sudden, a scream emanated from the main quarter's balcony.

"Noooo! Boys come, now!" The Dutchess screamed with all her might.

Quickly Santos released his grip. Dantias jerked, gasped for breath, rolled over, and pushed himself up to a seated position on the ground. While they stared at each other, shock and disbelief filled their eyes. Both breathed deeply, trying to calm themselves, each turned and saw the glow of the last rays of sunlight shining on their mother's weary, terrified face.

Silently they bolted up at once, ran past the guards, who were staring up at the balcony, without even a bow or kiss to the door post as it was custom as one would enter the palace, to show your respects, and they were on the main staircase. They ran as fast as they could and skipped stairs as they went. At the last railing post, they turned, rushed back where they had left their parents some hours before.

There they saw The Dutchess, who was kneeling beside the Grandmaster's bed, silently and profusely weeping. This was shocking in and of itself because they could not remember a time when they had ever seen her cry.

As The Dutchess looked up at them, she was astonished. Her two sons were without their top outer garments, one of them bled from their nose and had a cut above his left eye. The other's shirt was untucked, pants were dirty and streaked with mud. The dirt from the ground and sweat from his body had made a thin layer of mud in spots all over his chest and back.

Already in emotional anguish, she became overcome with rage, she jumped to her feet and bolted towards them so fast, all you could hear was the swish of her long dress. She stood in the middle of the room glaring at them.

"Have you both gone mad?! How selfish can you be?" she exclaimed as she landed a thick slap on the side of each of their faces. The brothers would not dare move, react, or block it, as they knew better than that.

They looked at each other with anger and hatred brewing in their eyes. Santos quickly responded first.

"Forgive us, Dutchess. We have acted like fools," Santos said in serious tone.

Dantias stood stiff and said nothing.

"Wash your faces, clean yourselves. Now. Do it quickly. Your father wishes you both at his side. The time has come," she said sternly.

Both brothers, without hesitation, walked to the washing bowl that was sitting on the table. Lifting the jar, they poured out water into the bowl and washed their faces and removed the dirt and mud from themselves. Then they dried their faces with the small blue towels that had been provided for them.

Santos noticed that his father laid motionless on his back, eyes closed, and breathing slow, shallow breaths. A slight, breathy, whispering sound could be heard from the other side of the room.

Each brother walked towards the Grandmaster's bed. The walk felt as though it took forever. Thoughts, memories, and emotions filled their hearts and minds. What could ever prepare a person for a moment such as this?

A small, lone violin could be heard, softly playing out in the garden, under the balcony ledge. It was a soft, soothing sound that quieted the storm that raged within their thoughts and minds.

Dantias stood at the left-hand side of the bed, and Santos at the right. As they slowly kneeled beside the bed, they could feel their mother's presence just beyond the foot of the bed, watching, criticizing their every move.

Then, Lord Houlton opened his eyes, looked upon his boys, and smiled. His hands trembled as he tried to raise them. Each son reached and took one of their father's hands.

Lord Houlton was now much too weak to speak, but he tried his best.

"You... you...you, both," he whispered.

"Yes father?" They answered together.

"You... both...are... my, boys. - I... I... have... loved you... and..." Lord Houlton breathed deep and continued with a weak voice.

"...and... taught, you, all... I... know."

"Yes Father, we are ever so grateful," Santos assured him.

"I... bless...you..." he said.

Dantias looked across the bed at his brother, looking for reassurance. Was the Grandmaster blessing only his brother, or was he blessing them both?

Santos responded to his brother with a glance and a nod.

"I... bless... my...my..." Lord Houlton spoke even softer now.

Dantias stared at his father, emotionless, as they waited to hear what he would say next. With the little strength he had in his arms, Lord Houlton lifted his sons' hands, as if he were trying to clasp their hands together.

With a wheezing sound, he said one word,

"To...to-geth-er."

Then, The Grandmaster's arms fell to his side, and he breathed his last.

Dantias pulled his hand away from his brother's, stood quickly to his feet, and he walked out of the room.

The Dutchess surprisingly did not make a sound.

Santos began to cry quietly. He leaned his head onto his father's hand and stayed kneeling at his bedside weeping.

The candles and lamps glowed softly in the room as the violin, with its song of sorrow, wafted in from the garden.

Grandmaster Houlton, leader of the realm, had passed on to the next life.

# CHAPTER 6

"You will regret this!" Dantias screamed at his mother as he ran out of the house.

Things had changed since the passing of Grandmaster Houlton.

The Dutchess had exerted and received full authority over the Houlton Dynasty.

The Council of Kingsmen had agreed that one of the sons, or both, should be next in line to rule as the Grandmaster.

However, the law stated that the former Grandmaster must bless their successor or successors with a declaration. Since there was no audible, official declaration over his sons, even though the order had been implied, all the Grandmaster's authority, lands, belongings, voice, and chair in the council was now passed to his wife, The Dutchess. She was now one of the top reigning authorities of the realms.

As Dantias ran, the palace guards watched in disbelief. The Dutchess stood firmly in the doorway, with a stern and stricken face. No emotion was etched on her face, no remorse, though one single tear ran down her cheek. She looked on as she watched one of her chosen sons run out of the palace, down the path leading to the back gate, Dantias' preferred passage in and out of the palace.

Dantias wiped tears from his eyes as he ran through the dimly lit back province of the Houlton Dynasty, his father's grounds. Dantias' rage grew ever stronger, driving him to run faster. Never had he felt so betrayed, never had he felt so much anger. He ran to find Namid before it was too late.

**(Earlier that day, late morning)**

"No, stop, you know I don't like those," Namid said with a laugh.

"Oh, come on, just try it. You can't say you don't like it if you've never tried one," Dantias insisted as he tried to get her to taste a bichoso cake.

They are cakes, but an acquired taste, due to their texture and acarid-like filling, which leaves a strong flavor in the mouth after eating them. They were a favorite treat of Dantias's, which he ate every Sunday afternoon after they visited the temple.

The custom was every Sunday morning, as the sun showed its first light, they would go to reverence service, and then after there would be a family lunch in the central park, followed by dessert at the baker's cake shop.

The cake was so tart that it tasted quite sour.

"I do not wish to even try it, it smells horrendous," Namid said firmly.

"Well, you're missing out, they're quite good," Dantias said as he smiled, tossed it into the air, catching it in his mouth and eating it in one bite. There was a slight twitch of dissatisfaction in his eye from the tartness, so she still was not convinced it was worth trying.

It was time for the yearly Market Fair once again, which was two years since they had begun their not-so-secret, forbidden romance. They were in love and therefore both oblivious to the consequences. Walking now ever so much more with confidence, on occasion even in public. Now they displayed their love in the late afternoon of the day, enjoying each other's company at the Market Fair, where everyone and anyone could and would be present. It is the only time of the year where all borders are open, and no one is restricted.

The Market Fair was a fun and intriguing event that took place every year over the course of two weeks. It served as a world fair with each realm represented.

There were booths, rides, performances and special presentations. There were theater productions, choirs featuring the best singers from each realm, alongwith bands and musical groups representing the best of the best in each realm with all kinds of instruments and styles of music. There were poetry readings, dance exhibitions, and spectacular art displays.

Every cultural event represented the best artists from each realm. It took months to be selected to present at the Market Fair.

Each realm held localized competitions and once the winners, were selected by the Market Fair committee, they are given the highly honored invitation, a bronze ticket, to present their work at the fair. The Market Fair was the largest event within the Realms, next to the Planetary Games, which were dedicated to the best and most skilled sharpshooters, creature riders, and sporting games of each realm.

"Where do you want to go next?" Namid asked.

"Well, we've seen almost everything and been on nearly every ride and you will not try the bichoso cakes. So, you tell me. What would you like to do?" Dantias replied with a smile.

"Yeah, it has been quite the day. I'm impressed that you have gone this long. Thought you would have given up after that Hlok beat you at the hammer smash game," Namid laughed.

Hlok was a friend from the metal-forging Clydesdale-clan. Though two years younger than Dantias, Hlok was twice as big, much taller, and stronger than Dantias. Hlok had been able to lift the mineral and special metals bags as they were brought out of the mines, from an early age. It had been no competition, physically speaking.

"Yeah, it was dumb for me to even try. Those guys have been bigger and stronger than me since we were eight years old," Dantias replied with a smirk, "Let's get a drink and see if we can catch one of the last showmen."

"Sounds like a plan. There's one more performance up around the path, in the Theatre Dome, we might just make it. Hopefully, the line isn't too long," Namid replied.

Just outside the dome, there was a drink shack. Dantias grabbed a couple of drink bags, paid, and quickly got in line as the last few people went in the dome through the side doors.

The Market Fair was wonderful because every event was free to access, all day, every day.

As they walked up the path, just outside the door, Dantias noticed one of the volunteer workers had a different type of badge on his shoulder band. The workers always wore a blue and red band to identify to the attendees that they were there to help, give guidance, or assist anyone who needed help. They were also there to help keep events orderly and organized. The Kingmen had established a system where each realm had come to respect the others and there truly was truly unity, and no crime existed in any of the realms. At least none that was ever reported anyway.

This volunteer worker had a different colored armband, his was gold, which was like to the ones the palace guards wore.

Dantias pulled up the hood on his outer garment, covered his head, dipped his head down, and walked with Namid inside.

From the shadows the Grand spokesman bellowed as the lights grew dim.

"Ladies and gentlemen! Prepare to be amazed, dazzled, and astonished! What you are going to see this evening, is the best, the most wonderful show of creatures and talent that have ever been joined under one roof! Are you ready?!"

"Yessss!" the crowd roared as they erupted into cheers.

The dome was an exceptionally large arena, designed with seating for close to 2,000 people. With rows of 100, encircling the main stage in center. There was a wooden path leading to the main platform from the far side of the dome, the path looked as though it disappeared behind a large, thick red, and black curtain from where the performers, one by one emerged.

The lights and sounds inside the dome were of exceptional quality. From the ceiling, ropes held up massive sets of lighting and audio tech equipment in place. Each light looked as though it was an individual laser beaming straight toward the main center platform. Other lights moved with color, others flashed to the beat of the loud music, all in perfect synchronization. It was extremely exciting.

"It seems we got in on the best show of the day!" Namid yelled, her voice drowned out by the deafening music.

Dantias smiled at her, not able to hear a word she said, even though he was sitting right next to her.

Presentation after presentation, each of the realms was represented with the most beautiful displays of artistry and skill.

Acrobats, behemoths and quantum trainers and their riders, excellent singers, and amazing dancers, each more impressive than the last.

**(Meanwhile outside behind the Theatre Dome)**

"Hey, Aryan tie him down! He's going to get loose!"

As Aryan turned and looked over his shoulder, he noticed that one of the performers did not tie the correct knot on their quantum's rope, it had easily pulled off the post. Quickly he jumped over the fences, slipped through the bars for the corral and just barely managed to grab the loose rope.

"That was a close one buddy, good catch!" Aryan's father called from across the way.

Aryan was from the Pinto/Worker clan. His family was dedicated to the breeding, training, and presentation of the quantum. It was a trade handed down from generation to generation, all the way back to his father's, father's, father. The family and their riders were the best in the realms.

Every year, Aryan and his family would bring about 20 quantum and their trained riders to the Market Fair for one of the most spectacular parts of the show.

The riders not only could they ride with no hands, standing on the back of one, and on the back of a quantum's tail. Riding a quantum was extremely difficult because they are tricky creatures, that always looked for away to get a rider off their back. However, when they have total trust in their rider, they allowed a rider to take any riding position, riding on the tail being the most challenging due to the animal's walking style and movements, it required expert balance.

A young Pinto girl, with a beautiful, milk colored face, ran over to Aryan.

"I'm so sorry...I was over getting dressed and my makeup done because I go on stage next. I didn't tie him off properly," she explained.

"That's okay, I got him before he got loose," Aryan said.

"So, they going to let you ride in the show this year?" she asked flirtatiously.

"Me? Ha, no. Not this year. That's your job. I'm just the trainer you're the performers. It's not my thing. I'll leave the lights and the fame to all of you," Aryan answered.

"Oh, come on, you know you're the best. I don't know why your father won't let you ride and show off your talents? People would come from all over just to see you ride. I can ride my quantum because he trusts me. But you, you can ride about all of them, you have a gift," she explained.

"Well, thanks. I appreciate the flattery, but it's better this way. I train them,you ride them, and we all get paid. Now you better get moving, you are on after them dancers and drummers are done," Aryan responded.

**(Back inside the Theatre Dome)**

The Theatre Dome suddenly went dark, and a thin layer of smoke crept into the arena, as a subtle musical swelled, and slowly the lights glowed yellow and intensified.

The most elegant dancers emerged, one by one from the shadows. They were from the Mareviteaus Realm, the underwater people. What was most amazing that this graceful race had the ability to breathe underwater and on land. They moved gracefully as they flowed in and out of their choreographed circle. Their clothing glowed ever so slightly, like the invertebrate creatures of the deep oceans. As they spun faster and faster the music intensified, and tribal drums thrummed in the distance.

There was once again a flash and swirl of lights and a loud boom as 10 tribal drums boomed all at once. In the blink of an eye, the dancers were gone, like a magic trick. A circle of strong young men from the Bisonteus Realm were suddenly on the platform, pounding their drums in perfect synchronization.

As the rhythms got louder and louder, the vibrations so strong that the audience felt the bass drums in their chests. As a curtain opened and about 20 quantum and their riders trotted out and formed a circle around the drummers. Each one stood upright on the back of their beast, with blue and yellow smoke lanterns one in each hand.

There was no other place one could see such an amazing show with so many of the realms together, showing off their abilities and talents.

One of the drummers that was closer to the center of the group of massive buffalo-like young men stood out from the others.

Dantias pulled a small spying glass cylinder from his pocket, which he had taken off his laser blaster earlier in the day before he left the palace. Looking through it he could see the drummers even so much closer. Just as he had suspected it was him.

"Hey, look! It's Kiowa!" Dantias spoke loudly, leaning over to Namid and handing her the slender tube.

"What? No, really?!" she responded.

Dantias smiled at her and pointed towards the platform some 70 rows down. She looked and was surprised that it was him. He was distinguishable from the rest, not only because he was taller and more muscular than the others, but because of his braided hair and three silver beads in his beard. He was the eldest son of Kingmen Lord Hyram II.

"How great is that? We know one of the performers and he's one of the best ones at that!" Namid said with great emotion.

Namid and Kiowa had known each other since they were both young. Every other month, the Bisonteus traders would come in from the outer borders to share and trade on Market Street where Namid's grandfather and father had their trading station. They always brought golden-purple honey they harvested from the coalatia trees, dark purple trees with the hardest of bark, which was the most difficult to penetrate. It took great expertise and care to harvest the honey without damaging the trees or disturbing the beautiful Tyrianciacols that live there.

The Tyrianciacol, a flying behemoth, slightly larger than an eagle in size. Its body was covered in scales, which gave the appearance of thick, short feathers. This magnificent beast had a short, pointed beak that it used to pick open tree bark. This allowed it to feast on bugs and honey with its long, thin tongue. Its dragon-like wings and raptor-like legs allowed it to soar, with short forearms that have three clawed toes hanging beneath its wings for gripping. A long tail flows behind it, curling up beneath it when at rest, adding to its undeniable presence.

The Bisonteus people had been harvesting the honey for generations. As the honey was a regular part of their diet, their skin and hair always had a slight purple tinted sheen to it.

Dantias met Kiowa years prior since when he began to sneak out to see Namid and to buy sugar beads.

"Do you think they will tell their story of the Tyrianciacol Dragon?" Namid whispered loudly into Dantias' ear.

"I sure do hope so! That's such a great legendary story!" Dantias yelled back.

The quantum changed formation and speed and ran even faster. The riders back flipped simultaneously onto the quantum that was running behind them. This may not have seemed like a complicated stunt, but it is so difficult on so many levels.

First, there was the coordination of flipping off one quantum and landing on another. Second, the posture required to execute the stance. Third, the landing of the feet into the small planks on the saddle, and finally, making it seem like it was all so easy. Only those who had experience with quantum would even consider it.

A quantum will trust only one rider, rarely two. For this stunt to be executed properly, one must not only train with fellow members of the team for hours, and days at a time, but also with the other quantum, so that when the rider lands onto it will not try to buck or push them off.

This was an utterly amazing display of dedication, training, and timing. Then, suddenly, the drummers made a thundering sound on their drums and the riders came to a halt. The riders, and the quantum bowed, and they walked out.

Out came performers from the highly creative and talented Bisonteaus Realm playing flute-type instruments, and stringed instruments that looked like Namid's bow, but with several more corded strings wrapped around them forming a harp.

Then, just asDantias had hoped, they started telling the story of the Legendary Tyrianciacol Dragon. He had heard it recited before by the traders on Market Street one late afternoon.

With a swishing sound, out flew from an opening in the bottom of the floor, small trained Tyrianciacols. The wild ones could never be trusted to fly around people. Out they flew. One, then two, then five. They were such beautiful soaring creatures. At this size they were smaller than baby quantums. The majestic creatures flew with the rhythm of the drums.

To the audience's surprise they began to tell the story through song in perfect harmony. The men sang low, and then Bisonteus women, who were gliding down from the ceiling, wearing harnesses around their waists, sang the high and middle notes.

The lyrics to the tale were captivating:

(Verse 1) *In a land where legends roam. There's a tale that's carved in stone, Of a creature fierce and bold. A dragon with a heart of gold.*

(Chorus) *Oh, hear the tribal drums resound, As the village stands on sacred ground, This ancient love, this ancient war. The spirit of the dragon soars.*

(Verse 2) *In the twilight's golden haze. The dragon flew through ancient ways. A guardian to those in need. A beacon of hope, a noble creed.*

(Chorus) *Oh, hear the tribal drums resound. As the village stands on sacred ground. This ancient love, this ancient war. The spirit of the dragon soars.*

(Bridge) *In the fire's glow, their spirits rise. Echoes of ancestors fill the skies. With every beat of the native drum. We honor the legends yet to come.*

(Verse 3) *Through battles fought in days gone by the dragon soared across the sky, with fiery eyes and fearless might He fought for justice day and night.*

(Chorus) *Oh, hear the tribal drums resound. As the village stands on sacred ground. This ancient love, this ancient war. The spirit of the dragon soars.*

(Bridge) *In the fire's glow, their spirits rise. Echoes of our ancestors fill the skies, with every beat of the native drum. We honor the legends yet to come, we honor the legends yeeeet to cooommme!!*

With the loud blast of a single horn, the drums hit, boom, boom, boom! The crowd stood to their feet cheering, it was the most spectacular show the crowd had ever seen.

# CHAPTER 7

(EARLIER THAT SAME DAY IN HOULTON PALACE)

"It has been now one full year since my husband's passing. We must learn to work together, and again, I highly stress that each realm must keep its borders closed. The Market Fair is well on its way, serving as our annual unity event. If we allow for more crossing over, order will be disrespected," stated The Dutchess firmly.

Since the passing of Grandmaster Houlton, she had been installed as High Dutchess.

Although it was in accordance with the laws, the other members of the council had not been happy with the way things have been run over the past year.

"My great masters, I know that we have not seen eye to eye on every issue as of late."

"If any," said Kingmen Cotodus of the Amphibtius Realm, as he leaned over whispering to Lord Hyram II with a smirk.

The Dutchess glared at Kingmen Cotodus as she otherwise ignored the interruption and continued.

"I know we have not agreed on each issue as of late, but rest assured, the realms will continue to have a greater order and peace if they stay within their borders. Unity is a priority, but we cannot go back to the days of old when all people were able to go between realms freely. For the sake of our culture, for the good of the realm, we must leave the borders as they are as my late husband, your trusted colleague, stated in his last written report."

The Dutchess began to recite the report from memory, "For the good of all and the unity of the realms; I, Grandmaster Houlton, concur with the council of Kingmen that it is in the best interest of all, that the borders remain closed between realms."

The Dutchess paused before continuing, "True unity is up-holding what our great Master helped establish, we can not lose that."

"Well stated Dutchess. However, I fear we are lingering upon such trifle matters as these, when there are much more impor-tant things we should discuss," Aylo Kuang, Kingmen of the Terrartius Realm explained as he stood to his feet. His shiny techno suit glimmered in the sunlight that shone through the windows.

"What matters do you refer to master Aylo Kuang?" asked The Dutchess with chilling destain.

"The fact is that for a year now, you have been leading our council in the name of your late husband, Grandmaster Houlton. I do understand that the law approves of this and which I have no quarrel with," Aylo Kuang stated.

"Then what seems to be the issue at hand my sir?" The Dutchess asked staring him down.

Kingmen Aylo Kuang made his way around to the head of the table, stopping at the front right-hand corner.

"The issue at hand is this. That every member of this council, and each person in the Houlton Dynasty; from those who work in this palace, on these grounds all the way up to your very own sons, had understood, and I believe this includes you as well, High-Dutchess." His tone became sterner as he took a deep breath and continued, his voice full of conviction and frustration. "Believed that at the passing of our great leader and friend, your two sons would take their rightful place and lead this council into the new era."

Santos who had been present at every council meeting since the passing of his father and was seated in the far corner of the room, stood to his feet, and prepared to speak. However, before he could get one single word out, his mother spoke directly and firmly to the whole council, not just Master Aylo Kuang.

"My dear Kingmen, thank you for bringing this great concern forward. I too care about this issue, deeply in my heart. Ever since my late husband's passing. I wish to address the issue now," speaking as if she was asking permission to continue. As the other members began to nod in agreement and as Kingmen Aylo Kuang returned to his seat, she began to speak.

"My dearest colleagues, great men of wisdom and justice. We are a team that is insearch of the well-being of all, are we not? And what is the path to assure that what our ancestors have foreseen, comes to fulfillment? That we, the Council of the Realms, keep and hold to what we know is true. That each of us is important, and the diversity of this group assures us that peace and unity will always be upheld.

As you have revealed with such great wisdom and security my great Sir Aylo Kuang, that in which each of us has thought about and or questioned, but have never so bravely stated as you today, the relevance of the issue at the question is why The Dutchess is helping to serve and work alongside us, we who need no instruction, in place of the Houlton Dynasty's rightful successors? This is a true and bold statement.

You, the great men of the council have not considered the one thing that I hold dear to my heart, the longing of one whose whole life was to serve the great and wonderful Grandmaster and prepare his sons to one day take their rightful place, fulfilling the ancient prophecy that two heads will govern as one. Is this not a difficult, trying burdensome task? Oh, yes, but I received it willingly, keeping in the forefront of my mind, that if I were to fail, the future of us all could be forfeited. Who else was to walk such a fine line of honor, duty, and readiness? Who else has sacrificed their desires and dreams, with the only desire to see that, one day? One glorious day, all their hard work, patience, and passion would birth the future of a great nation, if you will permit me to say my sirs, a wonderful world.

I have held all this so dear. With the only thought, desire, and hope, that through the preservation of this council, that I, with your assistance, my great masters, preserve the position of Grandmaster for those who carry the Houlton name. Therefore, keeping with the great tradition, that our ancestors established, only a member with pure blood of the house will lead a Dynasty.

This, my great sirs, is my only wish and agenda. By my service to this great council, we all can work together in keeping the bloodline pure and the Council secure and unified." She paused dramatically. A silence filled the council chambers.

"Or I am in error my great lords? And for that, please forgive me," The Dutchess said lowering her head as she finished her grand statement and demurely returned to her seat at the head of the table.

Each Kingmen looked at one another in unspoken agreement with what they had just heard. Then in one motion all of them stood up and in unison responded, "Here, here."

The entire council knocked their knuckles on the table, stating their unity and agreement. The Dutchess then stood again to her feet and with a humble gesture curtsied and bowed her head towards them all.

At this moment a palace guard slipped into the room and made his way quietly to The Dutchess's side, leaning towards her, he whispered into her ear. She turned and looked at the guard without emotion. He bowed his head and quickly removed himself from their presence.

"My dear sirs, it has come to my attention that my services are needed elsewhere at this moment. I beg your forgiveness, but I must retire for the day. I do look forward to our next meeting next week," she spoke ever so kindly.

"Of course, High Dutchess, we are at your service. May you find yourself well," said Aylo Kuang.

Each Kingmen nodded to her as she quickly glided from the room, not even acknowledging Santos as she left him behind.

The Dutchess walked quickly down the hall, and out the doors to the front courtyard where four palace guards greeted her. She then stepped up into her awaiting wind carriage and took off through the front gates accompanied by her personal squadron of guards, and down the road.

Santos, stepped out onto the terrace, with the sunset in his eyes watched, as she drifted away.

# CHAPTER 8

(PRESENT DAY—EPIC WAR)

S antos, standing on the second floor landing pad, which used to be a beautiful terrace above the most immaculate gardens. He looked out over the horizon as the suns were setting. He stood in silence, pondering. The data report kept haunting his mind.

"At what point did everything seemed to go wrong?" He thought to himself.

His suit's intercom tracker beeped. Then, he heard a voice over his com-link communicator, "General Santos, over."

Santos, paused, and sighed, not really wanting to answer.

"General Santos, over. Do you copy?" the voice said again.

"I'm here, copy," Santos answered. "What is it Hammer?"

"Sir, we may have a situation. You might want to come down here and see this for yourself," Hammer stated.

"I will be right there," General Santos confirmed.

Turning his back on the sunset, he walked down the hall and followed down the wide staircase that he knew so well. He was instantly flooded with nostalgic thoughts and feelings as he touched the railing and walked down each step. It was all too familiar, yet nothing in the palace was like it once was. The beautiful marble floors and large wooden doors, the halls adorned with the most detailed tapestries, was now the established mission control base for the Iron Horse team. Their place of security and refuge during this ongoing war.

Santos turned the corner and walked into the secondary armory and control room.

"General on deck," called a soldier with a stern, respectful voice. The entire room stood up at attention, and acknowledged their leader.

"At ease team, as you were," Santos said as he approached the long table.

The table was covered with articles. At one end there were monitors where several members of the tech team were watching the base's perimeter cameras. In the middle of the table were arm shields that were not working properly. A few soldiers were trying to determine the glitch and get them to work properly again. The soldiers looked up out of the corner of their eyes as Santos got closer, trying not to draw attention to the issue before them.

"What seems to be the situation?" Santos asked, directing his question to Hammer as he stood at the far end at the opposite side of the long table.

"Well, the last hit was a massive one, sir. My team sheltered in place until we were able to retreat and regroup here. On our way back in, we discovered this and immobilized it, and then brought it back with us."

Santos looking down at the veloci-pod, lying on the table. Its eyes were wide open, but now they were a deep shape of purple in color instead of blood red. Hammer's team had it tied down with cables. Each cable was bolted and screwed to the table, just in case the veloci-pod tried to move.

Hammer continued, "We noticed that the eyes glitched on and off, and instead of turning red like the others and exploding, they turned purple, and the pod just froze. We decided it was worth the risk, and took action, jumped on its back, held it down, and applied the quick technique that The Professor briefed us on the other day, and well... seemed to have worked."

The technique that Hammer was referring to was something The Professor had briefed the team on two days earlier. The Professor had discovered a flaw in the veloci-pod's inner receptors.

Behind the eye socket on the left side of the head, there was about a one-inch gap, and precisely in that spot, about two inches deep into the head, there was a circuit board that connected to the brain mainframe of the veloci-pod. If a knife, or piece of steel was inserted into the circuit board, you could overload the circuits and cause a brief system shutdown and then as the pod rebooted its system memory, it would be disconnected from the Dark Princes' mainframe.

"Is it safe? How do we know that the Dark Prince isn't watching us right now and hearing everything we are saying? He could be tracking us at this very moment, you could have just given him our precise location soldier," Santos spoke sternly and with a nervous twitch in his voice.

"That is quite impossible my dear boy," an assured, noticeably confident voice explained as it came around the corner from behind a weapons locker.

Santos didn't even have to turn to see who it was. That voice always had brought him peace of mind. It was his loyal Professor.

"I checked it and did a system diagnostic myself. The interlink between the veloci-pod and the Dark Prince's ship is intact but deactivated. We are deciphering the code as we speak. A truly quite commendable effort made by Hammer's team. Resulting in, well, what could give us a great advantage. Work smarter, not harder as I always say," The Professors aid proudly.

"What advantage can this give us exactly?" Santos asked, now with a spark of hope in his voice.

"Well, if we can decipher the code, which I am confident that we will. The first viable option would be that we could connect to the interlink and then tap into the rest of the veloci-pods, turning them all off altogether. Or there's the second possibility, but we will not know until we have the source code from the pod itself."

"Well? What then?" Santos was losing a bit of patience as The Professor seemed to drag out his explanation, as he so commonly did.

"Or, if the code was decoded completely, we might be able to tap into the mainframe of the Dark Prince's flying fortress and either shut it down or at least paralyze it for a time. Until they block us out of their systems of course. But that could potentially give our location away, along with any info we have on our system as well."

"A situation General, as I said earlier," Hammer stated.

"How long till you know?" Santos asked, looking straight into the eye of the veloci-pod.

"Well, it's been about an hour, and we have about one-quarter of it decoded," The Professor said confidently.

"Okay, keep it going. Moving forward I always want two guards on this thing. It is never to be left alone, understood?" Santos said. They all nodded, including the others within earshot.

"Hammer, gather the others. Team meeting in twenty minutes, upper hall. We must have a plan in place when the Professor and the techies have that code deciphered," Santos said with greater confidence.

"Yes sir. On it. Meet you up top in twenty," responded Hammer.

For once in this war, it seemed that things could finally turn around.

**(402 AWOR- Back At the Market Fair)**
**1 year Before Iron Horse is established.**

"What an amazing show that was!" Namid said to Dantias as they were exiting the Theatre Dome.

"Which part did you like the best? I just love the music, the riders, and oh how amazing it would be to fly so graciously one day through the air riding on a Tyrianciacol!"

"Ride a Tyrianciacol? You know that's unheard of, right?" Dantias said with a smirk and a laugh.

"Well, I can dream and imagine, can't I?" Namid answered sternly.

"I need to find a rest station and use the ladies' room," Namid said as she changed the subject.

"The sign says there's one around the corner, towards the back," Dantias said pointing up at the sign, leading her by the arm slightly as they held hands.

There were people everywhere as it was the last event of the day. The Market Fair was ending after its almost four-week run. The crowds were a bit larger than on a normal evening. Even if people had already been there, it was an annual tradition for many to attend the final events, eat at the food stands, or just visit the Market Fair one last time on the final day. They were shoulder-to-shoulder with everyone else as they walked through the crowd.

"I'll just be a minute," Namid said as she walked inside the rest station.

Dantias took advantage of the moment and went to the gentleman's side as well.

He stepped back outside to one side of the ladies' rest station door and waited patiently.

A couple of minutes turned into 10, then 15. Dantias did not think much of it as to there was an extensive line of ladies waiting to get into the rest station. He just assumed that it was the crowds that kept him waiting.

After about 30 minutes he began to get concerned and began to ask others in the line if they could ask up ahead for Namid.

"Excuse me, I am waiting for my girlfriend. Could you investigate and see if she is okay?" Dantias asked a tall, slender Terratrius lady.

"Oh, why yes. What does she look like?" asked the slender lizard-like female.

"Well, she is from the nomad pale-foot clan, a bit shorter than me, but light tan skin and dark hair. Goes by the name Namid." Dantias answered.

"OK, wait here. I will check," she replied.

He waited and waited some more. Dantias has almost started to panic when he saw the tall and slender lady come out and walk towards him shaking her head no.

"There is nobody by that name or description in there. Sorry," she said with a shrug.

"What? That...That is impossible. She went in there just before me. I saw her go in there," Dantias responded, indirectly blaming her for the circumstance.

"Do not get upset with me, I am just telling you what I know. The girl you are asking about, is not in there," the Terratrius woman said sternly and now openly bothered.

"No, that cannot be. I saw her go in there!" Dantias pushed through the crowded line of ladies.

"Namid, Namid, are you in there?" he pushed through the line even more, making his way up to the door.

"Namid, can you hear me? Are you in there?" he stood at the side of the door.

"Hey, you cannot go in there! This is the ladies' rest station; you cannot go in there!" several very bothered ladies shouted at him as he pushed past them up to the door and barged in.

"Namid, where are you? Are you in here?!" Dantias was losing control now and walked through the ladies' rest station. Screams could be heard as he walked past one stall, then another, and another, reaching his way all the way to the back.

"You cannot be in here!" Ladies screamed at him as they ran in and out of the stalls. Dantias did not care now what was proper.

He was determined to find out where Namid was and what was going on. He stormed towards the door where he entered. As he walked out so many murmurs, complaints, and looks of disgust along with stares of rejection from every lady that was waiting outside.

"You appall me, young man! You should be ashamed of yourself for acting in such away," an Equantius mother said to him guarding her young daughter as he walked by.

Dantias stormed off, walking down the path in which they had come only sometime before. Pushing through the crowded street he yelled out her name.

"Namid! Namid!"

As he walked back towards the Theatre Dome's side doors, two guards, on each side pinned him between them. Then two more were behind him and one guard was walking in front of him.

They boxed him in and forced him to walk with them around to the back side doors of the dome.

There, they pushed through the crowd, much less in this area because the event had finished for the evening.

"Here, now," shouted one of the guards to the others.

Then in an instant, they forced him down to the ground, in the middle of the circle of them, slipped a back over his head and three of them grabbed his arms, twisted them behind his back, applied restraints, and lifted him off the ground.

Dantias tried kicking and struggling but it was to no use, seven of them and only one of him. He tried squinting to see through the fabric of the bag over his head but could only see light movement as they carried him.He started feeling dizzy and dizzier. Not only because they were carrying him so quickly but because of the smell. He breathed deeply, trying to catch his breath.

"What is that smell?" He felt even dizzier.

"Must be Elders Weed," he thought.

Elders Weed was a thick grass that grew out in the Nomadic planes, just north of where the pale-foot clans lived. If you dried the weed, burned it, and mixed it with oils, it could be applied as an ointment, with healing properties. However, if you put enough of it on a cloth, or inside a bag and breathed it in in a closed space, it could cause dizziness. If it were concentrated enough could cause one to hallucinate or even go unconscious.

"Hey! Let me go, do you know who I am?! This is an outrage!" He yelled at the top of his lungs, but all that was heard was just quite mumbling under his breath. In his mind, he was crying out for help, but due to his current circumstances, he was just fumbling for words.

Only two guards carried him now, one on each arm, the others followed behind Dantias' feet dragging in the dirt as they kept watch to be sure they were not being followed.

Cough, cough, sniff, snort. Is all that could be heard as Dantias jolted awake. His nostrils burned from some sort of smelling salts the guards had putin his nose, causing him to wake up. Still drowsy, he could make out a couple of silhouettes through the mesh cloth covering his head. As he tried to move, he realized that he is seated in a chair, a wooden chair. His hands are tied behind his back, and he feels the rope threaded through the back of the chair. His feet are tied as well, each leg tied separately to each front leg of the chair. He hears mumbling and talking behind him, at least two male voices. The guards who snatched him he thought. There is still a lingering of Elder's Weed inside the hood, but now with a penetrating sting inside his nose with every breathe, from the smelling salts. He heard footsteps come closer and closer. Then suddenly the hood is pulled off. It took him a minute to focus his eyes from the darkness due to a light in the room shining directly at his face. As his eyes adjusted to the light a familiar silhouette stepped out of the shadows in the corner of the room after the door closed quietly.

"You may feel confused, but before you speak let me tell you that this is for your own good. Due to your insolence, your very own actions have forced my hand," The Dutchess explained in a stern and even more direct manner than usual.

"Where is she?" Dantias asked.

"She is of no concern now of yours," said The Dutchess.

"Where... is she!?" Dantias yelled as he moved in such a way that the chair jumped off the ground.

"As I said, you brought this upon yourself, and her... and her people. You will not forfeit your position for some, some... nomad girl," The Dutchess said with great frustration.

"I am your son. What have you done? Look at this. Tied up like a criminal? And you, you, are thugs! Who do you think you are? Do you just do whatever she tells you? Have you not any decency? Any of you? You couldn't have spoken to me, asked me to go with you? You had to treat me as a common criminal!?" Dantias yelled.

"Oh, come now, you are taking this out of proportion. Just stop this yelling," stated The Dutchess

"Where am I?" asked Dantias. The only answer was silence.

"Where... are...we?" he insisted.

"We are at home of course. In the back of the maintenance building," she said with a smile.

The maintenance building was at the very back of the property of the Houlton Dynasty. Very few people ever visited this area because it was secluded, old, and outdated. There was little use for this building nowadays, only the switches to turn on and off the outer border pylons could be found here. Since most of the pylons had been fitted with automatic timers about eight years ago, the building mostly served as a warehouse and tool building.

Dantias looked up at her with nervous, almost scared eyes.

The Dutchess was a very keen, intriguing, and ruthless woman.

Earlier in the council chambers, word had come to her that Dantias and Namid had been seen at the Market Fair.

This was not the first time she had received a report such as about her rebellious son.

Earlier, as she rode away in her wind carriage, she had the guards take her the long way around the property, then take a side path to the back of the Dynasty's property limits, to not draw attention as to where she was going.

Santos and anyone else watching her leave would just assume she was headed to the city center perhaps conducting some other tasks or going to another destination.

"How long?" Dantias demanded.

"How long what?" she responded.

"You know exactly what I mean," Dantias stared glaring right at her.

"Oh, how long have I followed you, you mean? Well, that's not the point, but you should know that I am not ignorant of this place or the happenings here," she said.

For much of the time Dantias and Namid had met secretly in the front part of this very building. Regularly, Dantias would come home late, entering the south rear gate, his explanation being, that he was out checking the border pylons. So, after observing this on several occasions, The Dutchess sent her personal guards to follow him and confirm his whereabouts, without Dantias even knowing. Time after time, Dantias assumed that he was cleverly hiding their secret relationship. The only ones he was fooling were himself and Namid.

"Ok, you win. Let me go. Untie me. Now!" Dantias demanded.

"Yes, of course, my dear boy. But first, you will understand this. You are now the heir, along with your brother of course, to the Houlton Dynasty. You will act accordingly. There will be no more excursions, secret visits, or things of the like. Am I understood? This is behind us. We will move forward. This never happened. Am I clear?" The Dutchess spoke pointedly .

She nodded to one of the guards to untie his hands. As one hand was being untied Dantias asked once again.

"Where is she?" Dantias demanded as his hands were now untied.

"At least have the decency to tell me where she is, Dutchess," Dantias said with a kinder tone while two guards untied his legs from the chair.

"Don't worry, all is in order. Come now, let's leave this place, these memories, it's all behind us now. We have your future to plan for," said The Dutchess as she extended her hand toward her son in an inviting way.

Woozy, depressed, and incredibly angry Dantias stood to his feet. Pushing her hand away as he walked out. He walked through the wide maintenance building's main room, towards the front door where two other guards were standing.

The Dutchess, who was not far behind him, nodded to the guards, permitting Dantias to pass. As he walked outside, he noticed it was late in the day, early evening, which was strange because the guards had grabbed him late in the evening after the sun had gone down. His mother's wind carriage was a slight distance away and you could hear a behemoth as he swayed side to side, as they commonly did, while it was waiting.

Dantias turned around to question The Dutchess, she was now standing behind him.

"How long have I been here? What day is this?" Dantias insisted.

"Don't worry about all that, come now. Let us go up to the palace," she insisted as the guards circled him on each side.

Even on his best day, he could not take on all of them at once. Even though the Houlton Dynasty guards received basic training in the ways of the household, they were more politically positioned by title rather than real protection. The guards' job was mostly to overpower or intimidate. The reason is there had never been any real fighting or warfare as the Realms have always been at peace. Guards had little to no application for the battle tactics they had been taught.

Dantias and Santos on the other hand, had quite a bit of application, between the two of them. Even so, six guards were too many, and he felt ever so weak.

The Dutchess and Dantias stepped up into the wind carriage pulled by three larger quantum, there was a driver in front while a few other guards mounted their smaller behemoth and rode along both sides. As they approached the back part of the house Dantias spun the ideas around and around in his mind, getting increasingly angrier each time he thought about what had happened and the injustice his mother and the guards had applied to him.

They stepped down out of the wind carriage, and the guards continued leading the beasts back to their places in the housing stalls, located in a separate building back behind the side gardens. One guard followed as they walked up the path to the back door. They entered the family dining hall.

"Oh, Dutchess, for peace of mind, please allow me to know Namid's whereabouts. As a member of this house and future leader of this Dynasty, I desire to care for all our citizens. I cannot do that, if I don't have peace of mind, knowing that they are truly taken care of," Dantias said with a convincing tone. He had always been the more charismatic one of the two brothers. When he was a boy, he once convinced a palace guard to give him half of his daily panú rations.

"You need not worry about her ever again," The Dutchess said firmly, looking at him with assurance.

"Dutchess. What have you done?" Dantias asked nervously.

"Well, she and her family have been banished of course. Along with all her treacherous people."

"You can't do that! Not on your own. The Council wouldn't allow it. They must all vote in agreement. You can't just banish someone on your own, let alone a whole clan! They, they would never do that to anyone without an official agreement," he shouted.

"Oh, but they have my dearest son. I am the High Dutchess, with full support of the council now. Don't worry about such 'tedious' details, you mustn't concern yourself with such things. Not yet anyway," The Dutchess said with great confidence.

Earlier, while The Dutchess was giving her elaborate discourse to the council and before her leaving, each council member received a handwritten letter from her, inviting each of them to sign a partial law document.

A partial law is used to give the highest-ranking council member full authority over, clans, element/food portions, and there even exists a clause that permits such a person to apply the 'banishment' law. The authority given is for a limited amount of time, understanding that due to specific situations, it is not needed for all members to leave their lands and Dynasties for each decision.

When certain situations only affect one dynasty and not the others, this authority may also be applied. In this case, it is an internal situation, which impacts the Houlton Dynasty, thus giving The Dutchess full authority to have a clan reorganized, re-proportionated, or even banished.

"How dare you. You can't do that! Tell her she can't do that!" Dantias said as he looked at the guards for reassurance.

"I'm afraid it's already been done," she said with a smirk.

"You will regret this!" Dantias screamed as he ran out.

"Stop him!" The Dutchess yelled to the guard at the back door, another was walking around the corner just then from putting the wind-carriage in its place at the stalls.

The two guards moved quickly, blocking Dantias' path as he ran out the back door. They pulled out their electric lighting-staffs, a broad staff that had an electric tip, which had a turquoise blue glow to it, at the end. If you were only to get touched by it, you would be paralyzed for a least twenty minutes.

Dantias approached them running, not even concerned about their staffs. With a quick, yet subtle motion, he spun around low to the ground and with a 'scorpion tail' kick swept the first guard off his feet, then with a descending heel kick to the head, the guard was instantly unconscious. With two more steps he ran, and the second guard approached, then with a quick flying sidekick to the guard's chest, he was easily bested. The guard groaned as he lay on the ground trying to catch his breath.

As Dantias continued to run, the other palace guards watched from afar in disbelief. The Dutchess stood firmly in the doorway, with a stern and stricken face. No emotion was shown, no remorse, yet one single tear ran down her cheek.

Dantias ran, ran with all his might. Wiping his tears as he ran, he had to find Namid and her family before it was too late.

# CHAPTER 9

I t was late in the evening, the perimeter security pylons were lit. A single light beam could be seen turning on the top of each one, slowly searching and turning. If the light beam were broken for more than three or four seconds, an alarm blast would sound not just from one of the pylons but from each one, because they were all connected to each other and that would then trigger an alarm at the main guard house as well. Dantias slowly approached the edge of one of the pylons' beams of light. It was a tricky task to get past them, but something he had done multiple times before. You just had to be slow about it, but this time, time was no longer on his side. He had to be quick, just not too quick as that could trigger the alarm.

At the edge of the Houlton Dynasty's property, there were several lines of these pylons, interchanging between each other as they turned, as to never allow a section to not be without a light beam shining over it. The beams crossed paths with each other as they turned. Dantias had a trick though that he had used many times before.

When he was younger his father would allow him to go out with the guards that did maintenance on the pylons, so Dantias learned all the ins and outs of how they worked. So now, every time he wanted to sneak out and see Namid, he manipulated the pylons in his favor.

He carried a small light beam transmitter in his pouch that he had taken off an older model of one of the pylons. He re-programmed the transmitter to work in such a way that if he shined it on the head of another pylon, into the light eye circuit; it would blind the pylon and freeze it in position for a moment. If he did this in a zigzag formation, he could slip between the beams unnoticed. The trick was to time it exactly right.

Dantias laid low to the ground to not bring attention to himself, in case there was a guard, riding a quantum and out on his security rounds. He extended out his hand in front of him and flashed the pylon that was closest to him with his modified light beam transmitter. He pushed the button twice, sending out a mixed signal as he crawled on his belly toward the pylon.

Flash, beep, flash, beep, flash, beep, beep, beep.

It froze and turned off. He was up in an instant, ran up to the pylon in a crouching way,and as he persisted on to the next pylon to his right. He had a few minutes tops before it turned back on again.

His ear twitched back as he heard a noise off to his left, off in the distance. Footsteps, trotting of a quantum. Not one, but two, or even more. He could tell because they were not keeping the same rhythm. He had but mere seconds to get through the next pylon before the one he was kneeling at turned back on, and once they turned back on it was ever so difficult to flash the same one again because the relay inside the pylons does a code change when they reboot.

The guards, still a way off, were getting closer.

"So, what'd ya do yesterday?" one guard asked the other as they trotted along on their quantum.

"Ah it was my day off. I took the family to the last couple shows out at the Market Fair," the guard stated.

"Was it any good? I heard that last year's presentations were better," responded the guard.

"I agree, but the riders this year were surprisingly good, better than us anyway," he said as he chuckled.

Dantias flashed the next pylon.

Flash, flash, beep.Flash, beep. Beep, beep. The pylon emitted a sound and click as it froze to a stop.

The guards were coming closer. He made it through the first and second rows but still had three rows to go.

He flashed the next pylon, now to his left. As he slipped through it, he could see a dust cloud rising a bit in the dark from around the quantum's feet as they trotted. The evening was getting cooler, so a slight misty fog was beginning to rise off the ground. A little cloud burst could be seen from the nostrils of the animals as they exhaled, trotting along.

He was through to the next pylon. He heard a clicking sound and a long beep behind him. That was the sound of the first pylon coming back online. Its light beam blinked as it came back on and began to turn once more. No going back now. Two more rows to go and he was through.

The guards were approaching the first pylon Dantias had snuck past.

The second pylon he had gone past flashed brightly as it reset, beeped, and began to turn once again.

"Did you see that?" one of the guards asked the other.

"What?" he asked.

"One of the pylons flashed and they started up again. Like it was off," said the guard.

"Ah, it was just stuck and then got unstuck again. You know how those things are, they're always acting up," said the guard with disinterest.

Dantias flashed the fourth pylon with his transmitter.

Flash, flash, beep. Flash, beep. Beep, beep.

It was off and Dantias was quickly up next to it, squatting as low to the ground as he could. Only one more to go.

The third pylon flashed brightly behind him, the guards were now parallel to his position, four rows away.

"There it was again. Don't tell me you didn't see that?" the other guard said.

"Yeah, saw it that time," his counterpart said reassuring him.

Just then, a third guard -an officer- came toward them, riding from the opposite direction and blowing a whistle. They turned to receive him, flashing their handheld lamps at him to reveal their position.

"Now's my chance, while they're looking away," Dantias thought as he flashed the fifth and final pylon, he waited anxiously.

Flash, flash, beep. Flash, beep. Beep, beep.

It was off and froze to a stop. Quickly he rolled past it and was up on his feet, he ran in the dark. His breath could be seen right in front of him as he breathed deeply with every step.

"What's going on?" one guard asked the other as he approached.

"Probably some stupid new rule from The Dutchess again, I'm so sick of that woman," his partner stated abruptly.

"The boy is gone! He took out two guards up at the palace and is trying to escape. The Dutchess wants him back, now!" the officer raced towards them and shouted in a profoundly serious tone.

"What now? He didn't get to bed on time? Little rich boy needs his mommy?" one of the guards said sarcastically.

"Ah just let him be, he's better off away from here anyway."

The fourth and then the fifth pylon flashed a bright beam of light as they reset, beeped, and clicked back on. The last pylon got stuck as it made half a turn, making it seem as if it was blinking or signaling to that very spot.

"There, look. Last row!" the officer said while looking just past the flashing pylon and saw Dantias' breath in the air in the distance.

"There he is! Let's go!" the guard officer ordered as he lunged out into the pylons riding his quantum.

"And you thought this was gonna be a quiet night did-ya?" the other guards looked at eachother, one nodded and rolled his eyes, "Let's go then. Ya, come on!" he said as he kicked his quantum in the side to get him to go from a stand to sprint.

"Oh man... this is not good!" Dantias said aloud to himself as he ran.

The three guards rode quickly in the direction Dantias was running. The sensors on the harnesses of the quantum flashed as they ran through the pylons. These sensors worked as a fail-safe switch allowing the riders to ride through the pylons without triggering an alarm. The sensors were much more difficult to hack because they were coded to the rider's DNA and name. Only specialized palace guard quantum riders were ever given one. There were only 12 riders, 12 sensors in all and they were registered and counted every night.

They were quickly gaining on Dantias as he ran – he had about a 100-yard head start. He knew there was no way he could outrun the guards, so he quickly dropped to the ground. The grass was about knee high here just at the edge of the palace grounds before it tapered off into the sandy dirt that is found in the rest of the province.

"I can hide here if I lay low and breathe slow," he thought, as he dropped into the grass, trying to slow his breathing. Deep breath, hold, slow out through the mouth.

"Breath. Control. Relax," he could hear his father's voice in his mind as he calmed himself.

"You see him? Where'd he go? Find him!" the guard officer yelled at the other two.

"Just wait, standstill," one of the other guards said, "Watch for his breath. Watch the grass."

They pulled their quantum to a halt, eyes scanning the tops of the grass, waiting for Dantias to let out a small cloud of breath.

Dantias laid as still as possible. Back on the ground, looking up to the sky as he controlled his breathing. He could hear the steps of the quantum as the guards began to walk them slowly in his direction. One of the guards rode just past his feet, only an arm's length away. Another passed about 10 feet away from his head.

"That means the next one will be riding just over me in a couple of seconds," Dantias thought to himself.

As he turned onto his right shoulder, he could see the grass moving as the rider got closer. He pulled out a small knife, held it in his right hand, and waited for the rider to get just a bit closer.

He could feel the temperature of the air change slightly from the body heat of the beast as it came closer. Dantias dug the toe of his boots into the ground, readying himself to lunge up and out of the grass.

Dantias jumped up, one step, then two, he leaped in the air past the quantum's face, the animal spooked and jumped back. As the rider turned, surprised and a little scared, Dantias mid-air realized it was his mother's palace officer guard, one of the three captains, he regretted what took place next, but the action was already in motion, unable to stop now. His knife swiped the side of the officer's neck, slicing it clean open, while grabbing the opposite shoulder with the other hand, pulled the officer off his quantum, sliding slightly off its tail, landing on the officer's body as they both hit the ground.

"What...? What...have... you..." the officer took a deep breath but said nothing else as he bled out. A loud screech of the officer's quantum was heard as it ran off into the distance, back towards the palace.

The other two guards heard the noise and spun quickly around, like a top. In an instant, they circled Dantias as he knelt beside the lifeless body of the officer guard.

"Well, well, well. What's this now? Looks like you're in a bit of a predicament boy," said the guard in a sly tone.

Dantias breathed deeply but controlled his breath and looked up at them both as they rode circles around him at a safe distance.

He took another deep breath before opening his mouth and unleashing his rage, "Come on, let's get this done. I'm not going back, I gotta find Namid, and not you or anybody else is going to stop me!"

"Whoa, whoa, whoa. What's all this about now? Who? Look I don't care who you're looking for. We got a report that you took out two guards up at the palace and now killed an officer. Killed! There ain't been no killing in these lands for hundreds of years. You got some big problems friend," said the guard as he and his partner looked at each other before they came to a stop, one on either side of Dantias,as he stood to his feet.

"Look, if you let me go. I will be sure to repay you. If you help me get free from the tyranny that is taking place in these lands, I will give you great rewards. I am the only one that can do that. Are you content with the life you're living now? Do you not desire more? More for yourselves. More for your families. I could help you to never work as a servant again. I can make you Lords," Dantias spoke with a very convincing tone and sureness.

"And how's you gonna do that? You're down there and we're up here. We have our orders," one of the guards said.

"Well, so did he," Dantias said as he stared into their eyes.

There was a slight pause. The guards looked at one another and nodded quietly to each other.

"So, what's next then? The Dutchess wants you back and about now the officer's quantum is returning to the palace grounds," the other the guard said.

"Look, I must find Namid," Danitas said with frustration.

"Tell us then,"one guard said gesturing to Dantias to explain what had happened.

As Dantias recounted the events of the evening a quantum bent his head and started chewing on some grass.

"You see, that is why I must find them," Dantias continued, "I must find them before they are banished. Then, I must stand and stop this tyranny before this whole land is impacted by The Dutchess."

"If you help me,you have my word. All will be put back into order. I have that authority, I am a son of Grandmaster Houlton, the late Lord of the Houlton Dynasty. My mother, The Dutchess, is taking measures into her own hands, this cannot be. It goes against all that is good and established in the law," Dantias spoke with great conviction.

"Ok, kid. Let's say we do help you. What's your next step?" a guard asked.

"You let me go and give me one of your quantum. I will ride out and be sure that the nomad tribes do not leave. I will tell them the news of what has happened. I know they will stand with us. You will return to the palace and explain that you were unable to capture me. I defended myself against a striking blow from the officer guard, leading to his death. Leave the body here as evidence of my escape. Do you know snakeweed?" he asked.

"Yes, of course. I used to run in the plains as a boy," one of the guards said.

"You find snakeweed, grind it up, and then take it to the palace kitchen. In the cupboard, on the second shelf, there is a small, tin canister that has tea in it. This is the tea that The Dutchess prepares herself every morning and evening," Dantias explained.

"How do you expect me to get in there to do all that?" the guard asked as he laughed at the boy's plan.

"Just do as I say, it will never be traced back to you," Dantias reassured him.

The past several years Dantias has not been content at home, under the watchful eye of his mother.

He was not as evil as one would think. He was simply tired of all the politics, rules, and hypocrisy that he felt his family projected to the world.

Many times, he had thought, and planned, of ways to do away with this great stress and pressure but never acted upon this.

Although Santos was like him in every way, this is where he and his brother part ways. Santos has always been the one to walk respectively, even when he did not agree with the methods or the way of doing things in the Houlton Dynasty. Santos was loyal and obedient. Dantias on the other hand had always been more outspoken, questioning and even defying authority at times to find, what he thinks would be a better way.

"Just get into the kitchen, go to the cupboard, and on the second shelf put the snakeweed in her tea. Just do as I say and all will be fine for you. You have my word," Dantias insisted.

One of the guards slid off his quantum and handed the reigns to Dantias.

"Okay kid, but if this goes bad. I ain't taking no heat for you. We will bring the whole law down on you and banishment would be the least of your worries," said the guard.

Dantias slipped upon to the quantum and with a swift kick to its side, they sprinted away.

"I hope you know what you're doing. If we get caught, that is the end for us. I got a family ya know. I cannot go down for anything like this. Who will take care of them?" the other guard said nervously.

"Don't worry, just let me do the talking. If it goes south, it will be on me, not you. But if that kid does what I think he is gonna do. You and I got it made. No worries at all," said the guard to his partner.

"Come on, let's head back, come on."

The guard pulled himself up on to his partner's quantum, and once they were sharing the saddle and began to make their way slowly back to the palace.

# CHAPTER 10

D antias rode as fast as his quantum could run.

The quantum are very distinct behemoths, not only because they can run three times faster than a person, but they have adapted to the land in which they are bred or born.

The Houlton Dynasty is an arid area with the occasional heat wave from time to time. The quantum, which are born there have a high tolerance to heat and don't need to drink as much water. Their nostrils have also adapted and grown microscopic hairs and skin flaps inside the nose which prohibit excessive amounts of dust particles from getting into their lungs.

In the drier arid regions, their skin sags just a bit and this allows them to retain moisture and stay cooler longer. Even though they are herbivorous, they do like to eat small bugs from time to time, crunching them with their back teeth as their front teeth have small grooves in them, like small blades that help cut the foliage as they graze.

Riders must always be careful because just a small little nibble from a quantum could cause one to easily lose a finger.

The quantum thankfully also had the ability to see as clearly at night as they do during the day. Their eyes have a second, slightly thinner, eyelid, which protects their eyes during the bright sunny and dry days. At night, the second eyelid retracts, allowing extra light to enter the eye and a membrane on the inner eye gives moisture to it to keep their vision clear no matter what the circumstance may be. The quantum was not able to see far away, but they see very clearly all around them.

Dantias raced through the night. The suns had long set, and the night was now cold. The wind blew colder as Dantias rode further into the night. Though he did not notice the cold as his mind was set on one thing, one thing alone, to find Namid and put a stop to the banishment.

As he arrived at the Nomad settlement on the furthermost plain, Dantias was shocked and outraged to find the area completely empty. Usually, there were tents and families as far as the eyes could see.

This was one settlement of the nomadic clans. There were more clans, but no one truly knew how many, because the nomads purposely didn't register all their family members to keep a low profile. Dantias knew of Namid's clan, and two others, but had heard stories from her grandfather that there were more than 15 clans. Each clan had a multitude of workers, traders, and even warriors. Though it wasn't custom in the rest of the Dynasties to have warriors as they lived under the laws of peace. The nomads also practiced the old arts, passing them from one generation to the next.

Dantias jumped down off the quantum, still holding the reigns. Kneeling to the ground he looked for footprints, for any sign to show which direction they could had gone. He searched for a clue, broken over grass or shrubbery, marks in the dirt, anything that could give him a bit of hope in finding them.

The nomadic clans are experts at hiding. If they don't want to be found, it was almost impossible to find them. At a moment's notice the whole clan could pack up all their belongings, tents, and goods they may have, put it on a few behemoths, and be gone. They traveled in such a way that they hid their tracks, making it exceedingly difficult for them to be followed.

Over the years, Dantias had learned a few of these techniques from Namid's family, but his mind was distracted tonight. He couldn't concentrate clearly; he was a few feet away from his quantum as he frantically searched about the area where the camp had once been. It was late, cold, dark, and he was exhausted.

The quantum walked slowly chewing on some bush leaves.

Suddenly, the sensor on the quantum's chest made a click and a short beep sound. His ear quickly twisted back and then his head turned with a snap. Dantias rushed over and took the animal by the reigns and pulled him close. A small beeping noise was coming from the sensor, meaning there was a transmitter close by. He took off his outer garment, laid it on the ground, holding the top of it, one side in each hand, he dragged it across the ground as he walked slowly backward. He moved side to side in a sweeping motion all around the area where the quantum stood. The dirt moved slightly as he continued to brush and sweep it away. He was losing hope, feeling frustrated once again, and then as he moved a small sensor was revealed. The little red light on it blinked. He quickly knelt to retrieve it, but as he did, he noticed there was a thin string tied to the bottom side of the sensor. Dantias lifted it with great care. As the string rose from the dirt, it traveled a few feet and then stopped, tied to something stuck deep into the ground. He rushed to his knees and began to dig.

Snugly, inside a shallow hole he found a disc plate. He pulled the plate out of the hole and turned it over. As he held the plate in the palm of his hands, he could see a short message written on it.

*"We have gone to the meeting place. I pray you find us well." -Tala*

It was a message left for him by Namid's grandfather, who had practically raised her. Her parents died when she was incredibly young. Sadly, many of the nomad clans had lost family members at that time due to a terrible virus that had spread through most of the clans.

"This is not my fault. I did not banish them. It was The Dutchess," he thought to himself.

As he looked down, he noticed a piece of an arrow at the bottom of the hole, which pointed straight ahead of him. That had to be the way they had gone. If they are followed the path to the meeting place, an old sacred burial ground for the nomad clans, at the pace of their behemoth, he could catch up with them easily on his quantum. He climbed back onto the quantum, and with a quick kick to its side he sprinted off.

**(Present Day – Epic War)**

Santos stood at the far side of the meeting table. The table which was once used by his father and the council of Kingmen. It had lost its shiny luster. The great hall also looked much different now than it did then. There was a time when the room, the table, and chairs,had a great presence to them. The white walls had turned to a darkened gray, the tapestries that had once hung on the wall were now dirty, faded, and several of them were torn with threads unraveling on the sides.

"Gather around," General Santos called, as the other team members walked through the door.

Hammer, as usual, was the first one to report, followed by Bliss, and then Ace. The Professor was already standing behind Santos going over a readout on his digital monitor.

"What have you found out boss? Got the code so we can blast these jerks?" asked Ace in his usual sarcastic tone.

Hammer smirked as Bliss rolled her eyes.

The Professor turned and stood at the right hand of General Santos, with a concerned look on his face. Santos turned to him and gave The Professor the opportunity to update the team on what was taking place.

"I can reassure all of you that we are on the right track. We now have more than half of the signal decoded," explained The Professor.

The Professor looked Ace straight in the eye, indicating that he required his silence for a moment as he knew Ace was about to speak up. The Professor continued.

"But we have learned that as we decode, the signal code changes ever so slightly. Meaning, that the last part of the deciphers may take a bit longer, at least until we can find the chase code, within the code. Thus, blocking it and stopping it from changing further," The Professor explained.

"Thanks for the update. Please keep us posted," General Santos said as The Professor walked out of the room.

Santos turned to his loyal team.

"While The Professor and his techies continue, we need to have a plan in place. Once we break that code, we can shut off the signal, and finally have the upper hand in this war," he stated.

"Or control it," said Bliss.

The other team members turned and looked at her, with puzzled stares.

"What do mean?" asked Santos.

"You said we can shut off the signal once we break the code. I only said, 'Or control it,'" repeated Bliss.

"Control it?" Ace asked.

"Yeah, take control of it. Don't turn it off. That's brilliant," Hammer said with a smile.

"Hammer, could we do that? And if we can control it. What could be controlled?" asked Santos.

"Well, in theory. Everything that is powered remotely from the Dark Prince's shuttle," answered Hammer.

"Could we control the ship itself?" asked Santos.

"I doubt they use a remote code for the ship. But the fighters and the veloci-pods," Hammer assured him.

"Ok, let's say we can control those veloci-craps. What advantage can we take from it and how do we apply it? I mean, we just have a bunch of pods running around, or can we use them as weapons?" asked Ace.

"Well, as I understand it from The Professor, we could use them just as the Dark Prince does. To attack. All the same functions they must attack us, we could use them to attack them," responded Hammer.

"Now we're talking! How are we gonna do it, boss?" Ace asked with great enthusiasm as he clapped his hands.

"This is what I propose," Santos explained as he rolled out his digital map.

A digital map was like a paper map, but slightly thicker. It was an amazing technology that The Professor and his team produced a few years before. It gave the user a 2-D view, like a paper map would, but also had a 3-D function that allowed the user to see the notes, plans, terrain, and layout of the 2-D area. It was even possible to program future outcomes based on the data entered, creating strategic battle simulations. General Santos had a digital map that he was updating through his arm data link. The team all leaned on to the table as Santos began to explain.

"As you can see, here are the rolling hills just beyond the border. I want a perimeter set up there. Our intel tells us that the Dark Prince lands his fortress just beyond the ridge between attacks. There, he replenishes supplies runs system updates and reloads and repairs the veloci-pods. That's when we must hit him. While they are landing, and not a moment after. If we attack while they are updating and reloading, we run the risk that the code could change and the veloci-pods could download updated code, which we would not have," Santos explained.

"What about the guards and the other fighters? They're always on watch while they restock," asked Ace.

"That's where you come in," Santos continued.

"While they are descending and about to land, we upload our modified code, taking control of the pods and fighters. Then, we shut the fighters down, and don't let them get off the ground. The pods, become ours. Then, Hammer and his team, will bring in the heavy loaders, just off the first hill from – here," Santos excitedly pointed to the digital map and showed the animated simulation.

"Then while Hammer brings in the diversion with the long guns, Ace and his riders will come in from the other direction straight on towards the Dark Prince's landing station," explained Santos.

"But that's the most heavily guarded area boss! It would be suicide. They're quantum, not tanks brother!" Ace exclaimed.

"That's why the mission Bliss will undertake with me is of the utmost importance," Santos said as he turned to look at Bliss.

"I will take the pale-foot troops along the bottom of the hill to draw out the veloci-pods, while you take your sharpshooters along the top of the ridge. Your team will give us cover below, while you break off through here, pointing to a small tunnel halfway through the hills. Go through there and to the other side and you'll find a terminal, there is a docking port link, one of four. It's easy to see because there are solar panels on the top. Those terminals are used for communication," Santos explained as he pulled out a modified arm com-link transmitter. "You can use this to connect and upload the new code."

"If this plan is done correctly, down to the second, The Professor will have access to the veloci-pods. The fighters will be landed, the pods will turn and attack. My team will be on the ground, Bliss's team will provide cover from above, Ace's team will breach the Dark Prince's land defense, and then Hammer will bring up the rear. How about it?" General Santos asked.

They group looked around the table at each other, smiled, and nodded their heads in agreement.

Santos gave one more order as he clicked his arm comlink, and the rest of the team's coms beeped,

"Then we agree. Sending you the stats and info on your arm com-links now. Take this info, meet with your teams, and brief them on every part of this plan. Remember, if we get this right, we could stop this attack and end this war. This would bring peace and justice back, not only for us, but every clan and Dynasty, and the Dark Prince will be defeated and will face the consequences for all that he has cheated, lied to, and entrapped. I'll keep you posted on The Professor's progress, once we get that code, it'll be time to go. Let's make it work team!" General Santos spoke with authority.

The team responded with the usual, "Hoorah!" as they pounded their fists on the table in unison two times.

# CHAPTER 11

D antias rode through the night, as the sandy wind spurted and blew up into his face.

The first sun was just breaking over the horizon and the shadows were long. As he rode, he could see two large trees in front of him to his right, which marked the meeting place. He leaned into the quantum, and they glided together as he rode on.

Even though he and his brother were gifted quantum riders, Dantias had always been the better quantum rider. Especially after the time, Santos was bucked off one. After that, Santos lost all interest in riding ever again. The memory flashed through his mind, and he laughed aloud to himself.

Approaching, he could made out a few makeshift cloth shelters. The clan had set up a temporary camp under the sacred trees.

Suddenly a blinding flash hit his eyes, then another, then another. He looked up and saw it was one of the nomad men sending him a warning signal. He had seen it once before with Namid, as they walked across the plains. A dust devil was coming. On the plains, it was usually a large one, or multiple medium-sized ones.

He turned and looked over his left shoulder as he rode and sure enough, there it was, just behind him coming straight towards him. It blew and spun as it barreled his way. Then, he realized it was not one, but two quite large ones that were about to become entwined as they moved.

His quantum ran hard, but then suddenly, it was spooked by the high wind and jumped to a halt. Sending Dantias flying over its head and into the air. He landed hard on his back, knocking the wind out of him. Dantias rolled and struggled to catch his breath.

Pushing himself up and he sat on his knees as he breathed deep, exhaled, then again and once again.

The quantum squealed as it ran off in the opposite direction. The dust devils were but 100 yards off and the wind thrashed him as it flung sand and dirt into his face.

The clan rushed to secure their things. They ran towards the trees and began to tie loops and harnesses to the tree trunks, using them to hold onto and secure the behemoths. It has been said that a strong dust devil had swept away a whole clan before; people, goods, behemoths, and all.

Dantias stared into the sky, expecting the worst. He was too far off to make it to the trees and there was no way he could outrun the dust devil. The wind was picking up speed, he pulled his outer garment over his head to cover his ears, face, and eyes. As he tried to stand, the wind pushed him back. He could see a silhouette through the hood he had made and heard how the scared quantum screeched as the beast was pulled up into the sandy tornado.

"I'm next," he thought.

Just then he was body slammed onto the ground by two men from the nomad clan, one grabbed each arm. They had run towards Dantias just after the signal flash was sent. They wrapped a rope around themselves and Dantias then dug quickly into the ground with their ground hooks, the nomads would carry with them.

The ground hooks served as an extremely useful tool in many different tasks. It was used to harvest fruits and vegetables, as an anchor to keep a behemoth from walking off, to climb trees, and if it was tied to the end of a strong rope, it could be used in an emergency as an anchor into the ground to keep one from being pulled or blown away from a strong dust devil.

While the dust devils blew over the three men, Dantias was exceedingly grateful that they had two ground hooks with them. As the wind ripped over their bodies, they held on with all their strength, their legs began to be pulled up into the air. Their clothing was ripped as the wind blew heavily upon them.

"Do not let him go!" one of the men yelled with all his might. His voice sounded as but a whisper in the middle of the storm.

It seemed like an eternity. The people prepared, tying hooks to the trees, behemoths, and ropes between each other. Then, just at the last moment as the two devils spun together, they dissipated. The men fell to the ground.

Dantias lay there for a moment in total shock, trying to make sense of what had just happened when he heard great laughter to his left and his right.

"Hahaha, what a welcome!" the men laughed as they got to their feet and dusted themselves off.

Dantias looked at them puzzled and then began to laugh. The three of them began to walk towards the sacred meeting place.

As they approached, Dantias could see that everyone from Namid's clan was there, dusting things off and making sure all were okay and in order. A few people dealt with the behemoth and quantum that were still tied up, giving them water, and calming them down.

"There you are my boy! I was beginning to be worried about you both!" Tala, Namid's grandfather called as he walked out to meet them.

Tala was an impressive figure, even though he was older, he had a strong and muscular build. He walks with a confident stride that exudes authority and commanded respect. His skin was a pinto shade of white and a warm reddish-brown. His face weathered, with a thick protruding jawline. Half of his face white and half brown, painted diagonally down the center leaving the skin around his eyes colored brown and his nostrils and mount colored white. His eyes were a piercing blue, sharp and focused, with a hint of kindness that belies his fierce exterior. His hair, a mane of thick, once dark black locks, which had with the years turned to gray. He kept it tied back in a braid that reached down to the middle of his back.

He was a protector, a guardian, and completely trustworthy. Tala loved his granddaughter deeply and would do anything to keep her safe from harm. He was fiercely loyal and dedicated to his family. He had been completely devastated by the loss of his daughter and son-in-law. This caused him to have an unwavering commitment to Namid's well-being.

When Tala was around, others could not help but show him respect. His mere presence commanded attention, and his unwavering integrity and strength inspired admiration in those around him. He was a natural leader, and his wisdom and guidance were sought after by both young and old.

Dantias walked closer, and as the other two men walked by Tala, they nodded to him and he to them as they passed, acknowledging their great survival feat.

"I knew you would find the message," Tala said with great delight. But then his facial expression changed, Dantias noticed that Tala had a puzzled look on his face.

"You came alone? Where is Namid, why have you not brought her with you?" Tala asked.

"I thought she was with you. I had come to find you both, to warn you of what has taken place," Dantias said confused.

"Did you not receive a message from The High Dutchess?" Dantias asked.

"What message? I have received no news or word from the palace," Tala answered.

"If you have not received word from the palace messengers, why have you come here?" Dantias asked.

"It is custom, that after the great celebrations of the Market Fair, we retire here for a season. To rest and rejoice. Give thanks to the Maker for family, blessing, and all the wonderful things that He has provided. It is our annual migration," said Tala.

With all the disturbance and stress, Dantias didn't think of that. That's how he had known of their meeting place, he had traveled there with them two years prior. Dantias was in anguish.

"If Namid isn't here, then where is she?" Dantias wondered.

"I must tell you what has happened. It is urgent, this news, which will not bring you peace," Dantias said controlling the panic in his voice.

"Come, we will sit under the shade of the tree and drink. You will tell me about Namid and all that has taken place," Tala said with a nervous tone.

He and Dantias proceeded towards the largest of the two trees nearby. Tala motioned to a couple of the women to bring refreshments to drink. As they sat together, and with a heavy heart, Dantias told Tala and two other elders from their clan what had happened.

How they were celebrating together at the Market Fair, and after the great show they had witnessed, they walked out to the rest stations, and how Namid had disappeared, and then how the guards trapped him. Every detail he could remember, he retold his tale.

Dantias explained how his mother threatened to banish their clan and all the other nomad clans as well.

He told them of his anger and how he felt betrayed by his mother, and how he wanted to fight her, but restrained himself.

He spoke of his escape through the pylons, the guards who had trapped him, and sadly the officer he had killed in his outrage to get find Namid. Then, how he took his quantum and had arrived there.

"I fear the worst." Dantias said as a tear rolled down his cheek.

"This is a very disturbing story, my boy. Very disturbing," Tala spoke with a heavy heart.

"We must organize a search party. We must prepare the men to fight. To find her!" Dantias said with great urgency.

"No, we will wait," Tala replied as the other elders nodded.

"What do you mean wait?" Dantias asked. He felt outraged.

"Namid knows where we are. She knows of our plans and annual celebration. She will find her way here," Tala said with confidence.

"But what if she is hurting, or being hurt? What if she needs help? She could be waiting for us to rescue her right now," Dantias insisted.

"She doesn't need you now. She needed you before, and you were not there. So now, we wait," said Tala.

"Are you blaming me for this? You think it's my fault she was taken?" asked Dantias.

"We cannot blame those who oppose us, only those who we confided in," Tala stated.

"It's not my fault that The Dutchess sent guards to kidnap her! They took me as well!" Dantias said very frustrated.

"The law of your house prohibits you to have a romantic relationship with a person of the nomad clans, correct?" Tala asked.

"Well, I guess so," Dantias replied.

"There is no one to blame, but the one who has disrespected and disobeyed," Tala spoke with a stern look on his face.

"I didn't cause any of this," Dantias sulked.

"It's been done," Tala paused for a moment then continued, "We will trust the Maker. He will protect and bring Namid home. Meanwhile you will stay with us. Our preparations and celebration will continue. We will speak of this to no one else. We will trust and wait upon the Maker."

When Tala finished speaking the other elders nodded in agreement, then the three turned and looked at Dantias to see his response.

Dantias looked at them in the eyes, full of rage, and clenched his teeth. His muscles flexed under his shirt. He paused, took a deep breath, relaxed, and then acknowledging they were right. He nodded and hung his head between his knees.

"Ok, it is settled then. Tonight, we celebrate life and family as a clan. Let us prepare," Tala said as he stood up, dusted the dirt off his clothes and walked away.

Dantias sat, wiped a few tears from his face, stood up and looked out over the plains. Hoping, praying that Namid would find her way to them soon as anger simmered inside him.

# CHAPTER 12

Two days had passed since Dantias had been rescued from the dust storm. The day was now gone but the clan's celebration continued.

Each family had now set up their respective tent and settled in for the season as the celebration commenced. The vibrant and lively celebration brought together the entire community. As the suns set on the open desert, the rhythmic beating of drums filled the air, and the sounds of joyful laughter and chatter could be heard throughout the camp. The aroma of fragrant spices wafts through the air, mingling with the sweet scent of freshly baked 'panu' bread.

The clan had gathered in three large circles, shared sugar beads with each other, and danced to rhythmic flute music as their colorful traditional garments swayed with the beat. The dance was a celebration of life, love, and unity, with each movement expressing gratitude to the Maker for the blessings bestowed upon the family and the community. As the evening progressed, the night sky was illuminated by the warm glow of flickering torches and the twinkling stars above, casting a unifying ambiance over the gathering.

Young children were playing, and their laughter blended with the music creating an atmosphere of pure happiness and contentment.

The elders sat together under the larger of the two trees, shared stories of the past, and imparted wisdom to the younger people sitting around them.

Then as the last sunset, the great campfires were lit, as was custom on the final night of the celebration.

Dantias sat off to the far side of the smallest of the three campfires He could not find the desire to celebrate under the circumstances.

Suddenly, the celebration came to an abrupt halt. Namid stumbled into the center of the gathering. Her feet dragged with exhaustion, her clothes were tattered, her face bruised, and her nose was bleeding.

A hush fell over the crowd as all eyes turned to her, their expressions a mix of shock, concern, and anger. The rhythmic beat of the drums ceased, and the once lively atmosphere suddenly turned silent, and the air filled by an uneasy stillness.

Tala's face darkened with anger and frustration as he strode forward to meet his granddaughter in front of the largest campfire. His normally warm and kind demeanor was abruptly replaced with a steely resolve as he looked her over and assessed the situation.

Namid stood weak and trembling, her eyes downcast as she struggled to remain standing. She was exhausted and broken.

In an instant, the women of the community sprang into action. They rushed to her side and offered comfort and aid. They quickly led her away from the center of the gathering, their voices murmuring words of reassurance and support.

Meanwhile, the men swiftly mounted their quantum, their expressions set with determination as they prepared to ride out and secure the perimeter of the camp.

Dantias jumped up and ran towards the tent where Namid was being cared for, when Tala stopped him.

"Leave her. She must rest. You must wait," Tala said sternly.

"I must see her. We must know what happened, where they took her. I must speak to her," Dantias replied insistently as he walked towards the tent.

Tala took him by the arm and looked directly into Dantias' eyes.

"You. Will. Wait," Tala spoke in such a way that it brought a deep fear into Dantias' stomach.

The celebration had been transformed into a scene of urgency and concern as the entire clan came together to ensure the safety and well-being of their community. The air crackled with a sense of solidarity and determination as they mobilized to address the unexpected threat that had disrupted their peaceful gathering.

**(At the palace 2 days prior)** - The **evening Dantias ran away.**

"What took you so long?! Where is he, did you not bring him back?" The Dutchess screamed at the two guards as they dismounted off the back of their quantum.

These were the same two guards that made an agreement with Dantias the evening he ran away.

"We looked everywhere Dutchess. We didn't find him," one of the guards stated while the other nodded his head.

"You are worthless, worthless! Must I do everything myself?" The Dutchess raged.

The two guards stood still and received their tongue-lashing. It was common for them to hear things of this nature from her. Many of the guards had heard similar words from her. However, it had increasingly become even more common since Grandmaster Houlton's passing.

Santos came rushing downstairs as soon as he heard the yelling in the back gardens. As he approached, he could see that his brother was not there, and the situation was getting progressively worse.

"You will organize a search group, and at first light, you will go out and find him. Bring him here to me and I will deal with him myself! Am I understood?" The Dutchess had entirely lost her composure, as she poked the guards in the chest as she continued to yell at them.

Santos stepped in taking the hand of one of the guards just as he bowed his back slightly in defiance and began to lift his arm towards The Dutchess.

"I will organize the search first thing in the morning Dutchess," Santos said as he shook the guard's hand. "Good work sirs, thank you for your excellent service this night," Santos reassured them.

"Just find him," The Dutchess said with in a stern tone as she spun away and stormed off into the palace, her flowing robes trailing behind her.

"It's been quite the day gentlemen. You should get some rest, tomorrow we will regroup and head out with the others at first light," Santos explained.

"Yes, sir," They replied in unison as they nodded.

As they too began to leave, one of the guards turned back and spoke to Santos.

"Say, my lord, it's a bit of a ways back to our quarters out on the edge of the grounds. Might I have your permission to pass inside and use the washroom?" the guard asked in his most courteous tone.

"Why yes, of course, it's late. Go ahead," Santos replied.

The guard nodded to his partner and walked into the palace. There was a washroom just past the dining hall, on the other side of the palace kitchen. The guard proceeded to walk towards it carefully and quietly.

Slipping into the kitchen, he flicked on his personal lamp and walked towards the cupboards. After opening four he finally found what he was looking for. On the second shelf, there was a small black canister of tea crushed into a powder just as Dantias had said.

The guard brought it down and set it on the small table that was in front of him, just under the cupboard, and unscrewed the tin lid that kept the tea powder secure inside.

The guard reached into his outer garments' left-side, inner pocket. His hand found a small handkerchief and he brought it out from inside his cloak. He glanced over his shoulder, to be sure no one was watching, and he unfolded the handkerchief, revealing five short strands of dried snakeweed. He quickly crushed it between his fingers, thankfully he had gloves on to not get the poisonous powder on his skin. He then proceeded to sprinkle it into the canister and mixed it with the contents of the canister. When he finished, he quickly dusted off the little bit that fell on the table, put the canister back into its place, and quietly closed the door to the cupboard. He then slowly tiptoed out of the kitchen to go back out and leave.

As the guard stepped around the corner Santos confronted him. The guard jumped back startled to find him.

"Did you find it?" Santos asked.

"Find what?" The guard answered stuttering.

"The washroom. You were going to the restroom were you not?" Santos asked.

"Oh, yes of course. It just took me a bit longer, sorry. Is has been a long day,and even longer night sir," the guard answered as he recomposed his posture.

"Please send word to the rest of the crew that tomorrow we'll head out at first light," Santos ordered.

"Yes, I will tell them my Lord Prince," The guard answered. He quickly made his way through the dining hall and outside once again to his partner. As they headed off to the guards' hall he winked ever so slightly to his comrade, gesturing that it was done.

Santos stepped around the corner into the palace kitchen, and looked around briefly, not noticing anything out of place, then he too went off to his quarters to rest. He expected the next day would be a long and stressful one.

**(The next morning after Dantias ran away)**

Early the next morning, the first and farthest sun, which had a purplish glow to it, came over the horizon. Its hue was a blend of violet and magenta, casting a soft, ethereal tone across the horizon. Despite its distance from the planet, its radiance was unmistakable, adding a unique and captivating view.

Santos organized his search party, which was made up of several of the palace guards and himself, to embark on a quest to find his brother.

The Professor came out of the side door entrance walking towards Santos. Looking around he noticed there was not a quantum for him to ride.

"And where is my two-legged beast?" asked The Professor.

Santos turned and looked over his shoulder at The Professor, he was about to swing up onto his quantum.

"I'm sorry my dear friend, but your services are not required today. I need you here in case Dantias returns before we get back. I can't leave him alone with The Dutchess, can I?" Santos said.

"I suppose not. Besides, you know I don't like riding these beasts anyway. Why would you insist me to ride along," The Professor said with a sarcastic tone.

"Well, get on your way, your brother has a day lead on you. Do you even know where to look?" The Professor asked.

"I have an idea where to find him," Santos said.

"Which way will you go first?" asked The Professor.

"I have a feeling that he may be out past the pylons out towards the rainforest, the lands of The Aprosmarteus Realm," Santos said.

"Good idea, they seem to take in anybody these days. You better hurry, once the Market Fair is over the paths and roads over there will be full of travelers returning home," said The Professor.

"Yes, sir," Santos said as he adjusted his right then left gloves before he proceeded to swing his leg up and over the leather seat on the back of the beast.

"Men, comrades. As you know, we are on orders to find my brother. Bring him back here safely and help re-establish order at the palace. This is not a joyride. This is no time for games. I expect your utmost attention, help, and respect. Is that understood?" Santos stated with a strong tone in his voice.

"Yes, my sir," the riders said in unison.

"Let us be on our way then, and put this affair behind us," Santos shouted as they took off.

As they rode out the back gate, Santos led the riders towards the east, in the direction of the rainforest lands of the Aprosmarteus Realm, as he had said to The Professor.

However, Santos knew his brother wasn't there, he knew full well where Dantias was. Santos knew Dantias with was in the North, with the nomad clans. The place where his brother had sneaked off to so many times before.

Even though Santos wasn't certain about Dantias' relationship with Namid, he knew his brother spent a lot of time with her and her clan.

His plan was simple, yet noble at that. He would ride out towards the east, then circle back around towards the north to the nomad's territories. They were always around there this time of year, and if they moved or migrated, usually they went east, thus allowing Santos and his search party to cross paths with them as well.

Santos was trying to uphold his brother's reputation, even though he didn't agree with his decisions most of the time.

The only thing is, that to follow that path, their journey led them through dense underbrush areas, a labyrinthine of rocky terrain, where there would be several, potentially dangerous, obstacles.

# CHAPTER 13

Santos and his companions, the strongest and best trained of the palace guards, kept a steady pace as they followed the smooth road out and around the palace's border. They had already passed the furthest, eastern pylons of the grounds, Santos did this so that the exit would be registered on the security record back at the main security room. He then began to take a slow turn to circle them back to the north.

"Hey boss, we ain't heading the right way if you wanna go over to them crazies?" asked one of the guards who was towards the back of the group. It also happened to be that he was one of the same guards that had found Dantias the day before and helped plant the snakeweed in the tea box meant for The Dutchess.

Santos slowed up and turned back, and allowed the others to catch up to him, as he was, he was six strides ahead of them.

"What did you say?" Santos questioned him as they got closer.

"I said, if you want to get to the land of the wilds, this ain't the way, you're leading us off track," the guard replied.

The wilds he was referring to were those who lived in the Aprosmarteus Realm, a land of all those who didn't fit in. The guards commonly called them wilds among themselves, since they were people who didn't follow any set rules.

"Yes, you are right," Santos said, "We're not heading towards the rainforest. I have reason to believe that my brother is not there, but instead, has gone north toward the nomad clan's territories."

"Okay, that's fine and all, but why didn't we set out that way in the first place? You take us around this way and we gotta go over towards the mining area, that's rocky terrain, it will take more time. Plus, as I assume you know, there are packs of them terrible sombru dragons over the mining ridge," the guard said as they caught up with Santos, all of them coming to a stop.

"I understand all that, but there shouldn't be a problem, we're traveling light, which means we can outrun them, and there's not very many this time of year, the miners reported very few sightings and hardly any danger. The mining crops were the best they've been in years,"Santos said.

"Well, you're the boss. I just don't like it, but whatever," said the guard.

"Where is your sense of adventure brother? We're traveling by daylight, and it's early. They won't be looking for us or be a bother. We'll be fine," said another guard reassuring him.

A sombru dragon  is the name the people gave to a quick agile animal with black scales, a smaller behemoth, which means "shadow predator". Their scales absorbed light, making them look shadowy.

Nobody knew who coined the name first, the Asno miner clan, the Clydesdale clan, or one of the half-blood clans. The sombru dragons are slender little creatures with strong bodies, allowing them to move swiftly through the underbrush. They have long tails to help with balance and sharp, curved claws that make climbing easy. The sombru dragons have a narrow, elongated head with smart, keen eyes with a hint of amber in the darkness, they can see easily in the dark mines and caves. For an Equantius, the creature was about knee high. Its jaws lined with two rows of sharp, serrated teeth, one row on the inside, and another that shows on the outside of the mouth, and with a keen sense of smell and hearing. They were strong hunters who can take down prey much larger than themselves with precise skill.

Despite its fierce appearance and predatory nature, the sombru dragon was also known for its social behaviors. It could mimic a few hundred sounds, with its resonating nostril and vocal chamber, making itself sound almost identical to other animals, using these sounds to set traps for prey, deceiving them, and making them a next meal. They were smart, resourceful creatures, using cleverness and agility to out maneuver both predators and prey in their dense, underbrush habitat.

As the day went on, the second sun shined bright, and they ventured closer to the caves and mines. Santos knew that as the path turned back, they would have to leave it to continue north, thus taking them up and over the hills where the Asno clan had built their homes.

Santos stayed ahead and led them out on a side path as to not draw attention to himself or the group. The last thing he wanted right now was to be spotted by the miners and need to stop and explain why they were passing through.

The Asno mining clan were serious people who like to get into everybody else's business. Even though they are genuinely kind, they were nosy and gossiped quite a bit. If you ever wanted to get the news out or be sure that one of the scrolls was shared with other clans, all you had to do was be sure the Asno clan heard about it, and the information would spread throughout the whole Dynasty.

Surprisingly, they were perfectly accurate as well when they shared the information. They had a gift for being analytical, and memorizing dates, times, and specific information.

The Professor's father was of the Asno clan, which explains his giftedness in taking notes and never forgetting a single fact.

Santos slowed down, making sure the others caught up to him. He wanted to be sure they were all together as they made their way past the caves, up and over the hills, and through the thick underbrush. As the others approached, they all loosened the reins, allowing their beasts to rest a bit before they continued. The quantum hung their heads as they grazed in the taller grass and shrubbery.

"Do you see anything on or over the hill?" Santos asked one of the guards, who had just looked through his digital scanning goggles.

"I don't see anything, but a few half-bloods smoking their pipes, over at the mouth of one of the mines," he pointed, "Looks like they're taking a break."

"Lazy bums," the guard said as he began to laugh. They all, except Santos, chuckled, shaking their heads.

"I mean I'm glad and grateful for all that metal they bring up outta there, and all that handy stuff they can make, well between them and the Clydesdale-clan. But dang brother, do they sit around a lot," said another guard as they continued to chuckle.

"Okay, enough. Focus on the task at hand. Stay together, don't go too slow. If anybody sees anything, speak up. Let's make this crossing quick and smooth and get over to the other side of that ridge before the eclipse," Santos said.

There was not one ridge really, there were three. One ridge where the mouths of the caves could be seen, the entrances to the mines could be found there. Several were natural cave entrances, that the Asno clan used to go into the hills and dig down deep to extract the metals and stones from within. Other openings have metal beams and wooden doors on them, created entrances, dug out, and some even blown open with small explosives, creating an entryway into the hills. Several small tracks and paths could also be seen coming in and out of the caves and hills, paths that the Asno clan followed with their behemoths, pulling up and out the carts full of the precious stones and metals they harvested there.

"Let's go men. Don't bring attention to yourself and stay alert. Everybody has their lightning stick ready, just in case?" Santos asked.

"Yes sir. Ready," replied the guards.

Each one gave a slight kick to their respective quantum, and they were off, trotting around, then up onto the first ridge.

The Asno men didn't notice them as they passed in the distance. They were relaxing and enjoying a hand of jinxbrum, a type of card game they liked to play.

Several Asno-clan workers could also be seen lighting up a few hanging torches and half a dozen hand torches that hung outside the caves. Even though it was daytime, the time of day was approaching when the suns and the moons would align and cross paths, creating a daily eclipse for about two hours, it was never an exact time because of the elongated orbit of the planet around the largest second sun. Even though a person could still see, and it wasn't completely dark as night, it would get dark enough to need a hand lantern or torch if you were out in the field and not in the city.

As they moved up over the first hill, the terrain seemed to shift ever so slightly. The grass was a bit taller, the brush a bit thicker and the next hill in front of them now marked a slow curved silhouette in the distance. The tangled undergrowth seemed to test their endurance as the quantum pushed through the thorny thickets and now twisted roots. The thick-skinned behemoth changed from a trot to a walk, working a bit harder to get through the brush that was now up to their hips. The leather strips on the legs of Santos and the guards protected them from the piercing thorns and scratchy thistle grass.

The search party moved cautiously through the denser brush and grass. Their senses were heightened by the eerie silence that was around them. All you could hear was the rustling of the grass as the wind blew through the shallow valley between the hills. The suns and the first moon aligned in perfect harmony, and then the second and third moon followed, leaving a long shadowless valley in front of them.

"Hand lanterns on," Santos said. Secretly he was questioning his decision as he had forgotten to calculate for the daily black-out.

"We'll be fine," he whispered under his breath.

Suddenly, the quiet breezy silence was broken by a shrilling cry. It sounded as if a baby quantum was crying out for its mother like it was caught in a hole, a snare, or was in some kind of danger.

All the quantum surged forward towards the cry. Santos pulled back on the reigns, bringing his quantum to a halt, but as soon as he would relax the tension ever so slightly the beast would lunge forward again, pushing towards the cries.

The screeching got louder, and louder. The quantum females in the group, began to cry out as well. The quantum became

increasingly agitated, pushing and searching about. It was becoming more difficult to hold them back and control them.

Then, at once, before they could react, dark devilish shapes
emerged from out of the brush.

"Sombru dragons! They're coming up out of the valley!
Look!" shouted one of the guards.

They flashed their hand lanterns frantically about trying to
catch a glimpse of where and how many they were.

Their obsidian scales blend seamlessly with the eclipsed day.
Their dark eyes reflected an amber light in the grass. Panic and
adrenaline surged through Santos and the rest of the search
party as they scrambled to prepare to defend themselves against
the fast onslaught of the other worldly creatures.

Every quantum screeched a terrific sound as they lifted their
heads and began to run in the opposite direction.

"Stay together, follow me, turn to me!" Santos yelled out trying to bring order to the instant chaos.

The dragons launched themselves at the search party, easily
rising above the backs of the quantum. With ferocious speed
and deadly intent, they continued to attack, one after another.

Like a flock of birds migrating or escaping a storm, the quantum began to run together. Santos the head of the v, two riders
at his right, two at his left, and three lined up behind him, they
raced diagonally towards the next ridge. Snapping and slashing
sounds could be heard just behind Santos, the sombru dragons
were trying to bite the feet of the quantum. Between the thick

grass, protruding roots of the brush, and the snapping teeth and claws of the dragons, one of the quantum stumbled, almost tripping over itself.

Each of the guards held their lightning sticks firmly in their hands, ready to hit and shock the little demons. As the sombru dragons leaped up and out of the grass, every so often a guard would make contact with one of them, shocking it and bringing it to a screaming fall to the ground. The quantum cried out with blood curdling screams, with an almost rhythmic timing. Hearts pounding and adrenaline coursing through their veins, they kept riding. Fighting and hitting with all their strength. The ridge was just ahead, and a glimmer of a purplish light could be seen around the sun as the moons covered it, overlapping one another.

Santos looking forward, yelled out to his men.

"A bit further, then we can have an advantage, come on!" his voice rang out.

Then three sombru dragons slipped through the brush like fish in water. There was a screech as two leaped through the air toward one of the guards riding towards the back of the formation. A fourth dragon bit his quantum's foot causing it to stumble while the others latched onto the guard's back and left shoulder, he screamed out in terror as the claws jammed into his spine and ribs. All a sudden a fifth sombru dragon latched itself onto the thick hind leg of the quantum, not able to pierce its hide, but making it trip and fall. The sombru dragons worked in perfect unison as a strike team, nothing could stop their powerful attack.

The other guards frantically kicked their own quantum to get them to run faster, but it was no use, the sombru dragons were upon them. Another two jumped out of the thick grass, side-swiping another guard, and taking him to the ground. Two additional dragons ran up from behind and the pack began to bite and rip the clothes and flesh from the guard's legs and body.

Santos cried out, "Faster, follow me!"

The fate of the search party was hanging in the balance as they were confronted by the terrifying shadow dragons, the riders were in a fight for their lives.

Arriving up at the top of the second ridge, the guards gathered around Santos, three of the guards were missing. They looked out on the valley and could hear the excited, rejoiceful screeches of the pack of sombru dragons as they feasted on the fallen. A lone quantum could be seen in the distance as it ran back, towards the direction of the palace. Its silhouette could be seen drifting away on the horizon as the first moon passed from its eclipse with the suns and the sky became a little bit brighter. A long shadow was left over this valley of death where groaning could be heard as the little monsters ate their prey, alive. Santos hung his head as he turned away and motioned to his mento do the same.

"There's nothing we can do, let's move on," Santos said. Counting himself there were now five in the search party. They all sat solemnly for a moment, with shoulders hanging low, they let their guard down.

With a blood-curdling shriek another sombru dragon jumped up out of the brush, this one was quite larger than the others. It grabbed Santos' arm and flipped him off his quantum. The remaining behemoths jumped and kicked, nearly throwing their riders to the ground. The men scrambled at the reigns regaining control. Santos quickly jumped to his feet, briefly examining his arm, only a ripped shirt and scratch that allowed a little bit of blood to trickle out on his clothes and then drip to the ground.

"Where did it go?!" Santos yelled out, as the other riders circled around to his position. Their beasts had been startled and had run out from their position.

"I don't see it boss!" one guard yelled back.

Santos whistled to his quantum, he had a bond with this one, as he had trained and ridden it before. The quantum, who had run off to the next ridge, lifted its head and faithfully began to run back to Santos' location.

Then another baby-like cry could be heard afar off. The guards gathered around Santos, waiting for the little monsters to come back. Nothing. The cry got louder. Then a click, click, chirp, chirp, screech! One of the mounted guards saw in the distance, six or seven dragon heads popped up out of the brush from where they were feeding on their fallen comrades. Another guard noticed a long tail coming quickly through the brush and tall grass behind them. It seemed the larger sombru dragon was calling them all to come right to where they were standing, ready to attack and feast again. They came ever so swiftly, running through the grass and brush, without even a sound. The sound of sticks cracking and grass swishing was the only sound that could be heard.

"Ride! Go now!" Santos shouted.

"We can't leave you sir!" the guard shouted back.

"I said, go! Now! There is no time!" Santos ordered.

The guards looked a teach other in horror, nodded, kicked their quantum, and jumped off into a sprint. The sombru dragons were closing in on Santos' position, he could hear them coming. One of the shadowy dragons lunged out, coming down upon Santos. Its silhouette could be made out in the sky, like a graceful ballet dancer it came at him soaring high above. As it came falling, claws and teeth ready to destroy the flesh, Santos extended out his left arm and grabbed hold of the quantum, who had not stopped running towards him. Santos whisked himself up onto the back of his behemoth just as the black demon landed, in the exact spot where he was standing.

One of the fleeing guards looked back, seeing the miracle screamed out, "That's the way my lord, woohoo!"

Santos pulled the quantum to a tight circle, not slowing a bit. The largest of the sombru dragons was right behind him, as the other seven quickly joined it in the pursuit. This was no training or practice riding; one mistake and Santos knew he'd be joining his fallen comrades. They ran; they ran hard. The others were a good hundred yards ahead of him.

"That's okay," Santos said to himself.

"Better me than them," he thought.

The other guards rode on, looking back and slowing their pace, looked on in terror as they saw the dragons closing in on Santos.

"Keep going, don't look back!" Santos yelled.

The relentless predators closed in on him, their feral eyes almost glowing in the dim light of the eclipsed moons. Santos urged his two-legged behemoth to go faster, the sound of its feet, crunching through the brush, could be heard with the pounding of his own heart. He didn't dare let go of the reigns and reach for his lightning-stick, too risky. The chase seemed almost endless, Santos not giving attention to the direction they were running, kept riding with all his might. Every muscle in his body tensed as he tried to outpace the relentless hunters.

The largest of the sombru dragons was now just on his right heel. Not able to grab the quantum, but with any slip or misstep, it would all be over. On his left three smaller sombru dragons had caught up to them as well, he turned his ears back and could hear the others snarling behind him.

There seemed to been eerie glow over the grassy landscape as the predators stalked their prey. The chase felt like a nightmare-wanting, hoping to wake up, but to no avail. Santos' heart raced with fear. Then suddenly, with a slash and snap from the monsters, the quantum cried out as they bit part of its tail, though the loyal behemoth would not stop running, it was unclear now if the quantum was running for Santos or to save its own life. The grass got taller and taller, thicker even. Santos' companions were steady in their pace, but he was getting even closer to them now.

"Could it be my quantum was running even faster?" he thought to himself. That would make sense due to the literal life-or-death situation right on their heels.

Up over the next ridge they flew, the thick brush had turned into a smooth tall grass, reaching now to the shoulders of the mounted riders.

All a sudden, the sound of horns blasting could be heard in the distance. Santos looked around quickly trying to make out from where the sound came. Again, a loud resounding blast of a horn.

The sombru dragons leaped and slashed, at the quantum once again, it squealed out in terror. Then, out of nowhere, with lightning-fast speed, a spear flew just past Santos' shoulder and slammed into the neck of one of the dragons that was chasing him. One spear, then another, it was like an onslaught of precise marksmanship. Santos couldn't believe it! As he turned and raised his head, he could see three, no four Bisonteus riders heading directly towards him.

With all the chaos, without realizing it they had ridden much further north and drifted into the grasslands of the Bisonteus

Realm, where Lord Hyram II had served faithfully as Kingmen for many years.

Santos kept straight as he rode and the Bisonteus riders passed him, not even looking at him. They were focused on their common enemy, the sombru dragons. These little monsters were no match for the courageous warrior clan, they have fought them off with ease, repeatedly. Santos finally caught up to his comrades who were now moving forward at a slow walk, allowing their quantum to catch their breath. Santos kept time with their pace as well. Relief came over them as they realized that they were now safe.

Two more Bisonteus riders moved towards them. A large shadow covered the riders as they approached. One of Santos' guards looked up to see a silhouette covering the suns.

"Would you look at that!" he said surprised.

The others looked up, shading their eyes from the suns with a Tyrianciacol, quite a bit larger than the ones Dantias saw at the Market Fair, soaring over them.

As Santos and his men smiled at one another, he looked ahead and noticed a familiar face, one of the riders was Kiowa, Lord Hyram's eldest son.

"It seems you are a way off your land, Prince," Kiowa said looking at Santos and assessing the situation as they approached.

The Tyrianciacol circled back around and slowly hovered down, as he landed on a perch mounted to the back of Kiowa's saddle, appearing as though Kiowa himself had wings, the wind made from his wings moved all the grass that was around them.

"It looks that way, my friend," Santos replied, "We got off track, due to all the excitement. I must say, that's a quite impressive companion you have there with you, my friend."

"Oh him?" Kiowa said with a smile, turning and giving the winged behemoth a small morsel he pulled out of a leather pouch that was tied to his belt.

"I didn't know the larger Tyrianciacol could be trained," said Santos.

"We call them Quetzal-Tate, it means wind dragon, and this one's been with me since he was just a hatchling. We train and raise them you know," Kiowa said proudly.

While Santos looked past the muscular riders, and their amazing, winged companion, he was looking for their land barriers. Tall wooden poles with red or blue flags on top of them, they are placed every several hundred feet, marking the separation of the Realms.

"I don't see the border markers anywhere around here?" Santos questioned.

"That's because you passed them over a mile ago. Our scouts saw you coming at full speed. We figured you had company who wanted to join you for dinner," the Bisonteus warrior laughed.

"Well, are we ever glad, even blessed, for your help. Three of our party had fallen, just back over there, past the second ridge," Santos explained.

By this time, the other riders were arriving, coming up behind them.

"Sorry to hear that," Kiowa said with a sober tone. Then he turned and spoke in a dialect of his language to the others of his clan, in return shook their heads with solemn looks on their faces.

"So, what are you doing all the way over here, and coming unannounced?" Kiowa asked.

"Well, that's a long story, but the short of it is, we are looking for my brother. He has run off and The Dutchess has sent us out to look for him," Santos responded.

"It seems that your plan isn't going quite as hoped," Kiowa stated.

"Why don't you come with us, eat and rest? You cannot continue like this," he said motioning to the search party.

"That would be ever so kind of you, I would be in your debt," Santos answered.

"Nonsense, you will owe my father!" Kiowa said as they all chuckled.

"Many of us are just arriving back from the presentations that our clan made at Market Fair. It is an enjoyable time to be in the camp. Come with us," Kiowa said to them as he turned, heading back in the direction he came.

He said a few words in their native tongue, and instantly two of the riders jumped to a run and rode their quantum ever so quickly back towards their camp.

"I must find Dantias before things get even worse. Men, some of them fathers, and all of them comrades have lost their lives for his selfishness. We are quite far off track, but am I glad to be with these guys," Santos thought to himself.

As the last of the moons passed out of the eclipse and continued in their orbit, streams of smoke could be seen rising in the distance. Fires from the Bisonteus' encampment.

Kiowa with his warriors, and Santos with the remaining guards rode side by side, towards the camp. Relieved but somber, they continued their way.

Bisonteus Realm

# CHAPTER 14

As Santos and his men followed the Bisonteus warriors, they ventured further into the Realm.

After about half an hour of riding, at an easy pace, they were greeted by the sight of mudbrick houses, their earthy tones blended seamlessly with the natural surroundings.

Although the camp had no paved streets or signs, it was organized, clean, and peaceful. There was a clear sense of order and purpose in the layout. The sounds of laughter and conversation filled the air, accompanied by the occasional long groaning sound of a behemoth or a joyous squeal of a quantum.

The landscape surrounding the encampment was flatter, which allowed one to see as far as your eyes would permit, with no disruption at all along the horizon. Just a few clusters of the large coalatia trees, which were harvested for the special honey. The striking silhouettes of several wind dragons could be seen in the tops of the trees as they flapped their wings in the distance, interrupting what would otherwise be a blank slate of a panoramic view.

"There are so many of them, and so close to your camp. Doesn't that bother you?" Santos asked.

"Not at all. We share the trees with them. There are more than usual though, as it is mating season. They come down from their dens in the far north and mate out here in the trees. We try not to harvest while there are so many, but they will migrate north in a few days. Not to worry my friend," Kiowa explained with a smile.

As the group got closer to the camp the men marveled at the intricately designed, handcrafted details on each home. Many were adorned with vibrant symbols of the clan's heritage. The camp was bustling with activity, families going about their daily tasks in an almost perfect harmonious rhythm that spoke of generations of tradition and community spirit.

The corrals on the far side of the camp were filled with the most exemplary behemoth. The quantum and behemoth of this realm looked physically similar, but there was no question as to what the beasts were, yet as they did have their differences in appearance. The most obvious difference was that they were larger in size and had longer tails than the quantum and behemoth of the Equiantus Realm. Their skin was even slightly different as well. Here the quantum had a slight bluish tone to their skin, while those of Santos's realm were more of a sandy tan color. This is probably because here the grass was thicker, taller, and much more plentiful than in other realms, here there was no lack of water or vegetation. Their presence added a sense of vitality and connection to the flow of nature around them.

While riding through the main path of the camp, the air was filled with enticing aromas and mingled scents of wood smoke, cooking fires, and fragrant herbs, giving a journey of the senses into the heart of the people's culture and traditions.

Children could be seen dancing and playing to the rhythmic beats of handcrafted drums. As they continued, heads began to turn, and many noticed the visitors that came following Kiowa and his warriors. Although others were welcome, it was not a common sight to see visitors from other realms travel through here.

Kiowa turned and looked over his shoulder gesturing and speaking to Santos, "This way, we are almost there." Santos followed in line, nodding in confirmation.

Veering slightly to the left, the group approached one of the humblest, yet respectable homes in the encampment. It was clear that this was the home of the clan leader, Lord Hyram II.

Constructed using mud clay bricks, straw, and wood, the quite large hut boasted a sturdy, circular shape, with a flat roof fashioned from wooden log beams and packed mud. The thick walls provided excellent insulation, shielding the inhabitants from both the heat of summer and the cold of winter experienced in this realm. A small, low, yet sturdy doorway served as the entrance, leading to a simple, yet very functional interior featuring minimal furniture. A central fire pit for cooking, which also added warmth to the interior, could be seen in the middle of the first large main room. The Kingmen's hut was adorned with intricate symbolic decorations and carvings, each telling a story of the clan's rich history and cherished traditions.

"My father will be here shortly, he is greeting and congratulating those of the clan who performed in the Market Fair this year. It was spectacular," Kiowa said with a smile as they all dismounted their quantum in front of the family's home.

"That is great news, I hadn't heard how the fair was this year, nor did I have a chance to go," responded Santos.

"Well, perhaps next time. Please come in and have something to drink as we wait for my father," Kiowa said.

Kiowa motioned to a couple of his men, and they stepped forward to receive the reigns from Santos' and his men's quantum. The reigns were passed over to them and they led them around back to the Kingmen's private corral.

"They shall have a drink as well!" laughed Kiowa.

Santos smiled as they accompanied him inside.

**(Houlton Dynasty - Back at the palace, late in the afternoon)**

"Have you not heard from them?" The Dutchess questioned one of the guards standing outside the front door.

"Good afternoon, High Dutchess. Heard from whom?" the guard responded with a question.

"What do you mean, whom? My sons of course. One is missing and the other left early this morning to go look for his brother. He's been gone since the first sun came up and now it's about to set and I have heard nothing! Where is Santos?" asked The Dutchess again, getting quite upset.

"I'm sorry ma'am, I do not know. The best place to ask would be at the communication quarters," said the guard.

"Then, why, don't, you, go, ask them," she responded with a very direct tone and almost hate in her eyes.

"Why yes, yes ma'am. I'll go right now," said the guard with a nervous tone as he quickly walked down the front path and proceeded towards the communications quarters located at one of the side buildings on the grounds. It was located right next to the security office and guard's barracks.

Then The Dutchess breathed deeply, patted her brow with a small white and purple striped handkerchief as she closed the door, turned, and went back inside. As she walked down the main corridors, she slowly came rounding the corner to the palace's kitchen. The guards were outside and since there were so few people the last couple of days, she dismissed the chef and kitchen staff, giving herself some needed peace and quiet.

"I shall make myself a tea, which will help me to calm down," The Dutchess said to herself as she looked at the main clock in the front hallway just adjacent to the kitchen.

The clock was a gift from her grandfather, passed down from generation to generation. Usually, a clock of this grandeur would only be passed from father to son, as it was from her great-grandfather to her grandfather, but the heirloom had skipped her father and went straight to her since she was the only granddaughter, and daughter for that matter, on both sides of the family. Her grandfather had a special liking towards her ever since she was born. He'd never say she was his favorite grandchild, but the whole family knew it, he treated her as ever so special, even making her parents slightly jealous of her at times, but especially her three brothers.

The clock was grand, with dark wooden tones with golden accents on the sides and front door, where the most elegant timepiece was seen just behind a panel of glass with gold, hand painted lilacs in each corner of the door. The face of the clock was a beautiful bronze with gold accented numbers. The hands would faithfully mark the second, minute, and hour, and only a slight tick-tik-tok, could be heard from the clock. Its subtle, loyal sound could be drowned out during the activities of the day, yet at night its sound would echo through every inch of the great hallways of the palace. The chimes of the clock no longer rang out, ever since The Dutchess ordered them to be silenced after the passing of Grandmaster Houlton, but that did not seem to take away the sentimental meaning of the clock for The Dutchess.

She walked past the clock, touching the classic adornments on its corners as she regularly did. She then turned towards the cupboards, the very same cupboards the guard visited the night before.

She proceeded to prepare herself a cup of tea. Opening the cupboard, she brought out the tin canister and laid out perfectly on the counter her cup, spoon, and the canister of tea. She then turned and proceeded to heat a bit of water in a pot, over the small fire that flickered on the nearby stove.

Outside the wind blew a slight breeze through the garden bushes and flowers, the second sun was beginning to set and left the usual light purplish glow in the sky and on the horizon. It was a beautiful evening sight as the sun's aurora shone and the gloss of the moons began to shimmer in the early evening sky.

The Dutchess served out two, level tablespoons of tea, poured the now steaming hot water into her cup, and began to stir it until all the powder dissolved. Then, she opened the first cupboard to the left, and she brought out a similar canister, but this one did not contain tea, but sugar beads. Removing the lid, and placing it on the same counter, she took out one and a half sugar beads, exactly. Crushed them between her fingers and sprinkled the sweet dust into the cup, stirring it in with the spoon she held with her other hand. When she finished, she laid the spoon carefully on the counter, not dripping a single drop of tea, and set her cup on a most elegant matching saucer of blue and white porcelain, it was handmade from one of the outer provinces, clans there had such wonderful craftsmanship. She lifted the porcelain pair together with both hands and walked to the doorway that led to the outer porch where she had spent many an evening, sipping her tea, feeling the breeze, and watching the last rays of the second sun as it found its place to rest.

Now seated in her favorite, wicker-woven porch chair, she took a deep relaxing breath and began to sip her tea. Little by little she continued to sip her tea, not knowing that it would be her last. The garden was the only witness of this moment. It was as if the bushes, shrubs, flowers, and a few small trees were watching this tragic moment in time. As the wind blew, the new moon observed the gentle, slow rise and fall of her chest. The moonlight and the last rays of the sun created a serene ambiance on that side of the palace.

The Dutchess continued to sip her tea, not realizing that with every swallow she was sealing her fate.

Snakeweed has no odor and is tasteless. It relaxed and slowed breathing until they faded into permanent sleep.

It was in that tender moment, her head relaxed to one side, and she breathed ever so slow. Her eyes with a slight silver glaze to them as the light reflected off them. With a slow deep breath, her body relaxed even more, then as she breathed her last breath, time stood still. Her hand, still clasping the teacup, conveyed a sense of quiet resignation. As her presence faded, the world around her felt hushed, and still, the breeze withdrew its touch. The garden was without movement. There The Dutchess sat, still and quiet, with no one around to notice that this evening was different from all the rest. The only noise that could be heard was the steady, faithful sound of the grandfather's clock. Tick-tock, tick-tock, it continued as it had for generations before. Then as her eyes slowly closed, The High Dutchess passed on from this world into the next.

### (Bisonteous Realm as the first sun is setting)

Sitting around the crackling campfire in the center of the room, a flickering glow washed over the men. Santos leaned against a sturdy log behind him as he sipped his drink. The flames danced upon his face as he stared into the fire.

"Do you remember the time we saw you on Market Street, and you convinced us to follow you back home?" Santos mused; a slight grin spread across their faces.

"I do remember, you kept whining about how you were going to receive such great discipline if you were caught," Kiowa said as he laughed aloud. The palace guards turned to see Santos' reaction to the banter. Santos smiled, not lifting his gaze from the fire, "Yes then you also talked me into going out to the Asno and half-blood clan's mining area, telling me you found a special treasure in the mines," Santos explained.

One of the guards turned to Kiowa, "Well, what was in the mines, did you find a treasure there?"

"Oh, there was treasure out there all right, just not the kind you'd expect," Santos answered lifting his eyes to Kiowa, chuckling.

"It is called, wisdom and experience my friend. The greatest treasure one could ever ask for," Kiowa said with a laugh as he glanced at Santos, gesturing with a nod that he should tell the story to the others.

"You see, this guy here, got me to sneak out two quantum from the palace corrals, ride out to the mines, and look for the lost golden relics of his people," Santos explained.

"As we rode out there, which was an adventure in and of itself, we snuck past the miners and hid out in the largest mine till dusk. When the workers went home for the evening, we found an old cart and decided to ride it down into the mine. We took a couple of lanterns and went deeper into the mine, down the main shaft riding in the cart. We kept going deeper in, it got darker and darker until we couldn't see any light coming from the main entrance anymore. This guy started shaking and getting so nervous he shook the cart and tipped us over," said Santos.

"Now, I wasn't the one afraid of the dark my friend. Don't leave out the details," Kiowa interrupted.

"Anyway, all we could see was our shadows up on the walls reflecting from the lanterns. Then we started hearing creaking sounds and strange noises. We kept on because he kept telling me there was a treasure down there. Then we saw a glow off in one of the side tunnels. So, what do we do? Go off and check to see if it's a piece of the shiny treasure," Santos chuckled.

"As we walked down the slightly curved side tunnel we got turned around, and as we walked closer to the shiny glow..." he paused.

"What? What was it?" one of the guards asked. Kiowa chuckled.

"The glow blinked at us." Santos looked at them with a slightly sinister grin. "That glow blinked at us. Boy did we turn, scream, and run out of there!" Santos laughed as he told the story.

"What do you mean blinked? Was there sombru dragons in there or what?" the other guard asked.

"Might have been, but we didn't stick around to find out. And let me tell you, I've never liked those mines till this day! Later, I found out it was a scamper, they lay in the dark mines sometimes and have deep rest," said Kiowa.

"A scamper?! Ah, they don't hurt anybody though. They're just a long, fat, and sluggish behemoth. They're good for eating annoying insects though," said another guard.

"Yeah, but when you're only 10 years old, nervous in a dark mine, knowing you shouldn't be there in the first place, anything like that will scare the wits out of you!" Santos exclaimed.

They all chuckled and laughed at the thought of young boys screaming and running out of the mines. "Did you ever get caught?" one guard asked.

"If our folks did find out, they never said anything. They figured we learned our lesson that day." Kiowa said with a smile. "Wisdom is a great treasure, acquired from experience."

Just then the front door to the house swung open and there stood a massive silhouette in the doorway. The men quickly stood to their feet, giving reverence to Lord Hyram II. He turned toward them, spoke to them in their native tongue and they all sat with a smile.

"So, what brings you here my prince?" Lord Hyram II asked as he gestured to Santos as he sat next to Kiowa in his usual place. Santos explained all that had happened since they left the palace grounds and how they came across Kiowa and his warriors.

"We are ever so grateful to Kiowa and his men, without their help, I truly don't know what would have become of us," Santos said, thanking them once again as he nodded with gratitude.

"We must be on our way, I have a feeling my brother has gone with the nomad clans, I need to find him at once," said Santos.

"Nonsense, you will not make it that far before complete darkness. The second sun is already setting, and you already know what can find you in the shadows. You must stay the night here, safe with us." Lord Hyram II spoke.

"I must agree with father. It is too risky my friend," said Kiowa.

"I do not wish to be a burden. Your kindness has been shown to me not once or twice, but now three times this day, thank you. We are most grateful," answered Santos.

The Bisonteaus men then proceeded to show Santos and his men to a side hut where they could rest for the night. Like the other huts the room was cozy and adorned with clan symbols and decorations, telling more of the history of their people, this time in the form of colorful hand-woven tapestries that hung on the walls. There were four cots, with similarly styled hand-woven blankets and three pieces of fruit on each, given as a welcome gift to the weary men. Off to the right was a door that led to a bathing house, where each of them relaxed with a hot water bath, with water that was direct from the warm spring located just a short distance from the camp.

As Santos, now refreshed, sat outside on a weathered wooden bench behind the hut. His eyes lifted upward, transfixed by the celestial display, he contemplated the events of the day. As he pondered with a small but satisfying snack in hand, he savored each bite, he couldn't help but think to himself, "What are you doing Dantias? What are you thinking? Where are you?"

Little did Santos know that a few hundred miles away Dantias was looking up at the very same starry sky. The two brothers had a connection in their souls, one to another. Yet, Dantias' thoughts were not towards his brother, but towards Namid. Dantias sat outside, a good 100 yards from Namid's tent, he began to formulate a plan. A plan that had been in the back of his mind for the last couple of months. A plan, from his point of view, which would set the record straight and bring all things into order.

Each brother, pondering, wondering, planning. Neither of them knowing that their mother, The Dutchess, had passed on and faded into eternity, that very same night.

# CHAPTER 15

(THE NEXT MORNING AT THE HOULSTON DYNASTY'S PALACE)

As dawn approached, the twin suns slowly ascended from behind the uneven rolling hills on the horizon. One sun emitted a fascinating purplish glow, casting a shimmery hue over the landscape, while the other radiated a dazzling, golden light, blending the surroundings with warmth and brightness. The dual display of celestial radiance painted the sky in a mesmerizing blend of purples, pinks, and gold, casting long, dramatic shadows across the land. It was a truly extraordinary and captivating moment.

A long glow began to spread over the palace gardens, the light glistened in the slight bit of dew that rested on the garden's beautiful flowers and almost tropical-looking, foreign plants.

The Houlton Dynasty's gardens were known for the beautiful and exotic plants that were throughout. Since the area was an arid environment, much care had to be taken to keep the gardens healthy and in all their grandeur.

Exotic flowers with intricate, colorful petals began to stretch out towards the sun, while other magnificent plants flaunted their huge, glossy leaves.

Even though the palace had many gardeners and experts in botany and horticulture, The Professor enjoyed tending to the gardens early each morning before fulfilling his daily responsibilities. It was a joyous and simple task for him. He lived in a small house, made in the same design as the palace, adjacent to the gardens.

He thoroughly enjoyed tending to the exotic flowers each morning. However, nurturing these extraordinary botanical wonders required a delicate touch and the most meticulous care since many of them were imported from the lush tropical forests of the Aprosmarteus Realm. Although these plants abound there naturally, without hindrance, here it is an art form to care for such plants.

The Professor, the caretaker, wearing his iconic weathered, yellowish, straw hat with a green leather band and sporting his wire-rimmed glasses, which seemed to just rest on the tip of his nose, moved deliberately among the vivid and colorful plants. He took his time on each plant, as if it were his child. His knowledgeable hands lovingly tended to each flower, ensuring that it received the perfect balance of sunlight, water, and nutrients. The Professor was an expert in addressing the unique needs of each exotic species, keeping a harmonious environment allowing each one to flourish and grow, to great, even enormous sizes.

As the second sun was rising the light glistened off the petals of the large pink and white orchid he held in his hands. This species of orchid was distinct from the rest because they had ever so small thorns growing on the sides of the stem. If these thorns were trimmed in a peculiar way, with the most delicate of care, it caused the flower to bloom even more, growing the flowers to the size of a man's head.

That flower, which The Professor had been tending to ever since it first bloomed, was now over 10 years ago. Each year increasing the bloom ever so much, to where now when it bloomed it was just over one foot in diameter.

After watering the beautiful flower and cutting away the leaves from around the plant's base. The Professor put on his gloves, lifted his plant shears, and ever so slightly began to remove the newly grown thorns on its stem. Snip, snip, clip, clip, he patiently trimmed.

It was like a relaxing therapy for him has he worked. He lifted his straw hat just a little as he looked down, concentrating on the plant. Then a slight smile came across his face as he adjusted his hat once more.

"Oh yes, I remember," he said with a smirk. Even though he was speaking to himself, it was as though he was conversing with the flower. The Professor had developed a friendship with the flower, after tending to it for now more than a decade.

"I remember very well," he continued, "The time where those boys came out here running around like crazy. You were but a little one, just budding out of the ground then."

After he was sure there was nothing more to do for his beloved flower that day, he collected his things, walked to his garden shed, and placing each instrument, water can and tool in its place. He then went over to the rose bushes and selected the freshest blooming buds to take up to the palace.

As a routine gesture, he would take flowers early every morning and place them in a vase on the family's dining table. So, as usual, he made his way up the path, leading to the back patio porch door, not knowing what he was about to find there.

The suns were now shining a nice glow across the sun-dripped gardens, a slight warm breeze brushed upon his face. As he held the small bundle of roses in one hand, he adjusted his glasses and then his hat with the other. Then humming a classic hymn as he walked up to the palace.

Approaching the back door, he noticed The Dutchess slightly slumped over in one of the patio chairs, an unusual sight at that time of day. It was quite perplexing, as she was known to be an early riser who would typically begin her day well before sunrise. This uncommon scene left him feeling uneasy, creating a disquieting atmosphere during this, what would have been a tranquil morning.

"It is now at least three hours after sunrise, she should be up and about by now," he whispered to himself.

Quickly he pulled open the back door, and walked through the dining room, laying the rose bundle on the table as he passed. Walking out onto the back patio he looked frantically around, assessing the situation. Kneeling on one knee at The Dutchess's side he began to believe the worst. Slowly cupping his right hand under her head, with his left he took off his straw hat and laid it on the ground next to him. As he held her head, he checked her vital signs and called to her.

"Dutchess, madam. Can you hear me?" he spoke nervously. He repeated, this time much more direct.

"Dutchess. Can you hear me!?" There was no response. No movement. No pulse. She was cold to the touch. He knew then that she was gone.

He paused but a moment, reflecting, questioning, his memory went to a similar moment when he held Lord Houlton's head in much the same way once.

"Oh, my dear Dutchess, what happened?" He whispered. Then he breathed deep and started down the inevitable path.

"Guards, come quickly! Over here!" he shouted. He called out again, his voice quivering ever so slightly, holding back his tears.

Even though The Dutchess was sometimes cruel or unjust to The Professor, he had served the family since before the beginning. He had grown to care for the Houlton family, each one of them, as they were his own, faults and all.

At once three guards came running around back, two from one side of the palace and one from the other, they rushed in to help.

"She's gone. I found her this way. Take great care. We must investigate further to understand this situation," The Professor explained.

"Take her to my consultation office at once," he spoke with authority.

The guards carefully lifted her and proceeded to take her away. Picking up his hat and dusting it off as he stood to his feet The Professor turned and allowing his eyes to dance upon the far horizon he thought and spoke aloud to himself. "Oh, my dear boys, what will become of all this?"

**(Nomad Plains – Early the same morning)**

As the suns began to rise and shine brightly in the new morning sky, it lit up tiny dust particles floating in the air that were stirred up by the smooth breeze over the savanna plains.

Dantias, was already awake, sitting against a nearby tree, the very same tree he sat at the night before, waiting for Namid to emerge from her tent. It felt like he had been waiting forever.

Then at once, the tent flap pushed open, and Tala stepped out first. He looked around and his eyes met Dantias', giving him a serious look that showed he wasn't pleased. Dantias stood to his feet, brushed off the dirt from his clothes, and began to walk towards him, preparing his mind for whatever was to come next.

As he got about halfway away Namid, along with two other clan women emerged from the tent. Dantias sped up to a trot but slowed down suddenly as she looked his way, shook her head, and turned her back as he approached the morning breakfast fire. He slowed to a slow walk, in disbelief, yet he did not stop.

As he got closer, he overheard Namid saying, "Why has he come? What good is it that he is even here?"

"Namid, I'm sorry but what do you mean?" Dantias asked as he approached to kneel at her side as she sat by the morning campfire.

She ignored him. He placed his hand upon her shoulder, as he had many times before, to greet her, with the intention of comforting her this cool, sunny morning. As he placed his hand on her shoulder, she jumped pushing him away and almost tripping over the fire.

"Don't touch me!" she screamed as she backed away from him shaking and trembling with fear and anger.

"You, stay way! Get out of here!" she exclaimed.

"Namid, what is wrong? I've been searching for you, waiting here for you since  yesterday. Ask your grandfather, he'll tell you!" Dantias replied.

"You... you..." she trembled, and tears ran down her cheek as she pointed at him, shaking her finger. Namid looked terribly upset, filled with anger, and hurt. Her eyes seemed to stare right through him.

What? Tell me. Where were you?" Dantias replied.

One of the women went to Namid's side, comforting her, giving Namid the courage to speak, a little more collected now.

"You... left me," Namid said.

"Left you? I..." Dantias was cut off.

"You do not speak to me!" Namid screamed as she interrupted him.

Dantias just stood there now, not understanding what was going on or what took place.

"You left me, and those men... they... they..." she couldn't even say it aloud.

"What did they do? Namid, please, tell me," Dantias said with great urgency.

Namid stood there, cold, with so much anger, deception, and pain in her eyes. Her eyes pierced him as she stared at him while tears trickled down both cheeks and her lips quivered, it took all her strength to control herself and not lose all composure.

# CHAPTER 16

(MARKET FAIR - THE NIGHT NAMID WAS KIDNAPPED)

The Market Fair was ending after its almost four-week run, so the crowds were larger than usual tonight. Everybody, it seemed wanted to attend the final events, eat at the variety of food stands, or just visit the Market Fair one last time. The crowd was shoulder-to-shoulder, and walking was slow going.

"I need to find a rest station," Namid said as they walked through the crowd.

"Ah, come on, it will take forever. Besides, there is an extensive line over at that one. Let's find one closer to the exit on the way out," Dantias insisted.

"It will only take a few minutes, just wait for me here," Namid said as they approached the line outside the ladies' rest station area.

"Fine, I'll wait," Dantias responded.

After a few minutes, it was Namid's turn to go in, the line was long and ladies from all the other realms were lining up behind them. As Namid went inside Dantias took advantage of the moment and went to the gentleman's side as well, which hardly had a line at all. He stepped back outside, and he waited patiently to one side of the ladies' rest station door.

"What's taking her so long?" he said to himself as he waited.

Then a loud blaring siren could be heard about 100 feet away, and 20 or 30 people began to cheer loudly, someone had won the grand prize at one of the game stands.

Dantias stood on his toes to try to get a glimpse of what they won when the game announcer began to cry out,

"Come on, come on, who's next?! Who will be the next winner on the last night of the great Market Fair?!" Dantias turned and saw that Namid had still not come out.

"I'll be back before she even comes out," he thought.

He then made his way through the crowd over to the game booth. "Come on, who will be the next big winner?!" As Dantias got closer the game announcer turned to him with a smile. "Is it you young man?! You could be the next winner! All you must do is knock down all the bottles with one single throw!" he spoke with such an assuring tone, "It's that easy! Many have done it tonight in fact. You could be next!" he said.

Dantias was hooked. He took his money out of his pocket, not even noticing that just a few hundred feet away Namid was calling his name as she looked around for him just outside the rest station, he began to play the game.

"Now where did he go? He told me to meet him right back out here," Namid said to herself.

"Well maybe he went in to use the gentlemen's side as well," so she waited.

After several minutes went by, she was approached by two, well-dressed, Equiantus men with a palace guard insignia wrapped on their arms.

"Good evening miss," one of them said as they approached her.

"Good evening," replied Namid.

"So sorry to bother you on this eventful evening, but Dantias has been called away, there was an emergency at the palace. He told us to come for you and escort you home," the tan-skinned guard said with a smile.

"I'm fine, thank you. I will find my own way home," Namid said with assurance.

"We must insist my lady, Dantias was animate and very direct when he told us to get you. If you like we can take you to see him, he is approaching his wind carriage at the east exit as we speak. It's not that far away, just past here," the guard said as he gestured to her to follow him.

Reluctantly she looked around, not seeing Dantias, nor any of the bystanders alarmed, and began to walk with the men.

"Oh, you just about had it!" the game announcer said with a chuckle, "Give it another try?!"

Dantias had given now more than a dozen tries with no luck at all. He shook his head and laughed at himself, realizing he had been had.

"No thanks, that's enough for one fair!" Dantias smiled as he picked up his outer jacket off the game's wooden stand. He had taken it off, just after his first three throws, since he was working up a bit of a sweat and to give himself a better range of movement.

"Well, have a good one then. Hope to see you next year!" said the game announcer.

Dantias nodded in agreement and walked back through the crowd to get back to the rest station area. Standing outside once again he stood waiting for her to come out. Little did he know, she had already left with the two undercover palace guards and was making her way towards the east exit at that very moment. Two others watched him from a distance as well, waiting for just the right opportunity to pursue their very own assigned task.

As Namid approached the exit a cold sensation went up and down her spine, she convinced herself that it was nothing, and she proceeded to walk out the gate, turn the corner, and approach the wind carriage that was waiting on the opposite street corner.

The first guard that had spoken to her, opened the door to the covered carriage inviting her in, then as she stepped up into the carriage a third guard appeared covering her head with a hood while the other two quickly grabbed her hands pulling them behind her back and securely tying them. Her heart raced as she struggled and even was able to let out a couple of screams, but the night was full of activities, and no one could hear her. The only sound that could be heard was that of the music, rides, and commotion on the other side of the fence.

Namid took deep breaths, gasping for air, kicking her legs, and yelling as loud as she could. However, instead of getting help, she was breathing in Elders Weed powder, which was on the inside of the hood and made her sluggish and sleepy. Her screams turned into whispers, then dizzy, mumbles, and then at once everything went black. The last guard climbed into the wind carriage, closed the door, and they drove away into the night.

Slowly the grogginess left her, and she began to regain consciousness Namid felt so much pain in her entire body. First in her legs, thighs, back, and up her arms that she now realized were above her head. The pain was like an intertwining hot wire that wrapped all around her, she could feel it from the inside out. As the dizziness left her little by little, all she could sense was an extreme pain in her wrists, above her head. Coming to her senses she began to piece together her surroundings. As her head spun, she looked up and found herself hanging by her wrists in a dark, musty room that smelled of old panú bread. There was an ever-low glowing light was on the wall to her right. She could feel a slight breeze upon her skin, looking down and saw that she was exposed and her clothing ripped open. A small puddle

of blood was just below her, being absorbed by the thirsty dirt
floor. As she breathed deep, she began to cough from the blood
she sniffed up through her nostrils. A squeaky hinge could be
heard in the dark, a door opened slightly to her left.

"Well look who's awake," said a man's voice.

Namid struggled to stand to her feet but to no avail, because she was hanging just low enough that her feet just barely
touched the ground. She could only manage to kick the dirt just
a little.

"You're something quite amazing, even unconscious you are
a fighter. See this? Got a black eye from you," the man leaned
towards her as he pointed into his own face,

"So, I gave you one in return. Plus a few other things. Ain't
that right, comrade?" he said as he turned to a shadow in the
corner.

"Just shut up. What you and the others have done is nothing
to brag about," said the voice from the shadowy corner.

"Ah you're just angry cuz you showed up too late," the first
said with a chuckle.

"Let... me... go..." struggled Namid in a forced whisper.

"You just wait now. As soon as we get word. You will be free
to go," he reassured her as he touched her face.

Namid jerked her head back and gasped in despair, her
heart racing and breathing deeply. With each breath, her
stretched-out side hurt even more.

"Leave her alone," the voice said from the shadow.

Just then the door cracked open, and a woman's voice could be heard across the room.

"What are you doing? Stop this nonsense at once. I said make a point of it, not to do this. Get her out of here immediately," ordered the voice at the door.

"Yes, of course. Right away," said the voice from the shadowy corner hastily.

The door squeaked shut, leaving the only dim light of the room glowing once again. The shadow emerged from the corner, pulled out a large knife, and cut the rope that was holding Namid. She collapsed to the floor. Hurriedly as she could, with the limited strength that she had, she pushed herself up to her knees and pulled her garments around her, scooted towards the light, and leaned up against the wall.

"Why have you done this?" pleaded Namid.

"You ain't wanted around the prince. If you woulda kept away from him, you would not be here right now," explained the man.

As the kinder-toned man came closer she saw that he was dressed in a palace guard's uniform. He slowly draped a hood over her head, and she struggled and fought back.

"Stay calm, now. It's over. I'm going to take you out of here," his voice had a comforting tone, but Namid did not trust him.

Though she decided it was in her best interest to cease to fight back.

"Come on, I'll help you," the other guard said.

"You've done enough, I'll take it from here," he gestured to the other man to stand back.

"Okay. You don't have to get so feisty about it. We were just following orders," the man said defending his actions.

"All of this was not part of your orders," the guard said firmly.

Just then the door swung open, and Namid could see another figure's silhouette in the doorway, this time recognizing a voice she had heard before. It was the same that invited her to walk with him to the exit at the Market Fair and convinced her to walk to the carriage.

"What's this?" asked the new figure in the doorway, "Where are you taking her?"

"It's done, she came in and gave the word. I'm taking her back out," the kinder voice now tinged with anger.

"I believe we have a difference of opinion. She's not going anywhere. We report that we took her home, but she stays here, just as we all agreed." said the guard.

"No, please," Namid whispered just loud enough for her helper to hear.

"That's what you both said, but I never agreed to it. She said it is done, so we're done. Now move and let me through," the guard said raising his voice.

"Look, comrade, you're in this, just the same as us both. Don't act all righteous with us now. We all have been part of it since the Fair. Hand her over and give the report that we all took her home," said the third guard as he gestured to the other who was now standing behind them.

"Move, now, or else," said the helper.

"Or else what? There's two of us and one of you. And when we're done with you, we're just gonna take her again anyways, so... let's have her," said the voice in the doorway.

With a slow sigh, and a glance over his left shoulder, the helper breathed deeply and in a single movement, a blink, he executed a spin kick on the guard behind him. As the guard in the doorway lunged forward to tackle him, he lowered to one knee while pulling out his knife from the back part of his belt and pierced him upwards, from the stomach up into the heart, stopping him instantly. As the lifeless body slumped over on the ground, his comrade shook his head from the kick, jumped up, pulled his knife out, and proceeded to stab him in the back. Ears cocked back, the guard flung his knife over his shoulder finding its target abruptly, bringing the other guard to his knees. He let out aloud gasp and dropped to the ground. All the while Namid, curled upon the floor, not moving a muscle. This whole scene seemed to last but seconds.

"Quickly, we haven't much time," the helper guard lifted Namid to her feet.

"Come on, hold my arm, and walk with me. I will lead you out," said the helper with kind urgency in his voice.

"Why keep this hood on me then?" she asked.

"You cannot know where we are, and if we are seen, it must seem as though I am leading you out as a prisoner," he replied.

He pulled the dead guard into the room by the feet, laying him on top of the other. Then he broke the light on the wall, and lead Namid out by the arm. He closed the metal door behind them and made sure to jam the door handle and lock it as he did. Thus, making it exceedingly difficult for someone else to open the door.

Namid stumbled as they walked quickly down a long corridor. She could see only silhouettes as the dim lights one by one shone above their heads.

Then, suddenly he began to pull her upwards, the terrain started to become increasingly steep as if climbing up a ramp. She tried to keep pace. Suddenly, she noticed that the air was becoming less dense, and less musty. She could smell the sweet scent of grass and hear the breeze blowing through it, a sound she knew quite well. Ever since she was a little girl what she most enjoyed was running through the tall grass, laying in the shadow of the large family tree, and watching the clouds drift by.

Abruptly, the guard stopped, squeezed her arm, and spoke very sternly.

"This is as far as I take you, turn and walk towards the hills, go quickly, and do not stop. There are sombru dragons out here. Keep going and you'll get back to your people," he explained to her, in a hurried tone.

She could hear the faint sounds of a quantum nearby. He then pushed her down and ran away. Namid turned and pulled her hands from behind her back from under her feet, and worked to untie them noticing the knot was very loose.

Quickly she pulled the hood off, to just barely see the guard as he ran and mounted a quantum, quickly riding off into the night.

There she sat alone in the dark, yet no longer afraid. She had lived many a night in the darkest hours, foraging, and building shelters, ever since she was a young girl.

Glancing up at the night sky, she easily found her bearings, she saw she was standing in front of the old, abandoned mines. Mines that had been dry for over a hundred years. She was out past the mining colony of the Asno clan. She then stood up, held back her tears, and began to walk towards where she knew her people would be, the Festival Tree.

Her clan always went there after the celebration of the Market Fair. She then ripped off a piece of cloth from the bottom of her dress, and used it to tie around her waist, to fasten her torn clothing like a robe.

Namid looked ahead and proceeded on her way towards the security of her home, longing to find the protective arms of her grandfather, Tala. Grandfather had warned her more than once about Dantias, but she had refused to listen because she was in love. She could hear his voice in her mind as she walked through the starlit night.

"Be careful my dear, I do not fully trust the Houlton boy. He could lead you to harm."

Amphibitius Realm

# CHAPTER 17

In the warm glow of the late afternoon suns, a small wooden table stood in the corner of the Houlton family's living room, its surface top was worn from years of family games. A chessboard lay set upon the table, pieces carefully aligned along the edges, pieces set almost frozen in the positions. A 10-year-old boy sat across from his father and starred at the board plotting his next move.

Their game was intense. The young boy's dark-skinned brow, frowned as he concentrated and pushed his pawns forward, coming one square closer to his father's king. The boy's heart raced with excitement. Each move was like taking a step in a great adventure. But then, at once, with a quick flick of his wrist, his father made his move and took his queen.

The young boy's face fell as he realized what had just happened.

"Not the queen," he whispered, watching the most powerful piece slide away and off the board.

"I thought she was safe," he said in disappointment.

His father's expression softened, clearly understanding his son's disappointment.

"It's okay," he replied, "The game is not over yet. Once the queen is gone, remember this: the knights become the most versatile players on the board."

The young boy looked up; curiosity now filled his eyes.

"The knight? But...how?" he asked.

"Because the knight has the unique ability to maneuver around other pieces. It can jump over them, change direction in ways that the others cannot," his father explained as he leaned in ever so slightly, his face a bit more solemn.

"In life, sometimes we lose our strongest allies, our friends, but it is in those moments we should be the most resourceful and adapt. The knight can surprise your opponent and create new opportunities where others can only see obstacles," said his father.

The boy considered these words, nodding slowly. He glanced back at the board, feeling a sense of renewed determination, and then made a plan in his mind. After a moment, he picked up one of his black knights, moved it across the checkered battlefield, imagined the piece leaping over his enemy's barriers, carved out a new path, then took away one, two, and three of the white pieces off the board. He laughed as he took each turn, and his father smiled.

As they played on, he no longer saw the absence of the queen as a setback, but instead as an advantage.

"Two most agile knights are better than one queen," the boy thought to himself.

Each move became a testament to his new understanding of resilience and strategy that he would carry for the rest of his life.

**(Present Day — Epic War)**

"Not the queen?!" the Dark Prince yelled out as he jolted awake.

Coming to his senses he realized that it had been a nightmare. It was the same reoccurring nightmare he had so many nights of late. The thought of a single finger flicking a white chess piece into a dark abyss.

"How did I become this?" he thought.

Looking around and seeing he was alone in his quarters, he stood to his feet, buried his feelings deep inside himself, put on his armored vest, and slipped on his robes and the metallic face shield he always wore to protect his brow. After putting on his boots and gloves he stepped up to the doors of his chambers. The door swooshed opened, and he walked down the corridor to take control of his post at the helm.

"Status," thundered the Dark Lord to his crew.

"Approaching the outlying border of the swamps my lord," answered Captain Amin, his right hand in command.

The Dark Prince's spaceship cut through the mist that clung to the Amphibtius Realm like a shroud. Towering above the gnarled trees and murky water, its silhouette resembled a colossal knight chess piece as it shifted direction and prepared to land. Forged from shadow and adorned with jagged spikes, which glowed with internal lighting beacons, the air crackled as the ship descended, the ground shaking beneath its heavy weight as it touched down on the soggy earth with a trembling thud.

The massive vessel emitted a low humming sound echoing through the silence of the swamplands. The sleek ebony body of the ship reflected nothingness, giving it a dark presence, a presence that sends fear through the hearts of all who see it.

Inside, the crew of the Dark Prince moved with military precision, the familiar sounds of armor and the rustling steps filled the air as they hurried to their posts. Each member wore the symbol of the prince on their right shoulder, a shadowy figure of the same flying fortress that now was their everlasting home.

Their eyes were focused with purpose, yet there was a hint of anxiety within them as well as the lower crew prepared to disembark. They knew the mission, a routine that was far too common the last few months, and the Dark Prince would not tolerate failure.

"Steady yourselves!" yelled a sergeant on the lower deck. He was a half-blood from the Asno clan, many of them loyal to the Dark Prince's mission.

"We're coming into the deep swamps now, they're probably not as welcoming this time around," he yelled out to his foot-soldier crew.

The land crew was made up of soldiers from the light-foot clan, half-bloods, and the other realms such as the Terrartius, the lizard-like people, and the Aprosmarteaus, the misfits realm.

"We're not here to just gather soldiers. We're here to inspire fear. Each realm must understand that the Dark Prince will bring true order to all!" shouted the sergeant.

From the upper deck, one word could be heard coming from the intercom, "Go!" the Dark Prince spoke with a stern, clear voice.

With a swift motion, the hatch of the ship lowered down, the blast doors swung open, revealing a thick fog that coiled around them like a serpent. The 50-man crew stepped out one by one, walking down the landing ramp. Grey silhouettes emerged from the mist. The air was heavy and filled with the scent of decay and damp soil. Even though they knew the locals could easily be eliminated by their force and numbers, still as light chill ran down their spines as they faced the eerie terrain.

"Form a perimeter!" commanded the sergeant, as the crew instantly fell into formation, their senses heightened. A group of five was dispatched to scout the area with their mission to identify the whereabouts of the locals, subdue any anti-forces, and then move in to arrange subtle negotiations.

As they moved deeper into the swamp, every rustle in the underbrush made the crew flinch ever so slightly. Not because they were afraid of the Amphibtius men, as their weapons were too primitive to do them any harm. What made them nervous were the swamp-dragons, which were like the sombru dragons, but with no upper arms, and more slender bodies. They could also slide through the murky waters almost undetected as their longer tails would push them slithering through the mud.

The locals were not often affected by the mud monsters, because of their understanding and great ability to maneuver the swamps, never really getting into or touching the waters.

The crew's forced motivation was to enlist every person they could find. As the war with General Santos and the Iron Horse team continued, there were losses, so recruiting must take place.

The soldiers knew that every ounce of fear they instilled in this realm, would add to the legend of the Dark Prince, the chosen one, who had gone into the 'Unspoken Realm' and emerged victorious.

The Dark Prince held the power to rule within his being, descending in his flying fortress that looked like a nightmare become real.

As they ventured further into the swamp lands, the houses of the local villager people were now distinguishable. The local villagers, the crew, and every creature could feel the Dark Prince's presence, his unyielding dark power that moved ready to reclaim whatever he deemed his.

As the crew approached the homes through the lightened fog, Lord Catodus emerged with close to 50 strong men and women, including his two grown sons. Taking their spears in hand, they formed a semicircle in the marshy opening in front of the homes.

A few other Amphibtius men, cloaks hanging down and spears also in hand, could be seen standing on the wooden porches that adorned the fronts of the home and market booths like a small castle platform giving them a slight upper hand.

The Dark Prince's crew slogged through the knee-high murky water, pressing in closer and closer. Lord Catodus looked about, making small chirping sounds and clicks to his followers. They glanced over at him, each one in their position, and nodding in confirmation.

"Well, well, who do we have here? Lord Catodus how are you this fine afternoon?" asked the sergeant.

"What do you need my sir?" asked Catodus.

"We have come to ask for your services, once again. The Dark Prince calls upon your loyal realm, to send warriors to fight alongside us as soldiers. We call out the strongest once more to aid the Dark Prince as we end this war!" yelled the sergeant so all could hear.

"You wish to have more men to send to the slaughter!" Catodus cried out.

"This time I say, no. We will no longer send our people to serve the Dark Prince. My last answer is no," Lord Catodus said firmly.

"No? We have had a great relationship these past 10 years. Many lives have been lost, from every realm, not just yours. It is the sacrifice we are willing to make to bring peace and order once again," persuaded the sergeant.

"No, no more. We have seen none of the benefits which we were promised. There has only been pain and loss," Catodus replied, standing straight with his spear in one hand as he pulled his hood down with the other.

The sergeant looked around at those who gathered, his own crew were standing relaxed yet armed behind him. He smiled slightly and then chuckled to himself as he moved his gaze left and then right.

"My sir, with all due respect, we need loyal, strong men and women to join us. Otherwise, this war will just drag out even more. No one wants that. It would be a shame to lose your strongest people right here and now. If somebody is to die, don't let it be in vain, let it be for the greater good!" said the sergeant with a stern look on his face as his gaze now was set straight on the short Kingmen.

"I'm not asking, I'm telling you. We need more fighters," the sergeant said as he pointed his blaster pistol at Catodus.

With a whistle and a quick chirp, chirp, several spears flew, one piercing the sergeant in the leg bringing him down to one knee and firing his blaster into the muddy waters.

Other Amphibtius jumped out of small, hidden tree perches above the crew, and landed on the Dark Prince's men. They used their weight to pull them to the ground, as water splashed everywhere.

One of Sir Cysilian's brothers pulled out his blaster pistol, pointing it at the toad-like warriors, and shot one in the leg, and then another in the head with pinpoint accuracy.

Suddenly, a spear came falling from above, slicing his face just below his eye. The griffin-like soldier quickly looked up, and there on a perch in the trees was another Amphibtius warrior. With a smooth jump, his wings lifted him swiftly into the air, and his razor-sharp hand talons grabbed the menace, cutting through his skin with ease, slicing him through the heart, and dropping his motionless body to the ground.

"Hold your fire, stop!" the sergeant yelled as he stood and pulled out the spear from his leg.

"We are here to recruit them, not kill them!" he yelled.

The Amphibtius chirped and whistled amongst themselves, then ran and hopped off through murky waters into the mist between the trees.

The horse-like sergeant sighed and then yelled in frustration. At once the crew, separated ways and, went running after them through the knee-high waters in opposite directions.

"You think you're clever you little mud hopper?" shouted the sergeant.

Catodus grinned as one of his sons handed him another spear.

The humidity of the swamp hung in the air, thick and heavy. You could hear splashing water and the rustling of foliage as the soldiers ran after the toad-like warriors.

One smaller group of the sergeant's crew assembled into formation as they trudged through the muck, their faces, set with determination as they pursued the villagers who darted and jumped between trees and bogs, desperate to escape.

The Amphibtius people, even though smaller and heftier, were much more agile and accustomed to the swampy terrain. They moved like shadows and expertly wove in and out of the thick vegetation. Every so often, a soldier would spot a flash of movement, a glimpse of a cloak, a pair of legs leaping over a fallen tree, or a shadow slipping behind a gnarled swamp bush.

A few shouts could be heard in the distance, piercing the stillness, as the other group of soldiers chased the escaping Amphibtiusans on the other side of the swamp.

Little did the crew know, the swamp had its own agenda. As they pressed forward, their footfalls became heavier, their boots filling with sludge and muck. The first crew continued, squinting as they tried to see where they went through the thickening fog. One soldier, driven by adrenaline, took a bold step and lunged forward over a rotting tree stump, and quickly found his foot sucked into a hole and in an instant was waist-high in the mud.

"Hey, help me out!" the soldier cried out.

Two of his comrades quickly reached out to him, one taking each arm to pull him up. As they did the ground gave way and pulled all three down into the mud. Panic rushed through them all as they frantically pushed and pulled down on the surrounding shrubs, as they were pulled down quicker and quicker. Another one of their crew picked up a nearby branch and held it out to them.

"Come on, grab it! Take hold!" he yelled at his sinking comrades.

It was no use, as they continued to struggle, they sank deeper and deeper into the muddy waters, until they disappeared with only a few air bubbles popping and burbling on the surface.

The remaining crew members looked at each other in disbelief, struck by the realization that they were not just hunters, but now prisoners in this maze of mud and mystery.

At the opposite side of the swamps, the other group of soldiers pushed through the murky waters, equally wet and muddy, with their boots filled sludge. They pressed on after the toad-like people out in front of them. While they walked through the knee-high murky waters, something shifted.

"Hey, did you feel that?" one comrade asked the other.

"Feel what?" another asked.

"I felt something move around my legs," he responded.

In the distance, chirping sounds, one of the secret languages of the Amphibtius people could be heard. The chirping got louder and louder as the crew walked forward through the misty terrain. Then at once, there was dead silence.

Alarmed, the crew of 10 stopped, blasters and pistols drawn, and looked around at one another as they watched. Then, one of the crew, at the farthest edge of the group let out a blood-curdling scream as he disappeared instantly into the waters.

The others nervously adjusted their position, as they realized that now they were no longer on the hunt, but being hunted. As they moved closer together, another comrade, on the opposite end of the group screamed out as he too disappeared into the waters without a trace.

"Watch it, watch your back! Bring it in!" the leader of the crew yelled to the others.

A grotesque shape suddenly emerged, its scales glistening in the dim light, its thin eyes glinting with malice. It was a swamp dragon.

These creatures had only been rumored in local lore but were now seen in the flesh. It lunged at the nearest soldier with tremendous terrifying speed. The soldier barely had time to react, his scream swallowed by the suffocating air as thin claws raked through the wet foliage. Chaos erupted as the remaining soldiers scrambled to get away.

**(Meanwhile, inside Dark Prince's ship)**

"Do you read me? Hello, sergeant. Do you read me?" one of the communications team called on the crew's communicators.

Captain Amin walked across the leader deck, towards him.

"What is the problem?" he hissed.

"The locals ran, and our crew followed in pursuit. But now, one by one their tracking icons are disappearing off the radar," he explained as he pointed to the screen.

"There, you see. Another one is gone. We also have been unable to reach the sergeant," he said.

"Pesky little... I'm on channel four," Captain Amin said as he grabbed a blaster off the rack on the wall and holstered it.

Captain Amin adjusted his face shield and tested his communicator as he walked down the dimly lit corridor. A red glow reflected off his metallic mask from the hallways' dim shimmering lights. Anger filled his heart as he slipped on his gloves. The swoosh of a door could be heard as he stepped into the hover-pod bay. Racks of veloci-pods were aligned on the walls, each in its own cylinder capsule. Each one of them like a torpedo ready to be launched.

Amin stepped up to a large pod that sat on a sturdy iron rack, which was waist high, just in front of him. He swung his leg over it and straddled it with expertise. He extended his hand in front of him and placed his fingers on both sides of the oval-bodied pod. A blue laser beam protruded out of the base and scanned his fingertips. In the blink of an eye, a robotic sound was heard as the machine turned on. A slight humming sound could be heard from the core of the machine. Instantly the iron base dropped into the floor, but the machine stayed in the exact same position, hovering over the floor. The arms of the veloci-pod clicked backward turning into handles to maneuver the speeder-transport. Captain Amin lifted his legs, taking the handles, moved them, one forward and the other backward positioning the speeder, ready to launch.

Then in a flash, a door on the back side of the ship opened and Amin shot out like a missile, his tail in perfect alignment with the tail of the veloci-pod, now in speeder mode, hovering and racing over the swampy terrain headed directly towards Lord Catodus.

"Enough of these stupid games," Amin thought to himself as he rode the speeder.

Slipping in and out between trees and brush with ease. His mask was equipped with an internal visor, and vision scanner that helped him measure, speed, and distances and even had a thermal setting that allowed him to see the position of his crew or other beings as well.

In the distance he could see people standing, he clicked the side of his mask, and it zoomed in closer showing it was the Kingmen, standing on the porch, spear in hand surrounded by his family and several others.

In few short minutes he was face-to-face with Lord Catodus.

The soldiers who were once in an orderly pursuit, were now in a frenzied hunt. It was a desperate battle against both fleeing villagers and the horrors of the swamp. A blinking red light and a beeping sound came across their comlinks.

"Regroup! Fall back! Let them go!" one of the soldiers cried out to his comrades.

One by one, two by two they began to trickle back to the spot where they had originally split up, but this time Captain Amin was there, waiting, seated on his speeder-pod.

Amin looked around, assured that the remaining survivors were there, behind him. One of his sergeants was holding his leg and leaning up against a nearby tree, so he turned his attention to the Kingmen.

"We came and asked very nicely for your help. In return you threw spears at us, lead my men into the swamps to be killed, and yet you continue to stand there, firmly in your pride. That doesn't seem right to me, does it to you?" Captain Amin asked sarcastically as he got off his speeder-pod, bringing him now just in front of the Lord's porch.

Lord Catodus spokeout, "As I said before, we will not..." with a mechanical-sounding swoosh the speeder-pod transformed, and in one single motion the head of the veloci-pod came out, with knife-like teeth bit off the Kingmen's head mid-sentence, while the Lord's wife and sons let out a shrieking scream of terror.

"You have brought this upon yourselves! Look what you have done!" Captain Amin screamed back at them as he held out his arms and motioned to the rest of the onlookers, "Call all your men back here, now!" he yelled.

"We must be on our way, we have spent too much time in this place," Amin said as he collected himself, "What barbaric and uncivilized methods," he said to himself as he clicked a couple of buttons on his glove, bringing the pod under control.

In a moment there were two more hovering pods behind him. He motioned to his sergeant to get on the one closest to him.

One of Catodus's sons was about to say something against this unjust situation when his mother grabbed his arm and said something only, he could hear.

The young man lowered his head, speaking to those around him, and began to make loud chirping sounds.

In a few short minutes, the trees and rooftops were laced with the Amphibtius warriors, as they came leaping in from different areas of the swamp.

The warriors reacted the same way as the Kingmen's son, heads down then lined up in formation, ready to follow the Dark Prince's captain. Amin smiled and laughed aloud so all could hear him.

"Thank you for your cooperation, my good people!" he exclaimed.

"May we all rejoice in the glory of our great Prince!" he announced as he tapped a couple of buttons on his glove, sending the pods back to the ship, and forcing the new Amphibtius troops to follow.

As they were led back to the ship and up the loading ramp, they reached a large room with rows of seats. A most strange commanding officer, from the oceanic Mareviteaus Realm, stepped forward and spoke in an almost gurgling voice.

"All of you have been chosen. You will all serve a greater cause. Resistance will not be tolerated. Your loyalty will indeed decide your future," he warned. The captives understood that there was no way out and that their destiny was to become part of this powerful force.

Some clung to the hope of one day returning home, while others felt despair. Their fate sealed, and like many before them, was now in the hands and will of the Dark Prince.

As the ship readied the take-off sequence, its dark shape blended into the misty shadows. A low rumble could be heard inside, signaling the power that was about to be unleashed. Doors and ramps slowly closed and raised, and then at once the engines roared to life, glowing with bright blue flames. The ground shook as the dark silhouette rose into the sky, trailing smoke, and fire as it sailed higher and off into the distance.

# CHAPTER 18

(402 AWOR - BISONTEUS REALM)

**B**eneath the vast open skies of the Bisonteaus Realm, Santos and his men adjusted the reigns of their quantum and prepared to depart for the Nomad plains, quite assured that he would find his brother there amongst the nomad clan.

"Well, my friend, so glad you were able to come for a visit, even if it was an unexpected one at that," Kiowa said with a chuckle as he patted Santos on the shoulder.

"I don't know what we would have done if you and your mighty men didn't arrive. I am profoundly grateful. And please, give my honored thanks to your father, I know he is a busy man," Santos said.

"Yes, he is. As was your father as well. Both are respectful men. We are continually reminded by his wise words and great leadership, he will never be forgotten," Kiowa said as he held the stirrup of Santos' saddle as he mounted his loyal stead, now relaxed, fed, and rested.

"Oh, since we are mentioning our fathers. I never did tell you that day, but your presence at my father's funeral was much needed, I deeply appreciate that and will forever cherish it," said Santos.

Kiowa nodded and smiled.

"Let's be on our way then," Santos held his hand high, palm facing Kiowa, as was tradition for the Bisonteaus people to greet one another and say goodbye. With a swift tap of his heels and a glance to his men, they spun their behemoths and were off toward the nomad plains.

**(Same morning; Pale-foot lands)**

As the suns shone brighter, Namid stood there, piercing eyes, tears coming down her face. Two of the women comforted her, inviting her to sit back down next to the morning campfire. Tala stood and walked in front of Namid, forcing Dantias' perplexed gaze towards Tala.

"Why must you bring greater shame to her and our clan, demanding that she tell you all these things? She has suffered enough. Let her be, go now. Allow us to heal with her," Tala said with a direct, yet compassionate tone.

Dantias, his mind reeling with thoughts, stood almost dumbfounded, hardly able to grasp what he had just heard. A surge of emotions flooded his being, anger, sadness, desperation, complete helplessness.

He came to his senses, turning and looking Tala in the eyes.

"Will you do nothing? Will you not demand an explanation of this injustice?" Dantias asked with a forceful tone.

Namid and the other women, seated at the morning fire, raised their eyes to the two men standing in front of one another. Dantias turned, addressing the rest of the nomad men and women who had gathered in a large circle due to the morning's commotion.

"What will you do? Will you allow this injustice to endure, this degrading of our people? This cannot be tolerated!" said Dantias.

The clan began to gather closer now and speak amongst themselves, nodding their heads in agreement. Tala seeing where this could lead his people, spoke up.

"This will lead us to only more pain, more shame. It is a great grievance that has come upon my house today, we are full of sorrow, but we must not take justice into our power. For as the Great Teachings say that true justice is the great Creator's alone, He will bring all things under His hand. Not us my brothers, we must forgive and look for peace," Tala spoke with passion.

"But do not the scrolls also teach us that, there is a time for joy, a time for love, a time for sadness, a time for peace, a time to bring justice and even war!" Dantias said now moved with anger as he walked the circle of those gathered there, shaking his fists.

"Will you just stand there and do nothing? Will you be quiet as one of your own struggles in pain? Come, ride with me! Let us bring this to the clans, let us ask the people what should be done!

Someone must attest to this heinous crime! Is it not written, that if one is in pain, all carry the same pain and shame?" Dantias seemed to be speaking now from his pain and not of Namid's as he pointed towards the area of where the palace was located extremely far away in the distance.

The crowd, began to speak up, nodding their heads in agreement. Their voices went from regular voices to a slow-growing wave, gaining force every time it washes out to sea, returning with greater and greater force. The people's reaction was like this, as the comments increased, the story caught fire throughout the crowd. People could be seen turning one to another sharing briefly the story and shame that had come upon Namid and Tala's family. Confused faces were seen in the crowd as newcomers approached, questioning, and asking what all this was about. These same faces, quickly turned to frowns and disgust, nodded in agreement that something must be done to right this wrong.

Tala looked about, seeing that the entire camp was gathered, and others were moving in closer. There seemed to be a certain energy that was growing, a contagious anger. The voices began to go from speaking to stern comments, to now outspoken shouting that something must be done. Namid, noticing her grandfather's appearance, stood to her feet, and quickly walked over to Dantias, pushing him in the chest and grabbing his shoulders.

"Stop this! Stop this now! Look at what you are doing, we are a peaceful people!" Namid shouted with a trembling voice.

"I must speak out; you have been wronged! I cannot stop this, I love you, I must stand for you and your house!" Dantias exclaimed.

"You love me?!" Namid exclaimed. She then got closer to him, standing face to face, looking up into his eyes.

"If you love me. If you care for my people, even your own Dynasty, stop!" Namid steeled as she looked sternly into his eyes.

Dantias paused for a moment, his eyes connected with Namid's, for a moment considering a future, far away, only with her. Then taking both of her hands and holding them, he breathed deeply and said, "One day, very soon, you will understand. Remember you told me once, that with my influence, with my heritage, I could make a difference?"

"Yes, but not like this," Namid interrupted.

"Look around you, this is only the beginning. I'm doing this for you, for us!" Dantias finished saying this he put her hands down at her side, quickly turned, screaming to the crowd, "Come, ride with me! Let us bring justice to your people, to our people!"

At once the crowd began to cheer in an uproar,  a group of people mounted quantum. They whooped and cheered, as they raised their fists in the air, ready to ride with Dantias wherever he was to go.

Dantias turned and saw one of Namid's cousins, a strong man with a stern focused face, and gestured to him to hand him the reigns of one of the quantum that was now close by. As he handed Dantias the reigns, Dantias spoke close in his ear.

"Are you with me, you and your brothers?" he nodded in agreement.

"Then let us spread the word, let us join the neighboring clan to us as well, for they are many," Dantias said with great confidence.

The light-foot clan was a strong, Arabian, nomadic people that lived just over the mountains, where the savanna plains end and meet with the desert hills, just before reaching the beaches that lead to the great oceans of the Mareviteaus Realm. This clan mostly kept to themselves but were also known for their quick tempers and readiness to argue, even fight. They were less than a day's ride away. If they sent a few scouts ahead, they could easily get word to them quickly.

"They will be willing, I know this," Namid's cousin said to Dantias.

Dantias jumped upon to the quantum, raised his fist in the air, briefly looked down at Namid with disappointment, but quickly turned away as he shouted, "Let us go! Follow me!"

In that moment Namid looked over at her grandfather, both knowing now that the actions put in motion would take them, their people, and even possibly the realm to a point of no return.

Dantias rode off into the distance with 100 riders, men and women who cheered him on and were ready to follow him to bring justice. Clouds of dust could be seen as they rode off.

## (Meanwhile, Entering the Equiantus Realm)

Santos and his men rode at a steady and quick pace. He needed to find his brother before things got out of hand.

Santos did not know all that had taken place, neither on the nomad plains nor back at the palace, but he knew he must find his brother.

"So where are we going my lord?" asked one of the guards riding alongside Santos.

"We're crossing over towards the nomad clan's lands. I believe that we will find Dantias there," said Santos.

"That's what you said the other day, and we got run down by those black demons!" the guard said directly.

"I know, that's why we're crossing through the Pinto-clan farmlands. We're not as likely to get caught off guard through here," Santos responded.

"Yeah, I suppose that's a better plan," replied the guard.

The Pinto-clan is a loyal farming community. Much of the produce that is sold on Market Street comes from their farms. They are also well known for their training of the behemoth, especially quantum. For decades, the Pinto-clan has domesticated, bred, and trained these special creatures.

As the riders passed by the large pole markers of the Bison-teaus realm, the tall grasslands slowly transitioned into the smoother and shorter grass found on the outskirts of the Houlton Dynasty.

They could smell the aroma of the farm's tilled soil with the sweet fragrance of wildflowers that grew there. Approaching a smooth path, it was as if the path was cut away into the grass, made by the continued traveling between farms. Following this path they turned a bend, the riders were greeted by the expansive view of fields of crops that stretched out like a mosaic tapestry, each patch, vibrant with life.

The lush green wheat swayed as a slight breeze blew through it. On the far side of the path rows of corn stood erect and strong, reaching the rider's shoulders, the golden tassels seemed to almost bounce above the long leaves.

Santos and his men felt a sense of peace rush over them as they rode, knowing that through these lands, they were welcome and without adversaries.

In the distance Pinto-clan farmers could be seen, some bent over in concentration, carefully tending rows of delicate seedlings, while others laughed as they lifted baskets of freshly harvested produce.

As their tradition, the Pinto-clan still did everything by hand, even though the technology existed to make their work less tedious, they insisted and believed that working by hand brings a cleaner, purer product to the market, plus edifies family relationships, bringing them together for a common good.

As the riders exchanged smiles and nods with several of the farmers, songs could be heard as they worked, and an occasional whistle and "Get up, let's go, hey!" as one of the Pinto-clan men could be seen guiding a rock-behemoth as it pulled a plow, tilling up the earth behind it. Here there was a certain unity that could be felt with the heartbeat of rural life.

As Santos rode through, he heard from behind someone calling his name, it was not hard to notice a Houlton prince passing by, especially unannounced. It brought attention.

"Prince Houlton! Sir! A moment of your time!" the voice shouted.

A Pinto-clan quantum rider rode up alongside Santos and his men. Santos turned to see who was coming, without missing a beat as they continued trotting on the path.

"Well, hello. What is the commotion?" Santos asked, he recognized the rider right away, it was Aryan, the known quantum trainer.

He and his family had helped train every quantum of the palace guards for as long as anyone could remember. Aryan's father has been known by the Houltons for longer than either of them has been alive.

"How have you been? How was your presentation at the Market Fair this year?" Santos inquired.

"It was well, as expected sir," Aryan answered, "Excuse me to pry, but I had a concern," he continued.

Santos turned and looked at him, acknowledging that he continued.

"On the last official night of the fair, a few of us always go out to the games to see what we can win. Ya know, like last night out kinda thing," Aryan explained.

"Yes, go on," Santos said, now intrigued.

"Well, we came across your brother, Prince Dantias, doing quite well at one of the games. He didn't see us, since we were watching from a distance," Aryan said.

"Did he win a prize?" Santos said sarcastically.

"That I don't know, but what happened after that is what I mean to tell you about," Aryan's tone of voice became nervous.

Santos raised his hand motioning to the others to stop, he pulled back the reins bringing his behemoth to a stop and coming to the side of the path. The others trotted on just a bit more to give the two privacies to speak. Santo's expression grew somber as he looked to Aryan sensing the change in the atmosphere around them.

"What happened, do you know where he is?" Santos asked.

Aryan paused briefly, collecting his thoughts, and contemplating what he would say next. Santos looked at him with a feeling that something was wrong.

"Actually, I might have some information that could help. That night I, we, heard screaming and yelling," explained Aryan.

Santos' eyes widened, "Really? What did you hear, what was it about?"

This marked a turning point for Santos, moving from not knowing anything, going on only a hunch, to having some actual details of his brother's whereabouts.

"Please, tell me what you know," Santos said.

"Well, all I can say is what I heard and saw from a distance. We noticed that Dantias walked back towards one of the rest stations on the back side of the Theatre Dome. I didn't think much of it really until we heard a lady scream, at him that he couldn't be in there and then a bunch of commotion. Dantias was yelling and pushing people around like he had lost something," Aryan explained.

"Namid," Santos whispered to himself.

That is the only thing Santos could think of that could cause his brother to react in such a way, "Was Dantias there with her? Did something happen to Namid?" Seemed there were more questions now than answers.

"Is that all, what else do you see?" Santos asked.

"All we could tell after that was there were palace guards that came around him, said something to him, and walked him out of there," Aryan said.

"Just thought you should know. Wish I could tell you more," he said.

"Thank you, grateful you told me," Santos replied.

Santos sat for a moment and pondered what he had just heard. It assured in his mind that they should keep on their current route. Knowing about their culture and migration he calculated they should be close to their celebration tree about now. Then at once he sat up in his saddle with confidence, tapped his be-hemoth with his heels bringing it to a trot, then a gallop, waved his hand to the others, and gestured they move on. Aryan kept right behind.

"I wish to ride with you sir if I am not a bother. I could be of some use," Aryan said as he adjusted his position in his saddle and tied a blue handkerchief around his neck, with the knot in the front. He did this every time he was preparing to ride and ride fast, it was as though his quantum could feel his rider's energy shift.

Aryan knew his behemoth and it knew him, the hours, and hours they had spent together, riding, training, and living life, they had been almost inseparable ever since he was a young boy.

"Fair enough, let's go. I don't want to waste any more time," Santos said.

"We can cut across the back fields. They haven't been plowed yet, so we won't have to worry about crop rows or uneven ground," Aryan explained.

"Show us the way," Santos ordered as he lifted his head, and acknowledged to the others that Aryan was leading the group.

As they rode, their pace increased from a gallop to a good steady run. They urged their behemoth forward, the sound of their feet hitting the ground in a rhythmic fashion. The path seemed to almost unfold before them as they cut across fields with Aryan leading the way. The lush fields of corn, barley oats, wheat, and wildflowers were swayed, filling the air with sweet fragrances.

Dust kicked up around them and swirled in the morning sunlight as they rode on. They passed by well-organized fields with immaculate layouts.

The workers paused their labor, squinted into the sunlight as they watched the riders go by with looks of concern and curiosity upon their faces. Whispers seemed to ripple through the fields, questions hung on everyone's tongues as they gripped their tools and baskets tightly.

The comrades, with one more now added to the group, leaned lower against their beasts, and raced along the paths that seemed to blur beneath them. They pressed forward and raced against time to find answers.

# CHAPTER 19

A small mountain range laid before Dantias and the group that now followed him. The mountains were larger than the rolling hills of the Asnos-clan's mines but quite a bit smaller than the larger mountains to the Southwest, where even from a great distance, the shiny and futuristic city of the Terrartius realm could be seen.

The mountains before them separated the plains from the desert, then connected to the sandy beaches and portals that lead down to the Mareviteaus Realm. If you followed the marked paths, you could ride up and through these smaller cliffs in just a few hours.

As they approached the base of the mountain, Dantias addressed his followers, raising his hand.

"Comrades and allies, I ask that only a few of you continue with me from here. Make camp here and rest for a while. I will ride on to meet with the clan, and those of them who wish to join us will ride back and rejoin you here. There is no need for all of us to tire ourselves," Dantias said.

The crowd nodded in agreement, while some 20 riders came closer to Dantias and agreed to ride on with him. A sternness was upon his face as he glanced around looking each in the eyes, seeing the same look in their eyes, and without a word they started on a smooth angled path leading up and over the green-sided mountain hills.

It would not be long until they were cresting over the top and then down the decline on the other side, transitioning into the sandy terrain of the light-foot clans' lands.

## (Santos' party approaches the Nomad plains)

It was mid day, both suns were at their peak in the sky as Santos and his group approached the nomad's encampment. As they drew closer, the vibrant colors of the tents come into sight. However, an unsettling scene began to unfold before them.

The air was thick with tension, which and enormous difference between the usual cheerful sound of the clan.

The group entered the camp unnoticed and unwelcomed by the elders, which was the usual custom in the nomad clans.

Santos noticed a group had gathered near the center of the camp; their voices raised in agitation.

Some of the groups were gesturing animatedly, their faces etched with worry and great frustration. Some of the women in the group were clutching their children and walking about anxiously.

While Santos and his group dismounted and began to walk toward the circle, he noticed a few of the elders including Tala, one of their wisest elders and Namid's grandfather, arguing severely.

It was clear that something had gone awry. Even the behemoth shifted uneasily, sensing the turmoil. Santos exchanged worried glances with Aryan and the others as they walked closer.

"We must stay calm my brothers," Santos heard Tala say as they approached.

"How can you stay calm now, we must act! Either defend your granddaughter or ride with the prince! It is that simple. Make a choice!" one of the men shouted.

Suddenly the arguing group turned and noticed the uninvited guests. Quickly two of the nomad men, walked towards Santos, not even greeting him, as without missing a beat, and demanding an answer from the Houlton son.

"Tell him, tell him we must do something, we must act! We must not just stay here! Tell him my Lord Prince!" shouted one of the nomad men as he gestured to Santos and then to Tala.

"Greetings my brothers," Santos said as he raised his hand in salute. Aryan and the other palace guards stood just behind him, waiting to see what would transpire next.

Tala turned, with relief, and quickly greeted Santos with open arms, embracing him and inviting him to come close to the circle.

"Bless the Creator you have come, I was beginning to think my petition had not been heard. Welcome my Lord Prince, thank you for coming!" Tala said.

"Your petition my good sir? I have not received or heard of any petition," Santos said.

Tala looked at him puzzled, almost confused. "I sent a rider early this morning to the palace, asking for reassurance and council," Santos looked at him intriguingly.

"Council and help, because of the turmoil we have endured from the Houlton Dynasty and the uproar created by your brother," Tala spoke plain and direct.

"I am sorry, but I know not of your petition. We have come because..." Santos said.

Tala interrupted him, "Then why are you here, if it is not to help bring peace to this quite terrible situation?" he asked with frustration.

Santos kept calm as he looked around and tried to discern what happened.

"My companions and I have come seeking answers and inquiring about the whereabouts of my brother, Dantias," Santos said clearly.

"Whereabouts? You mean to say, you know not of what has happened here? To my granddaughter, to our people?" Tala's voice cracked, as he spoke. As he spoke, he held back tears.

Namid came closer and held his arm as she stood behind her grandfather.

"I am sorry my dear sir, I do not. We have been riding since yesterday, in search of Dantias. We do not know what has become of him," Santos explained.

The nomad clan began to speak loudly, in an uproar amongst themselves. Santos looked about, understanding now that the situation was much worse than he could have imagined.

Tala turned to the people and yelled three short words in a native tongue, and then a great silence rushed through the tribe.

"Come, we must speak, many things have taken place in these last two days," Tala motioned to Santos to follow him and go sit in front of his tent.

Santos followed him in step, expecting the worst.


**(Desert plains)**

Seated with the clan leaders, the sun hung high in the sky, shining brightly over the sandy horizon and tranquil oasis, where the sound of gentle water trickled over a few smooth stones, which were built up to create a small pool. There were a few lush shrubs nearby and four tall skinny palm trees that, along with the tents, gave just enough shade to escape from the hot sun.

Dantias sat cross-legged on a hand-made woven rug, sur-rounded by the leaders. The scent of fragrant herbs could be smelt in the warm air. A few small campfires crackled nearby, while the clan's intricately patterned tents formed a colorful backdrop against the light-colored desert sands. Dantias, with determination in his eyes, addressed the group with a calm, precise voice.

"I understand your traditions, your way of life," he began, as he looked at each elder in the eye, showing them profound respect for their autonomy.

"I have come to ask you for your help. A great, tragic matter has come upon our brothers from the pale-foot clan," Dantias then explained what had happened.

The elders of the clan sat in a circle, their expressions were a mix of skepticism, curiosity, and frustration. Even though the two clans had similar traditions to the, they were less outspoken, less emotional, and deeply rooted in their solitary ways.

They were wary of outsiders who sought to disrupt the deli-cate balance of their way of life. Even though they agreed that these were terrible grievances. They had happened to Tala and his family, not to them. They held little empathy for others.

The eldest leader, a graying man with wrinkled lines carved deep into his experienced and weathered face, crossed his arms, and spoke.

"We have thrived alone for generations, not seeking help from or disturbing anyone else in our realm," he said firmly.

"Why should we stand with you or anyone else? What do you offer that we have not already provided for ourselves?" an elder asked directly.

Dantias took a moment to sense the atmosphere. He quickly sensed their stubbornness, the clan were kind people, but very much set in their ways.

Yet, there was a flicker of openness within their trust as they sat by the brightly lit pool, a symbol of life amidst the harshness of the desert.

"Greater strength," Dantias said with confidence.

The leaders exchanged hesitant glances, still holding fast to their individualistic mindset.

Dantias continued, pressing on, "Together, we can forge alliances not only for survival, but also to secure a thriving future. Things have changed, since my father's passing, our realm has not been the same. I, a member of the Houlton family, can assure you that all our people will be protected. By our combined forces, and a collaboration of knowledge, with each one staying true to their own clan's heritages, all of us will be enhanced in our ways and have a secure place as members of the new re-envisioned Houlton Dynasty."

The leaders listened attentively to each word and starred as Dantias continued to explain his vision for the future.

The tension in the air began to lift. The eldest uncrossed his arms, now intrigued by Dantias' vision. For them, the most important thing was the preservation of their heritage.

"This sounds well and good, but what of your mother, The Dutchess? Or your brother? Are they in agreement as well?" one of the other leaders inquired.

"I assure you; they are of no concern. I speak for the Houlton Dynasty. I alone have been given the task of unifying each clan and securing the future for our realm," Dantias said charismatically.

The elders began to nod in agreement. It was in that moment, as he spoke, that he realized that within himself he held the confidence to lead and bring unity to the realm.

"If I can sway the opinion of one of the most stubborn clans in the Houlton Dynasty, I could do the same with others as well. This could go much further than just the Equiantus realm," Dantias thought to himself.

Then in unison, the leaders spoke together, "For the justice of our people!"

They raised their cups filled with cool water from the oasis. With a sense of triumph, Dantias raised his cup as well as they all smiled and drank together.

Dantias then heard a rustling, then a growling, clicking sound come from one of the tents behind him. As he turned his head, he noticed a caged animal sitting in the shadows of the interior of the cloth-wrapped dwelling.

"Is that what I think it is?" Dantias asked.

"Oh yes," one of the leaders said with a smile.

"You have trained one of those black demons, how?" Dantias asked with surprise.

"We can show you," the elder said with a sneer.

### (Nomad plains)

Tala looked at Santos as he reacted to this devastating and troublesome news. Santos hung his head in shame, frustration, and sadness.

"How is it that those of his guard, the ones trained to protect the clans would or could even participate in acts so horrendous?" Santos thought to himself as his fists tightened.

It was early afternoon; the two suns painted the sky with vivid strokes of purple and gold. The group sitting in front of Tala's tent looked at each other and hoped for answers to this great turmoil. A few embers burned in the small fire in front of them. As Santos continued to ponder the situation, he could not help but feel overwhelmed by it.

"How could his brother rise in such a way, taking everything into his own hands? What did he desire to accomplish with this? And now involving another clan, who had nothing to do with any of this?" Santos' heart sank at the thought of what could become of all this.

One of the nomad men nudged Tala's arms to persuade him to address another issue. Tala nodded.

"My Lord, I do not wish to trouble you more with burdens, but we have another question," said Tala.

"Yes?" Santos looked up at him.

"Dantias spoke of the banishment of our people as well. That your mother, The Dutchess, had expelled all of us and we are no longer part of this realm, and are no longer considered as members of your family's Dynasty, is this true?" Tala asked.

Santos looked him in the eyes, thinking things could not be worse, then sat up straight and spoke to Tala directly.

"I know not of the banishment of your people. I have been in every meeting of the council with The Dutchess, and never once was there talk of such things. Be at peace my brothers, you are our people just as any other clan in our realm. You have my word on that," Santos said with certainty.

What Santos said was true, no such topic was spoken of during the council sessions with the Kingmen.

The Dutchess had only told Dantias this. Clearly provoking him to give away his secret leading him to show where and with whom he was spending his time.

Just as the fire's embers faded, their discussion was halted by the sound of hurried footsteps. A nomad scout, the very same scout Tala had sent to seek help from the palace, burst into their circle. His clothing was covered with the dust of the plains and his eyes were wide with panic, and he breathed heavily as he spoke.

"My Lords, my sir!" he gasped.

Surprise and relief came over him as Santos turned around along with the others.

"Oh, my Lord Prince Santos!" he gasped, desperation in his voice, "We must return to the palace at once!"

Every heart around the dwindling fire stilled, the shared sorrow was now replaced by palpable urgency. The scout's expression conveyed a serious message, one that transcended even words, a sense of terrible doom.

He continued catching his breath, "The palace is in dismay, and there is need of the Houlton Princes."

"What is wrong, what do you know? Speak!" Santos shouted as he quickly stood to his feet.

"I was not permitted to enter the palace, but I observed the chaotic movement son the palace grounds." said the scout.

"And?" Santos inquired.

"A great tragedy has fallen The Dutchess. I saw, from a distance, as they carried her into the hall," said the nomad scout as he lowered his head.

"Dead?" Santos asked.

"That I do not know, but I believe there is a great need for you there," explained the scout.

The last few crackling coals could be heard as a breeze blew the white ashes onto the ground, Santos' furrowed brow reflected his anguish as the gravity of the scouts words pressed down upon him, forcing him to confront an agonizing choice between the deep bonds in shared grief of the nomad clan and the call of responsibility drawing him back to the palace. One does not know what they are truly capable of until the situation presents itself.

It was in this moment, deep inside his being, as the embers of the fire faded away, that a spark was ignited in his soul to believe, in justice and in order. Santos was not motivated by the pressure of all he had come to know that day, but by his deep sense of right and wrong, justice and fairness. He raised his head and took a deep breath, all eyes on him, awaiting his next words.

"I will find out who wronged you, I will be an instrument of peace for all of our people," he spoke plainly and directly to Tala, as Namid stood just behind her grandfather.

"What about your brother? He said the same, and now he is rising other clans to exercise justice in the name of our people," Tala said.

"I cannot speak for the actions of Dantias, nor do I support actions that promote disharmony among the clans. I can say that the Houlton Dynasty is and will be one of support for all our people, standing for justice and peace. As I said before, I will personally find answers to these crimes and help bring about order. I am convinced that all these situations are not a coincidence, but instead connected to a greater scheme. All I can ask of you, now, at this moment, is for your patience and understanding as I move forward to discover the truth," Santos explained with greater confidence.

As Tala extended his hand in approval, they both shook arms. Then, the weathered elder turned to a few of his loyal men and instructed them to go with Santos.

Tala and Namid could be seen watching them ride away, as the suns shone brightly down upon them. A cool breeze blew in the same direction as Santos and his growing group of riders, as though the accompanying winds were pushing them on their way, as if the Creator was sending a sense of approval.

# CHAPTER 20

Dantias was now accompanied across the plains by a much larger group some of which were armed with their own swords, lassos, and short spears. They rode with confidence and a sense of power. Close to 100 souls rode their behemoths behind Dantias.

The Lord Prince smiled, feeling a sense of self-worth, that he, and he alone had been chosen by the Creator to lead the people of the Equiantus Realm. He was sure that each clan would follow him now.

As the group rode past the mountain range, down the into the hill country their numbers caught the attention of the Asno clan and many of the half-bloods as they came out of the mines. Several men could be seen taking up pickaxes and shovels as they began to trot along the riders as they went by. The growing army's energy began spreading to those around. Many began to join even though they really did not know why.

"What is all the fuss about?!" one of the Asno miners asked a rider as they came down the hills.

"Our Lord Prince Dantias has called us to ride with him! He is to bring order and take away all the corruption of the realm!" a rider called out.

While the group pushed forward Dantias began to think, his plan was developing as he went. He turned towards one of the clans leaders that rode closest to him.

"We shall call on others to join our cause! It is time to bring true unity to the realms! Follow me to the Market Fairgrounds. There are many who will still be there!" Dantias shouted.

"Let us go! We are with you!" the leader shouted back.

They then began to shout and whoop, one by one the riders turned and looked at one another, then joining in. The shouts and cheers were contagious amongst the crowd until all were cheering, some not even knowing why.

**(Meanwhile as Santos rides back to the palace)**

Santos also rode with a group of followers. Although he did not know the exact whereabouts of his brother, all he did know was he needed to get back to the palace as soon as possible to decipher what had taken place, and what had become of his mother, The Dutchess.

When they arrived at the palace Santos quickly dismounted and went in search of The Professor. If anyone knew what was going on it would be him.

The once peaceful courtyard brimming with life was now full of a palpable tension, which hung in the air. The dynasty banners, which flew the families crest, seemed almost dulled by the dire circumstances.

While Santos walked briskly through the palace halls, he looked about desperately for The Professor. Then, he saw him at the far end of the hall. The Dutchess was laid out on one of the long tables, with several of the dynasty doctors, the chapel minister, and a few guards standing around the table. The Professor turned as he heard Santos' footsteps, his demeanor uncharacteristically somber, his eyes clouded with worry, hinting at the grave revelation he was about to share.

As Santos stepped closer, The Professor intercepted Santos and drew him aside, away from the anxious whispers of the others.

The weight of his words bore down on him as he tried to explain to Santos the horrendous situation that had taken place within the palace walls.

"The Dutchess, your mother," he began, his voice low and steady, "has been poisoned."

Santos felt a shiver run through him as he heard the news. The very thought of it was unthinkable.

"How could this have happened? Who could have done this?" he thought, his mind racing.

The Professor continued, detailing how he had found her earlier that morning as he brought the usual cut flowers up to the palace. How he had the guards bring her back to the palace and placed on the table and how for the past several hours he and the doctors had performed several tests to find answers. Traces of a toxin were found in her bloodstream, leading to accusations of foul play.

"It was ever so delicate my Lord Prince. It was almost unnoticeable. As you know, I do enjoy horticulture..."

"The situation at hand Professor, sir," Santos interrupted.

"Oh, yes, so sorry my Lord," The Professor continued, "Well, you see I have a great record of plants, and natural herbs and well, we could not find anything out of the ordinary, so I took a blood test and ran it through my personal database of flowers, plants and there were traces of snakeweed in her system. And as you know, snakeweed if ingested, becomes a poison," The Professor explained.

Each word reinforced Santos' growing decision. He understood that this was no isolated incident, but rather a calculated strike aimed at the very heart of their society. This situation, Tala's family situation, all of it orchestrated to bring about disunity and strife.

**(Market Fair grounds just outside the Theatre Dome)**

As the crowds dwindled and the workers were packed up their booths, and crafts and loaded their behemoths to depart back to their clans and realms.

Dantias and his growing crowd of followers rode up to one of the platforms that had been used for outdoor musical and theatrical displays, jumped up onstage and began to call everyone that could hear to come closer.

"Attention everyone, please gather around!" Dantias yelled out from the platform.

There was a substantial number who were already riding with him, which got the attention of many others.

Due to the Market Fair being a gathering of talent and cultures there were people present from each realm. As the people gathered around the stage, Dantias continued.

"Today, I come before you not just as a Equiantus citizen. Not only as a son of the Houlton Dynasty, but as a man. A man who seeks justice for his people!" he shouted and took a deep breath before he continued.

"I have come upon the knowledge of a horrific crime. A crime not only held against one of my own people, but a someone who has been wronged in the name of peace! The realms speak of peace and unity all the while the most terrible crimes have been committed by the very people who have sworn to protect us!" Dantias spoke with authority and assurance.

"What makes you any different, aren't you part of it too?! Isn't the palace your home? Aren't you a prince?!" someone in the growing crowd cried out.

"Yes, I was part of this so-called dynasty of peace, until I came to see the truth. The truth behind their lies and corruption!

For too long have we turned a blind eye, believing in what our authorities have told us, enduring the weight of corruption as it slowly seeps into our society, becoming like a poison that taints our very essence!" Dantias shouted.

"Our beloved realm has been exploited by those in power, who are driven solely by their own desires. They genuinely care not for the well-being of the people, but are blinded by ambition, creating a world where deceit can thrive openly. If it has been present in Houlton City and the Equiantus Realm, it is only a matter of time when the other realms begin to follow suit."

Dantias continued his call to action, "The Council of Kingmen swore an oath to protect us all from such tyranny, only to permit injustice within themselves and allow for the robbing of a young woman's innocence to take place! I call on you, to come with me, to my own home, the palace and hall of Kingmen to demand justice be done! Justice is not merely an ideal. It is the very foundation upon which we must build our future! Each of us must stand together, in unity. Picture a realm, a planet, where every citizen feels valued, where the cries of the innocent are not blotted out by the higher class or those who seek to only have power over others. Imagine a world where integrity and honor lead and oppose deceit and oppression!"

"I understand the disillusionment that many of you feel. I know the rumors that stain our lands, rumors of doubt. The scars of betrayal run deep; I too carry those scars. Let us not forget, even the longest night will yield to the dawn's first light!" Dantias spoke with such charisma and confidence that the crowd was hanging on his every word.

The crowd murmured and whispered amongst themselves, nodding their heads in agreement. Dantias watched as his influence washed over the crowd like a small wave flowing from the shore on out the ocean.

He continued to speak, "Together, we can construct a system where true laws are upheld, and justice is upheld. A system where the strong rise to protect the vulnerable, and the decisions that are make benefit the common good rather than the highly privileged few!"

Dantias scanned the crowd for their reaction before he continued, "I am calling on you, you faithful and loyal citizens, those of you who feel that your voice has not truly been heard! I require your voices, your fervor, your commitment as we work together to take a stand and embark on this grand venture to transform our realms into an honest reality! Let us march forth in united purpose and in spirit, together we shall not only endure; we shall triumph! Are you with me?! I will lead you, I will take you to my home, to the palace and we will make a change together!" Dantias lifted his fists in the air as he shouted.

The convinced crowd cheered and clapped as Dantias mounted his quantum. One of the clan's leaders smiled and nodded as he looked around. They were amazed at response of all the people, including those who were not even from the Equiantus realm.

Dantias turned and rode through the crowd, other riders followed as the crowd parted cheering them on. Once the final riders passed through the crowd, all of those who were gathered marched and followed them on foot through the streets making their way towards the palace.

# CHAPTER 21

It was now mid-afternoon, and the twin suns cast their golden and purplish rays over the city, calm yet assertive, illuminating the streets.

Houlton City was occupied by many Equiantus citizens this afternoon, all oblivious to the actions, which had transpired on this dramatic day.

Each person was going about their own business. The Market Fair was ending, so those who were visiting the realm were spending the extra time to visit the local stores and shops. The visitors were admiring and purchasing articles of clothing, jewelry, and other handcrafted items they would not normally find in their own realm.

At the far end of the main street, a procession rounded the corner and began its way towards the palace.

Dantias rode at the helm of the determined parade, seated on a quantum, whose muscles rippled in the suns' light as it trotted. Its feet marched out a distinct rhythm as they made their way down the street, captivating the attention of the shoppers and citizens nearby.

As the procession surged onward, more people emerged from the shade of their doorways and shops drawn to this spectacle. Some of their faces lit with enthusiasm as they assumed it was a parade to celebrate the end of the Market Fair, they joined in, lining both sides of the streets, men, and women both, young and old.

Further down one of the side streets, Hlok was in their family's workshop along with his father and one of his younger brothers as they put the finishing touches on the leg of a custom iron table. As was the custom, the Clydesdale-clan always took advantage of the Market Fair season to make and sell their hand-crafted furniture and adornments.

The workshop had an enormous forge at the center, with a fierce orange and bluish flames fueled by a mix of high-quality coal and air that was pumped in through a pipe which was connected to a lever on the right-hand side. The heat radiated from it, warmed the air and casting flickering shadows on all the walls. Although the room was quite large, it had a close homely feel to it, due to the physical size of Hlok, his father, and brother, but also because each wall was encased with tools and trinkets. Even though the workshop was full, from top to bottom, it was strikingly clean with every single piece in its proper place.

Surrounding the forge was a collection of anvils. There were low and flat anvils for delicate work, and tall and husky ones for shaping larger projects. Each was well-worn with its surface decorated with the marks of expert craftsmen. The forge had been used for heating and melting the metals that they used to make amazing artisan creations for generations.

A strong and sturdy workbench stood against one wall, its surface a place that held a multitude of tools. Chisels of several varied sizes, files for smoothing edges, and a set of calipers, a family heirloom that was passed on from father to son for generations, which were used for delicate, precise measurements were neatly laid in order, accompanied by crumpled-up sketches and blueprints.

Hlok's younger brother could be found here often, doodling innovative designs for intricate furniture, gates with swirling motifs, or robust tables that tell a story through their form. It was a such table that Hlok was finishing as he heard the ruckus just outside.

"What's going on out there?" he spoke over the noise of his father pounding on apiece for an iron gate.

"What'd you say?" his father asked as he stopped hammering.

"Seems something is happening out in the street. All the neighbors are out," Hloks said as he set down his laser-torch.

The laser-torch was something he had invented, it could take the heat and fire of the forge and, with suction run through a pipe where it mixed into a small chamber of specific gases, making it even hotter, then as the pressure would build up, it pushed the fire through into a hammer's handle, making the hammer itself into a mini-forge that could be used to heat, melt, and craft whatever material Hlok was tooling. It was quite an innovative tool. His younger brothers coined the name laser-torch for it because if you pressed the hammer just right and flicked it with your wrist, a spout of fire would shoot out the head of the hammer, simulating a blaster's laser, you had to be quite careful while using it.

Hlok took off his leather apron and hung it on a hook as he stepped outside. There was a crowd of people walking, even some trotting, past their shop towards the main street. As he looked down the street his father stepped out and stood next to him, both massive and muscular in size, their shadows reached the width of their street touching the other shops in front.

"What is it?" his father asked.

"Seems to be some kind of parade or march of some sort," Hlok responded.

"I do not remember hearing about any parade. If there was one, it would have been yesterday. That is when the Market Fair came to an official end," his father explained.

"I'm gonna go check it out, and see what all the commotion is about," Hlok said as he started walking towards Main Street.

"Alright, just do not take too long. We gotta get this table out before tonight. They will be by later to pick it up," his father instructed.

Hlok nodded and gave his father a thumbs up acknowledging his instruction, but his attention was directed due to the commotion just three blocks ahead.

As he approached, Hlok pushed his way through the crowd coming to the main street where the parade was passing by. Curiously, he looked about. A few Equiantian children were pointing, their eyes wide with wonder, while elders waved.

Dantias was further down the street, up ahead of everyone else. He waved, and then with a raised fist in the air.

The marching crowd yelled out, "Justice for all!"

The atmosphere crackled with energy; an almost collective heartbeat of hope transcended the mundane activities of the day. With each step, more joined the movement.

The humming pulse of unity surged through each person as they marched behind Dantias and his riders. Although all realms mingled together as the parade continued towards the palace, most of the participants were those of the Equiantus realm.

As the crowd approached the palace gates, Dantias could not help but notice how beautiful and grand it was, a stark reminder of the generations of authority it represented. Still, he continued forward with his plan, his mission to confront.

As Dantias lifted his hand high, a beacon of strength and resilience, his voice soared above the crowd, bringing them all into a fervent chorus.

"Justice!" the crowd roared, their voices mingling with the wind.

Dantias stood at the front gate, staring up at the palace, the only home he had ever known, contemplating his next move. He relaxed his shoulders for a moment as he sat on his quantum, the rustling of the crowd behind him, yet no one spoke a word, even the behemoths seemed to understand the seriousness of the scene set before them because they too were still.

As Dantias breathed deeply through his nose, he raised his head to the sky, looked at each of the large statutes that stood on each side of the massive portal, in their carved marble eyes, almost as if he was challenging his father and every Houlton that had come before him. It was this indelible moment that would ripple through the very fabric of their realm, their way of life, preparing to challenge this symbol of power and authority that stood before them.

At a distance Hlok made his way through the crowd and pushing himself closer and closer to the front towering above the rest of the citizens. He was a good 50 yards off when he realized what was taking place at the foot of the main gates of the Houlton Dynasty's palace.

Rushing footsteps on the other side of the gate broke the silence as palace guards ran into position aligning themselves on the opposite side of the palace gates. Then, on the upper terrace, facing directly in front of the main street, the place where Kingsmen of old would give their discourses, words of encouragement, and instructions to the people of the realm, appeared Santos accompanied by The Professor.

Dantias' gaze drifted from the hand-carved statues that stood as motionless giants one on either side of the iron-framed wooden gates to the upper terrace where his brother now stood looking down at him. Their eyes met for just a moment in the silence of that defining afternoon. The wind blew across their faces and the snort of one of the rider's quantum could be heard just behind Dantias in the crowd.

Santos raised his eyebrows and tilted his head slightly to the side as he looked at his brother from a distance, almost indicating a silent question, "What will you do now my brother?"

Although Santos was relieved to finally know his brother's whereabouts, a quite different circumstance was before him now.

Then, as Dantias breathed deep and exhaled once more, he broke view with his brother and turned to the many followers behind him and raising his hand in the air.

Hlok stood at a distance yet at the same height as Dantias sitting on the back of his behemoth, spoke aloud to himself shaking his head, "No, not like this…"

Dantias' hand came down like an axe cutting through the air motioning for all who were with him to attack the gates and storm the palace walls. Then at once, like small insects on a sweet piece of candy, everyone, without personal reasoning, screamed,

"Justice!" as they all ran towards the gates and began to push and pound with all their might.

With doubt in his eyes, Santos turned and looked into The Professor's face, and searching for guidance as they navigate this defying path that lies before him. It was clear that they must find who was responsible for his mother's death, revealing the traitors in their midst, but first, he was forced to put order to this crowd that was rising against everything that his father stood for.

"Santos, my dear boy, leadership isn't about having all the answers," The Professor spoke as he placed a reassuring hand on Santos' shoulder, "it's about facing uncertainty. Even the strongest trees bend in the storm but do not break."

Now the pounding and screams for justice could be heard loudly just past the courtyard gates, hundreds seemed to have joined in now on this ambush of the palace.

Santos, took a deep breath, "I want to guide the people, but this, how does one respond to this? He's my brother."

"Your desire to serve the realm makes you a true leader. Don't shy away from the moments that make you great; use them. The courage to confront, not your brother, but your fear, can reveal your greatest strengths. I stood by your father for many years and his father before that, so believe me when I say, you are becoming one of the greats," The Professor said with assurance.

At that moment, Santos knew what he was to do, together, they would confront the dark forces that sought to disrupt the peace they had held for generations starting right here, at the palace gates.

"Remember, it's the heart within you that makes you a leader. Now, let's face this storm together," said The Professor.

The palace gates shook, they began to groan under the relentless pressure of the surging crowd. Yelling could be heard on the other side of the great palace walls, louder and louder, shouting off instructions to push this and pull that. Rock-behemoths, their massive bodies could be seen now pulling large, thick ropes, one end wrapped around their thick torsos, the other tied to the strong palace gates. The metals screeched, twisting, and slowly contorting as the beasts pulled.

"Pull, almost there!" someone shouted as people jumped up, hanging on the ropes, pulling with the behemoths.

Then at once, with a deafening crash, the gates fell to the ground. The crowd, became a chaotic sea of faces from each realm, poured into the palace grounds like a rushing wave.

Palace guards courageously defended their posts but were quickly overwhelmed. The guards, of course, were not accustomed to such things. Although they trained and prepared as guards, knowing how to fight in hand-to-hand combat and use a lighting-stick, they had  never been commanded to use such skills against others because the realms had become an utopia of peace, a few hundred years without war or violence. Some of them were trampled, others beaten back by the sheer force of the crowd's numbers.

Many people could be seen throwing lassos around the statues that were found in the garden, toppling them to the ground, their marble bodies shattering as they fell.

Then, at the forefront of the chaos, sat Dantias on his quantum, his eyes shining with malevolent triumph. His dark energy, growing, and seemed to feed the crowd's frenzy, urging them onward in this now destructive quest. The guards, now battered, stumbled backward as the mob advanced. Just when it seemed the palace itself was to be breached, a sudden, earsplitting boom shook the air.

Santos, from his upper vantage point, stood with The Professor and deployed emergency defense measures, a storm of tear gas-like bombs which rained down upon the crowd. The effect was immediate. Everyone, including the guards, was momentarily shocked, stunned, and disoriented. Dantias' beast let out a screech of terror, rearing up and tipping him to the ground, all the behemoths kicked and ran frantically looking for protection.

Unknown even to the palace guards, about four years earlier, special canon launchers were installed just above the palace's roof tiles, unnoticeable to the passerby, creating a defense system for the Houlton Dynasty grounds.

The guards, with lighting-sticks out, seized the opportunity and rallied together once again. They began to push forward, slowly regaining control of the palace courtyard. As the chaos slowly began to subside, the true extent of the damage became clear. The once-manicured gardens were now scarred and trampled, the statues lay shattered, and the palace gates were twisted and broken.

The suns now hung low in the later afternoon sky, casting a warm, golden, and light purple hue over the palace grounds. Dust and smoke swirled in the air, and mingled with the scent of sweat and fear, as the people regrouped standing to their feet, wiping their teary eyes and runny noses. As they began to reestablish some semblance of order, many of their faces smeared with dirt and fright, turned into expressions of determination, fueled by the desperation of the moment. Coughs could be heard ricocheting through the group as they steadied their breath, trying to calm both their bodies and minds.

Santos, now a pillar of composure amid the turmoil, his presence commanding the attention of those before him. Standing at the edge of the upper terrace he raised his arms slowly, a gesture that brought the disheartened crowd to listen. When he spoke, his voice boomed with clarity, echoing from the very place his ancestors had instructed from ages past.

"People of the realms, please listen to me!" His voice filled the air, rich and powerful, resonating from every corner of the terrace.

"You have come with a mission, a mission of justice, but you have been deceived! The justice you seek cannot be found in this manner. We all seek truth this day! As do I!" Santos' voice rang out.

"Peace, true peace, cannot be achieved through division. It is our unity that will forge the future you, and I, desire. Let us not be separated by confusion and anger but let us stand as one!" The Professor smiled as he saw a new leader being born.

"Unity?! Is that what you call it, Santos?!" Dantias' voice sliced through the air with a force of hatred, drawing the crowd's attention.

"Look around you! We have been silenced for too long! This so-called unity is but a chain around each of you, it keeps you blind to the truth we need to face!"

His words sparked a palpable tension, reflected in the faces of those around him. A mix of fear and an exhilarating sense of rebellion hung in the air. Dantias stepped forward, raising his fist high, determined to rally once again the spirits of those still holding on to confusion and doubt.

"Will you just bow a knee to this broken system? We are not puppets in your game Santos, not anymore!" he yelled as he shouted up towards his brother.

"Stand with me if you desire change, demand that truth and justice reign openly in each realm!" Dantias shouted, now receiving nods from his followers.

Santos felt the shift in the crowd, determined to not lose the momentum he had built, he tightened his grip on the balcony's edge, his brow furrowing with resolve. "Listen to reason, Dantias! You speak of seeking truth, but all you spread is lies!"

At that moment, a large group of the nomad clan came walking around the palace's furthest corner. Tala, Namid, and others from their grouped joined the others who had come earlier with Santos. They came through the back entrance to the palace. Aryan and Kiowa were also with them.

"Truth?! What truth?! Look what you have done!" Namid pushed through towards the front of her companions, facing Dantias with the Dynasty's palace at her back.

"I am seeking justice for you, for your people, for all of my people!" Dantias spoke aloud for all to hear.

"Your people?" Namid questioned him and his motives.

"You were wronged, your honor, tarnished, I am bringing all that is hidden to the light! It's time the people know what kind of unity our Kingmen have given us!" Dantias exclaimed.

"It was the palace guards, with the blessing of the council, which took the innocence of my one true love! Tarnished the honor of her people! All because I did not follow the rules of the Houlton house! Is this fair? Is it just? They turned on their own people, in the name of unity. I demand justice for these crimes!" Dantias screamed at his brother with hatred in his voice.

"You speak of truth! Why don't we speak of truth then my brother!" Santos yelled back, voice booming over the crowd.

Then from the shadows behind Santos, a palace guard emerged. It was the very same guard that had killed two of his comrades to free Namid that horrible night.

Dantias looked, eyes focused on the terrace, which demanded the attention of all who were present. Namid did not recognize him until he spoke.

"Here we have a witness to your truth," Santos spoke clearly as he gestured for the guard to come forward.

"Tell everyone what you know," Santos said to the guard.

"I and two others were told to find and capture the young nomad woman, called Namid, at the Market Fair. We were instructed to quietly take her away, to a secluded place," said the guard.

"And how would you know it was her?" Santos asked.

"We were told that she would be accompanied by Prince Dantias," the guard explained.

"Then what happened?" asked Santos.

The guard, ashamed, hung his head in silence.

"Then what took place, my sir!?" Santos demanded an answer.

"We did as we were instructed. We followed the couple to the fair, waited for an opportunity, then we invited her to go with us, leading her to believe that we were to take her to Dantias," he explained as his voice echoed out from the terrace.

"Is that all?" Santos questioned.

"No. Then we took her to a secluded place and..." the guard paused.

"Say it! Tell us what you did!" Dantias screamed, pushing a much ashamed Namid to the side as his anger overrode his empathy for his love.

The guard sighed, shaking his head, and began to speak.

"Then... then we tied her up by her hands, hanging her from a beam, and punished her for being with the prince," he said.

"You disgrace your bloodline... I'M GONNA KILL YOU!" Dantias screamed in a rage as he stepped forward motioning with his hands.

At that moment, all that horrendous evening's occurrences rushed back to Namid's mind, and she burst out crying, as she now recognized the guard's voice.

Dantias stopped and turned towards her, all eyes now on her.

"It was him," she whispered.

"What? It was him; he did this to you?" Dantias asked Namid angrily.

She wiped her eyes, composed herself, and looked him straight in the eyes, "It was him!" She said aloud. Looking up at the guard standing next to Santos on the terrace Namid spoke out, "It was him! He was the one who saved me! He defended me, killing the other two guards! Because of him, I am with my family! Because of him, I am alive today! This man freed me and let me go!" Namid spoke with authority.

"He must be punished; justice must be done! He is to blame!" Dantias exclaimed looking to the crowd for support.

"Justice? Justice my brother?! Let us speak of justice!" Santos spoke out to the crowd.

Now all souls turned their attention to Santos, by this time Hlok was now standing to the side close to the front as were the clans who had traveled with Dantias and the others who had joined along the way.

The guard that testified to that horrible night, in secret, also had revealed the identity of those who had poisoned The Dutchess. Even though one of them had already met his demise at the end of his blade the night he freed Namid, the other guard was there in the ranks.

Santos prepared to speak. He looked once again to The Professor for reassurance, and his loyal friend nodded in approval. Santos relaxed his grip, took a deep breath, and spoke with a voice of leadership. There was no time right now for a grieving son.

"The Dutchess is dead!" He declared.

The crowd gasped, looking around in disbelief. Tala stepped forward towards Namid taking her under his arm.

"After much investigation, we have found that The Dutchess was murdered! She was poisoned!" Santos announced.

As Santos was speaking, the accused guard stood with his fellow soldiers, none of them knowing that he was the guilty party. His heart began to race, and his anxiety began to rise. He wanted to escape the punishment that was certain, but he knew he had to be careful. While the suns slowly set, he spotted at the edge of the courtyard, where the shadows of the trees cast across the yard, a place to slip away.

The crowd began to mumble, and voices began to rise, a commotion began to grow, each person speaking to their neighbor about what they believed should be done, questioning and giving opinions of who they thought had carried out such an awful act.

As the crowd began to put their attention one to another, the guard decided to act. He took small steps back, trying to keep his body still and his eyes forward. Each step felt ever so risky, but fear of punishment pushed him to continue. He carefully edged back until he bumped into someone else.

"Going somewhere bud?" Aryan asked as he stood with two other trustworthy men.

"Uh, just gotta go to the barracks to get my lighting-stick, I must have left it there," the guard answered.

"Maybe we could help you find it?" Aryan said sarcastically.

"Hey, we got a deserter here Santos!" Aryan yelled aloud, which brought full attention to the guard in front of him.

Then a few men, along with the alerted palace guards standing nearby, took the accused guard by the shoulders and pushed him to the center of the group, now standing just in front of the terrace.

"Who is this?" Santos asked for all to hear.

Aryan stepping out just behind him answered back, "While you were speaking, we saw that he broke ranks and tried to slip away! Kind of curious wouldn't you say?"

The guard in question began to get so nervous and began to fumble over his own words, "I've done nothing! You cannot blame me for anything! Besides, it wasn't even my idea!"

"What wasn't your idea?" Santos asked.

"I didn't poison The Dutchess, I told him I didn't want any part of it, I have a family!" The guard began to nervously react, letting out the secret in front of everyone.

"Who poisoned her then? Was it someone else?" Santos asked in a non-threatening tone.

"He killed the one guard that poisoned her, the night it all went down!" The guard yelled pointing up at the terrace, "Besides we were just doing what Dantias told us to do anyway!"

Then suddenly, like a flash, Dantias pulled his blade from its sheath on the back of his belt and with one single motion sliced his accuser's throat. His blood sprayed Namid and Tala's faces as they jumped back in horror.

"What are you doing!?" Namid cried out.

"Justice! How dare he blame me for the death of my own mother!" Dantias exclaimed.

Hlok reached out his massive arms subduing Dantias and pushing him to his knees. He easily removed the knife from his hand, tossing it away towards the building.

The crowd was now mystified and dumbfounded, trying to reason everything that was taking place. Many, still convinced of Dantias' words began to shout and cry out for justice.

"We demand justice! Dantias, Dantias!" the crowd chanted.

Namid wiped her face and stepped over the guard's lifeless body and knelt next to Dantias. She whispered in his ear and asked, "Why have you done this?"

Dantias turned his head, looking up at her, and with sincerity in his eyes instantly responded, "For love. No one will keep us apart."

Horrified Namid stepped back, extending her arms behind her, searching for someone to hold her up before she could collapse to the ground. She quickly found Tala's hand, held it tightly as she stood completely shocked.

"How could it be that the one she had loved for so long could do something so unimaginable?" she thought to herself as she tried to harness her emotions.

"He did it. He's responsible!" Namid said as she pointed at Dantias as tears quietly ran down her cheeks.

With a loud whistle, an elder from the desert clan signaled to his men, still seated on their quantum, by motioning with this finger and pointing to the streets indicating that their present involvement had ended. With a swift kick to their beasts, they were immediately trotting off and, on their way, back to their desert home.

Santos stood with a look of disappointment and disbelief upon his face. The touch of The Professor's hand upon his arm brought him back to reality and the difficult decision that he must now take. He solemnly spoke aloud for all to hear.

"In light of this incriminating evidence, I am now forced to take action. Action that no one of the realm would ever desire to take, but must be taken," Santos said with sadness in his voice.

He then motioned to the guards to take custody of his brother. In an instant the crowd roared, deferring the palace guards' attention now to them instead of Dantias. The multitude began to push against the ranks of the palace guards as they cried out for justice.

"Release him! We demand justice!" It was if their minds had been washed by the dark charisma of their leader Dantias.

"Banishment!" Santos yelled out from the terrace. His voice resounded and echoed off the walls, even being heard far into the streets.

Everyone stopped in their tracks. Even The Professor turned quickly, too shocked at such a statement. A banishment was never something to take lightly, if one was banished, there was no going back. It was permanent. It would be forever.

"Banishment is what awaits all those who side with this criminal of the realm! Choose now, take a step forward those who wish to follow his path!" Santos spoke loud and clear for all to hear.

"Or..." He paused for a moment contemplating his next words, "Leave now and no crime will be held against you. Decide now. What will you do my fellow citizens?" Santos said persuasively.

Those present who were from other realms walked away first, making this situation now an issue of the Equantius realm.

Then slowly one, then two, then five, then twenty, groups of Houlton City citizens began to lower their defense and walk away, mostly in agreement but there were others, including the Asno clans who left with pure resentment in their hearts. The idea of injustice lingered in their minds.

"Someday, he'll get what's coming to him. All his manipulation and self-righteousness," one person said to another as they walked out of the broken-down palace gates.

Kiowa stood in an open area of the courtyard with sadness in his heart, watching as brother now was forced to turn against brother. Even though he understood the circumstances, he did not agree.

The Bisonteaus people believed and taught every generation that, "No matter what, good or bad, family stays true to family."

As he lowered his head in disapproval and slowly turned and he too walked away, followed by others of his realm who had also come with him.

Santos noticing Kiowa's response, felt overwhelmed, that perhaps he had gone too far.

A few of the guards began to remove the dead body while others approached Hlok signaling to him that they now had control over the situation, three of them taking Dantias by the arms and restraining his hands behind his back as they proceeded to take him away.

"Namid! It was for you! She was going to banish you and your clan; I couldn't allow it! It was for you, for us!" Dantias said desperately.

Namid looking him in the eyes, dropped her gaze to the ground and turned her back on him, in turn causing Tala and the rest of those from their clan to do the same, signaling a shunning. In their clan it was a demonstration that meant, "I no longer recognize you. I don't see you." Casting the individual out for good.

Dantias, devastated and confused began to shout illogically to everyone around him, "You see, this is what they do! They bring division! It's their way or nothing! I HATE YOU SANTOS!"

It took several guards to hold him back as he yelled and pushed about as they led him away to be restrained.

Later that night, extra guards were on alert at the front, broken down gates. The Professor lay in his bed, now back in his own house, next to the gardens. Thankful that the mob hadn't made it that far into the palace grounds.

Santos was in his bed, wide awake, thinking about all that had taken place. The sounds and voices rumbled like an earthquake in his mind. He took a deep breath as he began to recite the ancient laws aloud to himself, in the same tone and rhythm that his father would do when he would put him and Dantias to bed at night.

Dantias sat on the cold bench in a much colder cell in the basement of the palace. His hands in metal restraints, trembled with anger and frustration as tears ran down his face. He leaned over, holding his face in his hands, his cries which turned to sobs and then to anger as he awaited the inevitable.

A banishment ceremony, where there would be no coming back from. The glow from a torch at the end of the long corridor danced upon the wall of his cell. He sat still in the cold hopeless space.

# CHAPTER 22

It was late in the afternoon, a cool breeze whistled through the spaces of the metal roofed hanger where Santos and his Iron Horse team gathered.

"Alright, we all remember the plan?" Santos asked as he looked around the circle.

The air around them seemed to feel electrified, with a sense of great anticipation and purpose. Each member stood huddled together in a dimly lit, makeshift command center. With their suits and gear strapped to their bodies, plated armor with blasters and gadgets strapped to them, light greyish uniforms speckled with the dirt of their previous encounters, every face gleamed with determination. Each one of them reflected a blend of fear, hope, and readiness.

Santos projected a commanding presence as he moved through the crowd. Hammer with his team of heavy lifters. Ace with his large group Pinto-clan quantum riders and an exceptionally substantial number of nomad soldiers ready to follow Santos anywhere. As his sharp, focused eyes scanned the room, locking with those of his teammates who silently exchanged nods, he continued to brief them all with the details of the upcoming attack.

This was not just another mission. It was a pivotal moment that could change the fate of the war they all had been tirelessly waging.

Each soldier, each rider, could feel the burden of responsibility pressing down on their shoulders, as thoughts of what awaited them echoed in their minds. All eyes in the room were on their General as he walked about, not a single word was missed from his instruction.

Off to one side of the room The Professor, along with his team of computer savvy hackers, stood with his eyes fixed on the flickering screens in front of him. Lines of complex codes raced past like a river of indecipherable symbols. The glow illuminated the faces of his team, seated hurriedly at their computers, fingers swiftly moved over the keyboards, working feverishly to decode the encrypted message before it changed again. They only had but a couple more hours to gain the upper hand against their enemies.

"Dig deeper, think faster," The Professor spoke in an unusual tone. His brow furrowed in deep concentration as he barked his commands. With every moment that passed, the weight of anticipation grew heavier in the room. General Santos finished his instructions and as he walked towards the computers The Professor let out a shout of praise, startling those around him.

"We, have it? You broke the code?" Santos asked with some a little enthusiasm in his voice.

"Yes!" The Professor announced, "Well…"

"Well, what!?" Santos replied.

"Yes, and no. You see, we broke it down into three parts, stopping it from changing on the internal bytecode," explained The Professor as he pointed to one of the monitors, bringing attention to a few lines of code:

*- flghj ffuifqwuvi rzjnp; mlgvl btwqv /ztumh btarf hltqu jtyfv vshtk doqea wmzolerrsl plknj nmgtv çrelhp qmbcc fpstw erwqk çkiiqa zleyl cjppr ayedceg -*

"Explain it clearly, please," said General Santos.

"Of course, my dear boy," The Professor turned to Santos directly. "We stopped the code from changing, but there are still two or three more turns to give the resolution."

Santos' eyes widened signifying even greater clarity, The Professor continued, "What I mean is, only two more loops to decode and we will have it deciphered completely, thus giving us control."

Santos nodded, acknowledging The Professor's explanation. Immediately he turned to his team and the soldiers behind him called out with a booming voice, "Let's go! Load up!" Santos ordered.

"Maybe I didn't explain myself clear enough. We do not have it decoded yet," The Professor spoke nervously.

Without even looking back Santos responded, "You will. Call me on channel three when you do."

As Santos and his team headed out, united under one profound truth. They were ready to face the fight ahead.

## (402 AWOR - Houlton Dynasty Palace)

Dantias sat up with cramps in his back due to the hard slab of thick, cold steel protruding out from the wall, which was a sore excuse for a bed. Deep within the palace's damp basement, the cold stone walls constricted around him, the air was heavy with the stench of mold. A faint light fell from the high, barred window, casting steep, eerie shadows across the floor. He sat in silence as, above him, a murmuring storm brewed in the realm.

In the bustling capital, people tried to get along as before, but no one could get past the events from the day before. Merchants opened their shops early in the morning as they do every day but today was different. As they exchanged worried glances and whispers, many citizens questioned the Dynasty's true intentions, though they were more concerned with their own preservation. Meanwhile, rural farmers expressed their discontent over the pressures of the times, finally opening about their feelings of neglect by the Kingmen council.

"Can the council truly lead us? Can the Houltons be trusted?" one merchant said to another as he prepared his fruit cart on Market Street in the morning's first light.

"They have brought us this far, haven't they?" a farmer said to another as they brought out their wagons from the barn.

"As the morning's first light shone through the palace windows, Santos knelt beside his father's bed, dreading what the next few hours would bring."

"Oh, mighty Creator, I come before you with a heavy heart," tears fell from Santos' eyes, sprinkling over the large pillow he embraced in his arms as he knelt and began to pray.

"I seek your guidance. Here I am, at a crossroads, faced with a decision that will alter the course of the realm forever. Please give me the courage to do what is right, and help me to discern your will, trusting in your goodness despite the uncertainty that I face. Grant me strength for the journey ahead and remind me that you are with me. In your name, I pray. Amen," he finished as his head fell into his hands.

**(Hours later in the palace front courtyard)**

As the loud trumpet blast echoed across the realm, its bold call sliced through the mid-day air, summoning all to the heart of the palace. The grand courtyard, still in disarray from the day before, was heavy with the weight of somber anticipation. The suns poured their light, illuminating the details of the chipped walls and broken statues.

Santos once again appeared on the upper terrace, dressed in his official attire. Like his father before him, he seemed both regal and burdened, a man torn between the duties of leadership and the pain of family betrayal.

The crowd began to fill the courtyard, a sea of eager faces, murmured anxiously among themselves, their voices beginning to rise and fall like a late night's tide. The atmosphere buzzed with an energy; a collective breath held in anticipation of the unfolding ceremony. All clans were represented in the crowd, a gentle breeze blew across them, creating a stark contrast against the backdrop of the somber occasion.

At that moment, a heavy wooden door creaked open from the side of the palace, the guards came forth, their presence as tough as the ropes and metal restraints on Dantias' wrists.

Dressed in polished armor that reflected in the suns' light, three of the guards escorted the prisoner to the center of the courtyard facing the main terrace where their leader stood stoically. The guards led Dantias set in grim determination. Handcuffed and subdued, he was led into the light, the corners of his mouth twitched with a hint of defiance, but he kept his head bowed, his gaze fixed on the ground beneath his feet. Then from the other side of the courtyard, another group of guards pushed another through the crowd. The onlookers parted as they walked through, sounds of disapproval could be heard as they walked past with another culprit.

Surprised to find he was not alone, Dantias turned ever so slightly to see who it was that brought such a reaction from the crowd. It was the other guard, the witness who testified the day before. Dantias snickered to himself quietly at the irony of the situation as the guards brought him over and stood him next to the young prince.

"Fancy seeing you here," Dantias said to the shackled guard with a sarcastic tone. "Would have thought they'd let you go for coming clean."

"What's done is done, I joined the wrong crowd," the guard said with a sigh.

The mood in the courtyard shifted palpably; tension thickened in the air like a fog as Dantias and the guard knelt before the terrace where Santos stood. The heartbeats of the onlookers seemed to beat in a communal rhythm that pulsed with uncertainty.

As each clan stepped closer, recognizable faces could be seen in the crowd. Aryan stood with his comrades. Hlok could be seen towards the back standing with his father, towering over the rest who were gathered there. Tala stood with several people from the nomad clan.

Namid was not present, it was too painful for her to watch. She stayed back to mourn in solitude.

There were Asno-clan elders, other clans mingled amongst the crowd. The representatives of each realm, the council of Kingmen stood in front awaiting the ceremonies' outcome.

Taking a step forward, Santos cleared his throat and raised his hand, commanding silence. Dantias stood defiant, his eyes blazing with hatred. Santos' voice rang out across the courtyard, clear and unwavering as he articulated the charges against both the guard and his brother. Each word shrouded with painful precision, treachery, rebellion, the betrayal of familial bonds. As he spoke the crowd hung on every syllable, the severity of the accusations covered the crowd like a thick shroud.

"Good people, by the ancient laws of our realm, that of which I am now compelled to enforce, I hereby declare, Dantias Houlton and his loyal servant, once members of our community, citizens of the Equiantus Realm and a son of the Houlton Dynasty, to be banished henceforth! Their crimes against the innocent, deceit, and the betrayal of our trust have brought this fate upon themselves!"

As Santos spoke, the air grew thicker, the wind picked up, and the trees surrounding the clearing even seemed to lean in, as if to emphasize the gravity of the sentence.

The guards stood at attention, saluted the Kingsmen, and proceeded to escort the two criminals to the edge of the palace property. As they walked through the crowd eyes filled with tears and averted gazes marked the assembly, as they could feel the razor-edge of fate slicing through the ties that bound them all. Each declaration from Santos felt like a finality, echoing in the hearts of those who bore witness to the decree unfolding before them.

Santos lifted a scroll and unrolled it as he read:

*"Let the name of Dantias Houlton be erased from every book and scroll!"*

With each declaration Dantias' steps grew heavier and heavier.

*"Erased from all documentation and written history, erased from every monument of the Houlton Dynasty. Let the name of Dantias be unheard and unspoken, erased from the memory of all people, for all time."*

Santos then laid the scroll on a small lamp that was burning next to him on the terrace balcony, and the scroll ignited as a heavier flame burned. As he concluded, a heavy silence fell upon all who were present. The implications of his words – of judgment and separation settled over the crowd like a dark cloud, casting a shadow on a bright afternoon.

This moment was not simply about banishment; it was a pivotal juncture, that highlighted the fragility of loyalty and the painful choices born of love and duty. The suns shone fervently overhead, indifferent to the turmoil below, as the realm prepared for the unchangeable turn of events that were to come and awaited them all.

"Goodbye, my one-time brother," Santos whispered under his breath holding back his emotions.

Several mounted guards led Dantias to the furthest borders of the realm, there they untied his hands and removed the hood that had been placed over his head. Not a word was spoken as they raised their electric spears into the air, motioning that Dantias and his new comrade must be on their way.

With a swift motion, Dantias whirled around, grabbing one of the long spears, pulling the guard off his quantum and brought him to the ground, quickly two more guards responded and countered, but Dantias was too quick as he spun himself around and up onto the behemoth, blocking each move of the guards, faster than they could react. Bringing each easily to the ground next to their comrade.

Instantly, Dantias had gotten the better of them. He did not waste a moment, tapped his heels into the animal's side and rode quickly into the distance. The banished guard slipped up onto another behemoth and followed closely behind. Baffled, the guards stood to their feet, dizzied by what had just taken place, and made a sworn pact that they would never mention this to another living soul.

The suns blazed hotter as Dantias rode not knowing where he would end up, but vowed to himself, one day, justice would be brought upon all those who set their path against him.

# CHAPTER 23

The suns' gaze lit up the mountain crests, casting a glow over the rugged landscape as Santos' team prepared to launch their attack on the Dark Prince's ship.

The air was light yet full of tension. The only sound was the behemoth's soft breathing as Ace and his riders lay flat on the ground, caressing their beasts.

Each secondary team was in position. Ace was at the far end of the short valley. Hammer and his group were nestled in between the trees at the foot of the mountain's hill. Bliss, along with five others perched on the closest ridge. While Santos and his foot soldiers crouched on the ground a click away from Hammer and the towering beacon.

A smooth humming sound could be heard as it quietly echoed through the small valley where the ship would land and begin the process of reloading and recharging. That was where the Iron Horse team would strike. A small group of Amphibtius

troops could be seen walking around, pulling out hyper-con-
ductors, preparing for their Lord's descent on their position.

"You read me? Over," came Santos's voice through the
comms.

"Here," the team responded one by one.

"Okay listen up. Hammer, you're with me on the diversion,
once the ship lands, I'll break off towards the tower to hack the
system and upload the code. Ace, you take the valley straight
on into their camp with your riders. Bliss, you're our eyes in
the sky. Provide cover fire and take out any bogies that get too
close," Santos instructed. Even though they had gone over the
plan almost 100 times, the General repeated it once more.

"Don't worry, we got this boss. You're like a swamp dragon
with a knot in its tail. It's gonna be alright," Ace responded
jokingly, trying to lighten the tension.

"Yeah, just stay alert. Should be coming any minute," General
Santos replied, "Professor, how are we coming on that code?"

"Loud and clear, sir. We're down to one turn—any moment
now, we should have it," responded The Professor over his
comms from the hangar.

Suddenly, a great shadow was cast over the narrow valley.
The enormous ship descended, blotting out the sky. Its roaring
engines drowned out the tranquil sound of the wind blowing
through the trees. Gusts of air kicked up small rocks and dust,
stinging Hammer as they struck his face and chest while he
shielded his eyes. The Dark Prince's fortress loomed over the

trees, radiating an oppressive darkness. Up close, its size was staggering- it could easily be mistaken for a small mountain.

The weight of the moment pressed upon Santos' mind, magnifying his unease. The silhouette of the ship was swallowed up by the light, screaming doubt into his very being. He could feel his heart begin to race, the enormity of the threat testing his courage. Deep down, he questioned his ability to lead his team against such a monumental adversary.

"Were they ready? Would they stand a chance? Maybe I should just call off the attack?" Santos thought to himself.

Then at once, the ground shook around him as a large stream of air and smoke burst from the bottom of the ship, jolting Santos back to the task set before him. Loud chirps and whistles sounded just ahead of him as the toad-like men communicated with one another, running about, pulling hoses, and staking down pylons as their lights flashed.

As Santos and his team prepared for the confrontation, Santos glanced up at the colossal shape above, its hidden weaponry and fierce insignia hinting at an almost invincible power. He felt a chill race down his spine —was his determination strong enough to rally them against such darkness? The air crackled with tension as the dark ship was lowering into position. At that moment, he became determined, "It's now or never," he spoke aloud to himself, his words drifting away like teardrops in the ocean.

"We're on the move!" he yelled over his com-link as he and his team sprang into action, their hearts in unison as they charged to prove their strength against the darkness.

## (402 AWOR) - Houlton Palace Cemetery

At the far end of the palace property, was a small private cemetery where medium-sized monuments could be found. Each one a pillar with the engravings of past Kingmen, their wives and sons, honoring the legacies of the family.

The grave site was an oasis of sorrow, nestled beneath the trees that had been planted there, now 200 years ago. The trees usually offered shade from the piercing suns. Today, however, the sky was a stormy gray, an unusual sight over the savanna plains of the Houlton Dynasty.

The rains had come and now fell steadily, changing the land beneath into a soggy canvas, each drop a solemn note in the symphony of mourning. The vibrant garden seemed now muted as if the color had been drained away in response to the unpleasant occasion.

Santos stood slightly apart from the small crowd that had gathered there, feeling as though a thick fog shrouded his heart and mind. The bitter sweet scent of the wet soil mixed with the delicate aroma of wilted flowers that lay at the base of The Dutchess's pillar, clean white and elegant, the pillar stood as a memorial to his mother with her name etched on the front, standing firmly next to the identical one of his father, Grandmaster Houlton.

As the officiant's voice drifted into the oppressive silence, echoing in the heavy air, Santos heard few of the words. Instead, his mind swirled with concerns, memories, and thoughts of what was to come. His eyes scanned the ground as he meditated, ever slowly raising them to see the solemn faces of those who were present. His friends, allies, and citizens gathered under the oppressive rain, their shoulders hunched, eyes glimmering in the dim light of this rainy day. Each raindrop symbolized tears unshed.

When the service ended and the last few words were being given, Tala began to sing the song of mourning in his native tongue, initiating a slow procession of those passing in front of Santos to share their condolences.

Hlok stepped up just behind him without saying a word and laid his massive hand on his shoulder, a gesture of loyalty, to him and the realm.

As everything ended, the passed by on by one, with few words spoken, Santos felt the reality of it all crashing down around him, heavy like the storm clouds above. He was to become the new Kingmen- the heir to a realm now burdened by sorrow, deceit, and desperation.

As Tala's song ended, he, Namid, and some of the other elders gave their leave. Santos felt the rain soaking his clothes, chilling him now to the bone.

With the public now gone, making their way back to their lands and homes, The Professor stood just a few feet away. Santos noticed three of the Kingmen standing by a nearby tree, as though they were waiting to speak with him in private. He could see, Catodus of the Amphibtius Realm, Aylo Kuang of the Terrartius Realm, and Lord Systrico of the Marvevitieaus Realm, dressed in his land suit—each formally attired in traditional garb. Interestingly, the other Kingmen were absent on this gloomy day.

Santos glanced at The Professor, seeking an answer as to why they were waiting for him in silence, but all he received was a shrug—an indication that he, too, was uninformed. Santos walked toward them, half-expecting a word of condolence or a warm welcome. Instead, the abruptly stopped talking as he approached.

"Thank you for coming today my good Lords," Santos said. Pretending he didn't notice their odd behavior.

"Oh, yes, yes. Our condolences Santos, my young prince," responded Kingmen Aylo Kuang, speaking for the three of them.

"What can I do to be of service to you this day?" Santos asked them.

All three turned and exchanged glances before Catodus nodded, encouraging Aylo to address the young Houlton prince.

"Well, first I must say, we are sorry for the circumstances that you find yourself in on this, gloomy day," Aylo said as he held his claw and out catching a few droplets as they fell off the tree branches.

"We must inform you of the decision that the council has taken," he continued.

"What decision?" Santos questioned as his eyes bounced between the three of them.

Catodus and Lord Systrico hung their heads ever so slightly as Aylo Kuang continued.

"You see, as is custom, whenever a council member passes—whenever there is a death—the others are required, obliged if you will, to nominate and then vote on who the next Kingman will be," he explained.

"I would assume that it's easy for you, as I am the only Houlton that's left," Santos said trying to lighten the uncomfortable tension.

"Oh yes," Aylo chuckled slightly, "You see, therein lies the issue. We have decided to, um, not nominate you," Aylo said as his tongue slithered slightly in and out of his mouth.

"Well, if not me, then who would take my place?" Santos asked desperately.

"Well, as you know, there have been some, let's say, indifferent circumstances in your realm as of late, and honestly," Aylo paused. "We, um well, just cannot be related to such things. The other realms run the risk of being contaminated by the same.

We must have order if we are to flourish," The Kingmen said smugly.

"What, where's Lord Hyram and Sir Cysilian? Do they agree?" Santos questioned, now even the integrity of the council.

"They have decided to take their leave from the council leaving us to now make the difficult decisions on our own," Aylo Kuang answered as the three stood up a little straighter.

"Oh, I understand. We wouldn't want the reputation of the council to be, tarnished," Santos answered sarcastically.

"Please understand, it's nothing personal. We just need to always think about what is best for all in the long run," Aylo said affirming their standing, "Well, we take our leave, my young prince."

As the three gave a slight bow in reverence and condolence, the Professor quickly hurried beneath the tree branches, which hung low under the weight of the rain—mirroring the heaviness in Santos' heart.

"What is it? What did they say?" The Professor inquired.

"That... I'm on my own, my dear friend," Santos said.

"Oh, heavens..." The Professor hung his head as raindrops trickled down the lens of his spectacles. After pondering the circumstances for a moment, he turned and, with a slight smile, said, "What shall we do next?"—emphasizing the *we*.

The Professor continued, "Shall we make our way up to the palace for a little bit of something warm to drink?"

Santos looked over at him with amazement, "Haven't given up on me yet?"

"Never," The Professor responded placing his hand on Santos' shoulder," Besides, who's going to make sure you keep everything in order?"

Santos smiled as they both walked towards the palace together.

# CHAPTER 24

At the edge of the Houlton lands, Santos stood looking over the plains, an almost daily ritual now as he meditated and prayed to the Creator, the air once again hung thick as he felt the heaviness and destiny of the realm upon his shoulders. Sunlight peaked over the faraway mountain crests of the Terrartius Realm, casting ethereal shadows that stretched long across the untamed soil.

It was hard to believe that five months had passed since the Kingmen council had been disbanded. The announcement echoed in his mind, a haunting reminder that the hope for unity had been extinguished, and the people were now left to navigate the storm, alone.

He still hadn't heard a word from Lord Hyram II, concluding that he'd rather not continue in fellowship with him nor the realm.

Santos' heart felt like a stone in his chest, each beat a reminder of the immense responsibility that now rested on his shoulders.

The last report that one of the scouts had given him was that Dantias was a good four or five days away, putting him somewhere within the thick jungles of the Aporsmarteaus Realm. That could be the reason as to why he had not received news from Sir Cysilian. His mind filled with challenging thoughts.

"What if they never spoke again? What if they partnered with Dantias and tried to take the realm away from me? It would be better if they did. What am I doing here anyway? Maybe I should just leave and let someone else lead," Santos pondered, his mind foggy and filled with doubt.

Later that day, Santos found his way walking down Market Street, he could feel the weight of the uneasy glances falling upon him. The marketplace, once one of great memories, a place filled with life and laughter, now buzzed with hushed whispers and furtive looks. Merchants and sellers showcased their wares, but even the vibrant colors of the fabrics and the rich aromas of spices failed to lift the mood. Instead, rumors spread like wildfire with stories of impending doom and the downfall of the realm.

"Is it true? Have we lost everything?" whispered an elderly Pinto woman just beyond the produce stall. Santos caught fragments of their conversation, each word like a dagger to his heart.

"Enough is enough, I cannot allow such despair to take root within the souls of my people," he thought, "We must rebuild, even start over if we have to."

Clenching his fists, he felt the cool metal of the Houlton Dynasty ring left to him by his father. The family crest adorned the upper part—a symbol of courage and leadership passed down through generations. As he looked down at the ring, he was reminded of the strength within him. His father's voice echoed in his mind, reciting the ancient laws each night as he drifted off to sleep. At that very moment, a reassuring verse came to him:

"Do not fear, be of good courage, for I am with you; do not fret or be dismayed; I, the Creator, will guide you; I will help you and uphold you with my right hand."

Then and there, in the middle of the cobble-stone street, Santos vowed to gather the faithful, all the diverse factions within the realm. He envisioned a new gathering, one that would rise from the ashes of doubt and bring each clan together as one in strength rather than division. As he walked down the street, he saw a booth selling beautiful tapestries, like the ones that hang in the palace halls depicting the history and richness of the Equiantus realm.

"We shall weave a new tapestry of unity, one that is founded upon all those who have come before us, yet it will be distinct, like none other than has been seen before!" he said aloud, almost shouting.

Several merchants, startled, looked up from their tasks, some smiling to see the contentment of the young prince, others just rolled their eyes and pretended they heard nothing.

It was early in the afternoon, just after most citizens had eaten their family mid-day meal when Santos returned to the palace.

Santos had not eaten, he had too many things to get done. He had tasks, organization, planning, and announcements to send out. He was flooded with ideas and motivation.

The Professor knocked on the door to the council chambers, which was now Santos' personal study. Santos sat at the far end of the table writing frantically, erasing, tearing, and crumpling up papers and throwing them on the floor.

"My sir? Excuse me, my prince, may I enter?" The Professor asked as he slowly pushed open the large engraved wooden door.

Santos didn't give the slightest attention to what had been said, he didn't even notice that The Professor was standing right next to him. He was so enveloped in what he was doing, he was almost blinded by anything else.

"Excuse me, sir," said The Professor, still no response from Santos, "Santos!" Extending his hand that held a crystal plate at the end, revealing a piece of panú with a luscious, bluish-colored fruit placed neatly onit.

Santos quickly sat up, almost shocked by The Professor's direct announcement, "Oh,sorry. I was concentrating on the mission plan for the realm," he explained.

"You've been in here for hours, the suns are setting, and you haven't eaten anything almost all day," said The Professor as he laid the plate and a small goblet with a sweet lemon beverage on the table in front of him.

"Ah, yes. Thank you, my dear friend. It's just that I am so into this I couldn't think about anything else. But I just can't seem to get it right," Santos said as he sat back in his chair sipping from the silver cup.

"What is it you are doing my lord?" asked The Professor as he looked about, raising his eyebrows to the small disaster of torn, crumpled-up papers all around the table and on the floor.

"Well, earlier, I was walking down Market Street, and I seemed to have an idea that's more than just an idea," Santos explained.

"Perhaps a vision, my prince?" The Professor said clarifying.

"A vision?" Santos whispered, thinking it over. "Yes... yes. That's exactly what it was. A vision of the future, of the realm, of how to rebuild. A vision of how to bring peace, balance, and protection to our people. I saw a tapestry woven from the threads of each clan—almost like a banner," he explained.

"Like the ones in the hall my lord?" asked The Professor.

Santos looked up at him and smiled, "Yes, but not exactly the same," he continued, "The tapestry looked like the ones in the hall, which portray our rich heritage, but it was woven in a unique way. A new way, but with the same colors as the old ones. Does that make sense?"

The Professor motioned to the chair next to him as he began to sit down, "If I may?"

Santos nodded in affirmation.

"May I read what it is you are writing?" asked The Professor, Santos turned the scroll that he was writing on towards him.

Written on the traditional paper were a scattered plethora of ideas, words, and sketches. In the middle of the page was a sketch of a symbol, much like the family crest but modified in such a way that it held a military power portraying authority.

"This is most intriguing my Lord," said The Professor, "What is it you plan to do with all this?" he asked.

"I am going to reorganize the realm," answered Santos.

"Well, that would entail a great deal of planning and work, explaining why you have not come out of this room since you entered earlier this morning," The Professor said with a smile, "What else needs to be planned then?"

"You don't think that it's a crazy plan?" Santos asked.

"Crazy? Of course, it is. Probably one of the most challenging ideas I've ever heard of from a Houlton. That's why I like it. The realm needs their hope renewed, there has been so much tragedy as of late," The Professor said in a reassuring and encouraging tone.

"I just can't seem to get the final touch, you know, like the last few threads that just bring it all together and make the plan complete," Santos said as he took a bite of the fruit and ate the last bit of the panú.

"I know just the thing that may help inspire you, my young prince. It's time I show you," said The Professor.

"Show me what?" asked Santos.

"What makes a Kingmen, a true Kingman? It's not just a title you know. Anybody could call anybody whatever they want, but it is the knowledge that is shared between the lords and the realms that truly make one a 'Kingman'," The Professor explained, "And since you are the leader of the realm and the only honorable Houlton left, I suppose I can share the secret with you."

"What secret? What are you talking about?" Santos asked with a chuckle.

"I have served three generations of Grandmasters who sat on the council; you are now the fourth. Although I am not a Houlton myself, I have been entrusted with the secrets of the Dynasty, and now I will share them with you." He paused for a moment. "Please, follow me," said The Professor as he stood to his feet with a grin and walked out of the room.

Santos stood in turn and with the most puzzled look on his face, followed The Professor through the council hall doors, down the hall, and into the family dining area. As Santos made his way down the main stairway, he could see his old friend waiting for him in front of the cold fireplace. A half-burnt log was lying inside it on an iron rack. Santos came closer.

"Ok, this is the secret? Our fireplace? Sorry my friend but I've seen this my whole life," Santos said with a puzzled look on his face.

"What is seated upon the mantel?" asked The Professor, motioning to the two small statutes, one on each end.

"What, those? They're just statues of a couple of *wind riders*, like the ones craved on the master bed. Nothing too secret about that," said Santos.

"Oh, no?" responded The Professor adjusting his spectacles, pushing them up a little bit high on his nose, "What if I told you they were real? And what if I told you that they hold a secret."

"Real? Those are just stories for children, fables," Santos said.

The Professor's face was still, and serious.

"Take the left wing in your left hand," The Professor instructed. Santos obeyed.

"Now turn the wing towards you, so it's pointing almost down, towards your feet," instructed The Professor. Santos followed each command that The Professor gave.

A soft click echoed from within the wall. Santos glanced over at The Professor from the corner of his eye.

"Good. Now go over to the other one and turn it so he faces his comrade," he said.

The young prince took two steps to the right. With a mix of curiosity and suspicion, he reached out and grasped the statue, turning it with a deliberate twist so that it faced the one opposite. The fireplace shifted with a heavy rumbling sound, revealing a hidden passageway cloaked in darkness. A cool, stale breeze rushed up to greet him, carrying the scent of earth and whispering echoes of long-forgotten secrets.

"You see, this will inspire you I'm sure of it," said The Professor with a smile.

"Yes, but what is it? What's in there?" Santos asked.

The Professor nodded as he stepped forward and flipped a switch that was on the inside wall of the newly revealed passageway. Instantly a glowing light was seen, a style of lighting that was commonly found in the Terrartius Realm, now showing a staircase leading further down below.

"We added the lights, your father and I," said The Professor with a smile as he ducked his head ever so slightly, and with a fluid motion pulled Santos' arm encouraging him to follow.

The corridor was narrow and lined with ancient stones. As he walked into the small passageway and began to walk down the steps, his fingers brushed against the cool, rough surface of the aged bricks. With each step down the spiral staircase, Santos became more amazed.

"How could this have been here my whole life and never know about it?" he thought.

As they descended, the path twisted slightly deeper into the belly of the palace. The walls were etched with faded symbols of a civilization that had flourished centuries before – many of their meanings obscured by time yet holding an undeniable allure.

"Is this the...?" Santos began to ask while The Professor abruptly interrupted him, clearing his doubt.

"The ancient vault?" Why yes. Many years ago, the first Houltons who migrated from the Arabian clan, worked with the other realms and they built the palace over the ruins of the Great

Hall, concealing the ancient vault beneath," The Professor explained, "Making it the unofficial center of the realms."

Walking down further, about every ten steps or so another light would turn on automatically, illuminating more steps downward. Then as they approached the end of the passage, Santos paused before the grand entrance the vault. A great archway loomed above him, its stonework both imposing and regal, adorned with carvings that depicted scenes of valor and desolation. He could sense the weight of history pressing down on him as if the responsibility of his ancestors had been placed upon his shoulders. Letters and words, which he could not read, were engraved on two large marble pillars at each side of the entrance.

"What does that say? I can't make out the words or language," Santos asked.

"That's because there are few who can read or interpret it anymore. It's the language of the first elders, from the Cornua Cerviteaus realm. It is believed that there are only two or three still alive," answered The Professor.

"What? Where? I've never heard of them. What realm do they live in?" Santos asked.

"The last of them are the keepers of the 'Unspoken Realm,' and no one knows where that is. It has been rumored that a small hut was found deep in the great forests, but that was almost 100 years ago. No one has spoken of it since," The Professor explained as he gestured to Santos to open the door.

Taking a deep breath, he pushed forward on the large iron door, adorned with silver and gold clasps. Surprisingly, the door opened without much effort—it was perfectly hinged and balanced. The vault lay vast and cavernous before them, its stone walls lined with antique crates and ancient artifacts.

After stepping nearly ten feet into the great room, Santos heard a faint beeping sound. Suddenly, bar lights around the perimeter of the vault flicked on, casting a cool, even glow across the entire space. At the far end of the room stood a wooden table, partially broken at one end, suggesting it had once been much longer.

Mounted on the wall above the table was a massive wooden cubby filled with rows of scrolls, each one neatly placed in a small compartment. Along the outer walls hung incredibly old tapestries and paintings, interspersed with shelves holding sculpted busts—one representing each race and clan.

As Santos looked around, he noticed that several of the sculptures had broken pieces lying at the base, others had looked as though they were recently restored, cracked ears or hands, repaired with the broken pieces carefully placed back into the space where they had been removed or broken off. At the farthest end of the room, hanging just above a great sculpture of an Equiantus' head was an old painting set in a golden frame. Lit with special lighting, the painting held a character like the statutes on the fireplace mantel. The Professor smiled as he watched Santos discover the room for the first time.

"What is this? Why so much emphasis on these wind riders?" Santos asked with a smirk.

"I told you; they were real. This is a painting of one of the generals from the days of old," The Professor said directly.

"I'm sorry, but it's just hard for me to imagine," said Santos.

"Come here," insisted The Professor walking towards the table, reaching for a wooden box at the top left of the 'ark;' the name of the long case of shelves that held the scrolls. He took it carefully in his hands, placing it on the table.

The box was a deep green. Golden, highly detailed paintings, and insignias could be seen on the top, faded from years, centuries of use. A small latch could be seen on one side with a tiny wooden pole inserted through it, not allowing the case to open by chance on its own.

The Professor then reached for a pair of white, thin leather gloves that were lying on the table. He did the motion so smoothly giving the impression that he was the one who had left the gloves in their place.

As Santos stood closer The Professor turned on a small lamp that was positioned just perfectly for viewing and reading the scrolls above them.

Slowly and carefully, The Professor opened the wooden box, revealing its contents: a well-preserved scroll. As he took it out and laid it on a soft cloth on the table, Santos noticed that the bronze handles at each end of the scroll were slightly tarnished and had a greenish tint. The Professor, with the utmost care, began to unroll it, revealing the written words and the delicate hand-drawn illustrations that appeared as the scroll unfurled. Again, one is a picture of a wind rider with the most elegant calligraphy handwritten words written vertically down the scroll.

"This is the oldest recorded description of our people. Dated back over 2,000 years before the War of The Realms," The Professor explained as he continued to unroll and lay out the scroll.

"What does it say?" Santos asked in amazement as he looked at the artifact lying before him.

"Well, I am not a linguist. However, based on the several other translated scrolls, it has been determined that this is a story, a retelling of ancient events and the origins of the Equiantus people," The Professor said as he looked over the rim of his spectacles at Santos.

"Go on. Please," Santos said with a spark of enthusiasm in his voice.

"Well, according to this, the first generations we know of were warriors of the Equiantus Pegasius-clan, what we now call the 'Wind Riders'. Mighty men and women they were, of great stature and strength. They could soar effortlessly into the heavens, and none could match their greatness."

The Professor paused as he pointed, "See here— the writer, Eclesstius, seems to have been a teacher of sorts. He writes about *The Great One*, Elian Sanctius—one of the names that inspired your father. He is described here as a strong general in the king's arm, known for his bravery and great exploits," The Professor continued. "But then something tragic happened."

"Really? What happened?" asked Santos, now totally enveloped in the story. The Professor continued extending the scroll and winding up the top ever so delicately.

"As you can see, this picture depicts the casting down of a flying warrior, and according to what we can understand, not able to translate it word for word mind you, are that there was a moment of greatness. The winged warrior announced to all the kingdoms that he would become like a god, or like the God, depending on the verb translation you pick. Here it describes the way he was to go about it, flying as high as the suns and bringing all others under his dominion so that they may worship him as a god, or God, the non-created," he explained.

"What was the tragedy in that?" Santos asked.

"Well," He continued to spread out the scroll, "it seems that as he did so, he flew so high, higher than anyone else. There was a group gathered there, watching him on the ground, but then all a sudden, a flash of lightning came out of the sky, casting him to the ground, and covering all those present in partial blindness because the light was so bright. Then here it says something to that effect," The Professor pointed to a written paragraph,

"*Then when they all came to, they no longer had wings, none of them, all cursed and '-The Great One'- stood in shame, naked and exposed.*"

"The Creator cursed them?" Santos asked amazed.

"Yes, because they believed they could be greater than Him," explained The Professor.

"Then what happened?" asked Santos.

"That's the end of this one, the rest is tattered and torn at the end," The Professor said as he showed the torn edges at the bottom of the scroll.

He carefully rolled it back up and placed it back into the box that it was taken out of.

"But... there is this one," he said with a curious tone as he reached for another scroll from the shelves. "This one is dated a few hundred years later and is written in a language more similar to our own."

He handed it to Santos encouraging him to read it as he motioned to a chair next to the table inviting him to sit down.

"Here, you sit, put on these gloves, and read what you can for yourself while I go and prepare us some evening tea," instructed The Professor.

Santos sat down and began to read, the language like his own, yet with a few modifications or distinct ways of saying the words, but he was able to understand it.

After about an hour of reading and slowly unraveling the scroll he turned to The Professor, who was now tinkering with an old metal tool on the other side of the vault and said with an enthusiastic voice, "This speaks of the building of a new generation. Those who were cast down rebuilt a society from the ground up."

The Professor just smiled and without looking up from his project answered, "Go on, keep reading."

Santos read it to himself in a whisper. He read:

*"In our days, when the world was untamed, we built with our hands—stained by rich soil—as we labored under the suns. We worked 'as hard as a horse,' as the elders would say. But then, beneath the rocks and mud, we unearthed treasures—gleaming metals, sturdier than timber. This discovery sparked imagination and inspired us to craft new things with our hands and minds. We designed, drafted, and created machines that could do the work of a hundred men, all powered by the hot steam of water and burning coal. Innovation soon took root in our growing society,"* the writer explained. Santos continued to read.

*"From the inventive minds of our most diligent leaders arose the legendary Iron Horse—a powerful machine, a locomotive forged by the clans, symbolizing unity and strength. Shining in the day and gleaming at twilight, it embodied more than just transportation. It represented a profound connection among the tribes.*

*"As the Iron Horse roared to life, it allowed us to bring metals from deep within the mines with greater ease. It helped carve pathways across the landscape, opening trade routes and fostering the exchange of goods and ideas beyond our borders. Towns have since grown and flourished along its iron tracks, bringing harmony among the people.*

*"Through our industrious spirit, we have risen from the dirt, building a legacy now celebrated by generations. The Iron Horse*

*stands as a testament to our unity and progress—a symbol of shared dreams and a new era we have forged together."*

As Santos laid down the scroll he looked up from the paper and whispered to himself, "Iron Horse."

"That's it, the symbol, the connection!" said Santos as he turned to The Professor, now on the other side of the room opening a large cabinet on the wall.

"What are you doing over there?" asked Santos, with now more curiosity.

The Professor chuckled as he opened a long thinner door revealing a recessed compartment in the wall.

As Santos stood and walked over to him, he noticed several cases sitting inside and a few distinct weapons hanging on the inner walls, the light blue lights illuminated them so one could see them quite clearly.

"What's all this?" Santos asked The Professor.

"Defensive measures," he responded.

"You mean weapons? I thought there were none allowed in the realms, ever since the council of Kingmen was established anyway," questioned Santos as he took a short spear off the rack inside the hidden compartment.

"When the council was first established, the Kingmen agreed to share all technologies with the other realms. So, each realm gave up its right to weapons, developments, and so on. Make the council transparent if you will," The Professor explained. "Your great, great, I believe, great-grandfather added these articles into the vault," The Professor began to show Santos each item, one by one.

"Here are the dual blaster pistols from the Terrartius Realm, they've always been a little ahead of the times. Plus, did you know they were the ones who gave us the designs for our wind-carriages quite useful wouldn't you agree?" He handed one of the pistols to Santos for inspection.

"Then here we have a tomahawk axe from the Bisonteaus Realm, as you can see this one has been modified slightly, giving it a light-beam edge (similar to the guards light-sticks) allowing it to cut through even metal. Here is a harpoon gun along with an underwater breather from the Marevitaus Realm, and there you already have the traditional spear of the Amphibtius warriors. Each respectively representing their tribe, or um, realm as we would say," said The Professor.

"What about us? What about the Equiantus Realm, what technology did we share with the other realms?" Santos asked.

"We, well, we have it all," said The Professor with a smile.

"What do you mean?" inquired Santos.

"We have the greatest weapon of all... Knowledge. We are the only realm that has preserved and kept the scrolls. One or two have been given over the years to other realms, but the majority and the most important ones, we have them here. Including the original translations from... oh what was his name again?" The Professor said as he walked to the table once again, pulling out yet another scroll.

"Lord... Estracks, yes, that was his name. He and his colleagues translated a vast number of the scrolls into the modern language. Quite remarkable really," assured The Professor as he adjusted his overcoat.

"Ok, I think I know how to begin my dear friend. We shall send out a notice, to all the realms, inviting everyone to come here. A new beginning!" Santos said with great confidence.

As they placed each scroll and object back into its place. Santos and The Professor made their way back upstairs, closing the vault and its precious secrets once again inside.

They made a fire and sat late into the night talking, pondering, and planning for the future of the Houlton Dynasty, the era of Iron Horse was to begin.

# Chapter 25

E arly the next morning, the first sun broke light into the dawn. The air was rich with the scent of the newly planted flowers. The Professor having safeguarded the seedlings in his back patio.Santos, the only remaining Houlton in the realm, emerged from the grand archway of the palace and called all the palace guards together to join him in the main courtyard.

Dressed in his traditional formal attire, a detailed uniform of royal blue, with the Houlton family crest embroidered on his left shoulder with silverthread that caught the light. One by one, the palace guards began to gather, forming a living wall in front of him. As Santos stepped forward, he raised his hand, and an instinctual hush fell over the assembled guards.

"Brave men and women, guardians of our realm," he began, his voice resounding clear and warm, "Today, I've gathered you here today for a most special and envisioning announcement."

The Professor walked out onto the upper terrace, overlooking the gathering.

"As of today," Santos continued, "Effective immediately, I am disbanding the palace guard and all those who serve within."

Instantly the guards began to turn to one another in desperation, confused looks upon their faces, many of them even started to grumble and make a scene.

"What do you mean disbanded?!" yelled out a guard.

"This is outrageous, my family has been serving here for three generations! You can't do that!" shouted another.

Santos raised his hand, demanding silence. The crowd grew increasingly restless and began to move forward ever so slightly, attempting to intimidate Santos.

Then in a flash, Santos pulled out one of the blaster laser pistols he had taken from the vault, aimed it at the head of a recently erected statue, and pulled the trigger. A flash of blue light came out and hit its target, exploding the head into a thousand pieces, quickly the group stood at attention, scared out of their minds, they had never seen anything like that before!

"Good, now that I have your attention, you will allow me to finish," Santos said firmly as he walked in front of the guards. He stopped just in front of the first line of guards.

"As of today, I am disbanding the palace guard," Santos declared, his voice carrying great authority. "There have been acts of treason, crimes committed within your ranks, and doubt has spread amongst the citizens of our realm. Therefore, the palace guard, as it has been, will cease to exist!"

He paused, looking over the now humbled and downcast faces, before continuing. "In its place, a new team will be formed. A team of the best. A team made up not only of those of privilege but also of the finest from all corners of our people. Handpicked by me to become part of an elite force that will not only protect our realm from future threats but also foster unity between the clans. If you so desire, as I hope you will, you may present yourself here in three days' time. Clear out the barracks and take your personal belongings with you. May the best of us unite this realm as one—one clan, one family!"

Santos stood firm in front of the palace, solidifying his place as the new leader of the Equiantus Realm. "Thank you, that is all."

## (Three days later – Palace Courtyard)

In the expansive courtyard once again, an electric atmosphere filled the air as citizens from every part of the realm gathered together. Clans, and tribes, each boasting their own vibrant attire, intricate jewelry, and special insignias, converged to form a life-like tapestry that represented their diverse cultures.

The suns hung high overhead, casting a warm glow over the crowd. This place, which just weeks before had known devastation, shame, and deep family hurt, was now a place of curiosity and enthusiasm. In the middle of them all, stood Santos once again representing the future and new era of the realm. His polished armored suit was gleaming brightly in the sunlight, a direct reflection of the dedication required for the task at hand. With focused eyes that sparkled with determination, he surveyed the gathering, ready to ignite their spirits.

Raising his voice to cut through the murmurs of excitement he called for attention, "Come forward, everyone! Thank you for coming and responding to my announcement summoning you to the palace. Today marks the dawning of a new era, a new chapter for our realm and all its clans!"

His words resonated through the courtyard, echoing, and capturing the attention of those around him. He continued. "As of today, each clan, each person, whosoever that wishes, can put their name on this list, to face the trials and become part of the Houlton Dynasty army! Then the best in each category will be selected for further trials to see who will form part of my personal elite team, Iron Horse!"

The crowd swelled with anticipation.

Young Pinto men flexed their muscles, while older veterans huddled together, making comments of how their experiences have shaped their lives, filling them with determination. Nomads, seasoned in the art of observation, being one with nature, exchanged cautious glances, sizing up their competition with both admiration and resolve. Nearby, families could be seen standing with a blend of pride and concern, whispering words of encouragement to their aspiring protectors, their faces illuminated by a mix of hope and anxiousness.

Santos spoke passionately about the values that would define the Iron Horse team. There would be unwavering loyalty, the courage to defend the innocent, and the strength to unify the diverse peoples under one banner.

The palace courtyard seemed to throb with the collective energy. The echo of his words vibrated through the stones, mingling with small bursts of laughter and hushed whispers as dreamers and ex-guards alike shared their thoughts and desires with those around them.

As Santos ended, he turned and saw a familiar face in the crowd, as their eyes met, they both nodded and the seasoned man, Tala, walked towards him with a smile. Santos met him halfway, greeting him with the traditional salute of a raised hand, and embraced him warmly.

"I'm so glad to see you here my old friend," said Santos.

"Two days ago one of your riders came to our lands and presented me with this written invitation," Tala explained as he pulled out a folded letter from a leather pouch he carried at his side, "For this purpose we have come, myself, Namid and many of our people," Tala spoke as he motioned his hand to a small crowd of his people standing behind him.

"I am so grateful for your presence, thank you for coming," Santos said again.

"Yes, but I have not told you the purpose why we have come," Tala continued, "We have come because I have a question for you my young prince."

"What question is that?" Santos asked in return.

"If we are to be a people of peace, why then must an army or team exist? Why must you take our people and put them through these trials as you call them? What is your hope, what do you look to achieve?" inquired Tala with a serious tone in his voice.

"That is a direct and very important question, which deserves a truthful answer," Santos said as he turned to the whole crowd to address Tala's question.

"My good people, our brother Tala has brought out a most intriguing question to my attention, that I believe, deserves an honest answer!" said Santos loudly, drawing attention to himself. The crowd came to a hush as he spoke, everyone giving him their undivided attention.

Santos began to speak of the ancient scrolls, the information that he had learned as of late, careful to not reveal anything about the secret vault. He spoke and told them the story of *The Great One*. Elian Sanctius and his great exploits, fall, and how the Creator cursed the people. He went on to tell them how centuries later the people came together and built the - 'Iron Horse' locomotive and how it raised the realm from the ground up.

Santos continued casting, sharing his vision with all who could hear, each person now hanging on his every word, "It was the great machine, the one they called the - 'Iron Horse' that unified the clans and took the realm to new heights, a new era!

Once again, the Iron Horse is not a machine, but this time an ideal, a team will be formed, bringing us all together as in the days of old. Making us one with each other! If we stand together, we can face any trial, any oppression that may come our way!" Santos spoke with great conviction, heads began to nod, and eyebrows began to raise.

"I do not wish to burden you with more weight or worries, but I must tell you the truth! There is something that I fear, and I ponder it daily," Santos paused and turned to The Professor who was now standing just behind him for support.

"Go on, tell them," instructed The Professor.

Tala in turn responded, "What is this that troubles you, my prince?"

Santos turned, took a deep breath, and spoke with great confidence, projecting his words with boldness.

"Since the banishment of my brother," people were on edge at the possible mention of the name, but Santos was ever so careful to not say, so that he would go back on the very law he enforced, he continued, "I fear that he will return one day and try to take the realm by force! If we are not prepared, if we are not unified, I fear he may succeed!"

Many in the crowd began to show worried and perplexed faces, murmuring to one another. Just the thought of concerned most.

"Let's say he did, what could he do against all of us? He can't take on the whole city! Much less all each clan!" said a man from within the crowd.

"If we unite, NO he cannot!" Santos responded. "But as we are, each living their own life, concerned only about the day-to-day. Yes, he could and would destroy us! I know him better than anyone, and if I know anything about him, I know this, he will not give up without a fight! He will return demanding and taking what he believes is his birthright!"

Santos looked through the crowd before he continued, "So I call upon you, good people, men and women, young and old, to join me! Let us rebuild our realm! Let us return to our roots, as in the days of old, unite each clan, bring out the best of each, forming the elite Iron Horse team and the Houlton Dynasty army!" Santos spoke with honesty, clarity, and great conviction.

As he spoke one could feel the worries and fear begin to drift away. As he lifted his voice he began to rally their spirits, forging a sense of camaraderie among those who were present. Today marked not just the start of tryouts to become part of the elite; it represented the forging of bonds, the spirit of unity, and the collective aspiration to contribute to something far grander than themselves.

With hearts pounding in unison and determination in their eyes, they all prepared to take the first step towards this monumental endeavor, ready to embrace the calling of the 'Iron

Horse' and their new leader, General Santos, Kingmen of the Equiantus Realm.

The people, from every clan that was present, began to form single-file lines in front of the long scrolls that hung stretched out on the palace wall in front of them. Each scroll, adorned with an elegantly drawn letter at the top, awaited names to be inscribed upon them. They were instructed to write their first name on the scroll corresponding to the first letter of their name.

The morning breeze rustled the papers, creating a soft sound that mingled with the stirring voices of the people. Santos observed now from a distance, his heart now filled with joy as one by one, people from the Pinto, Clydesdale, and Asno clans and many others approached the wall with firm expressions, eager to pledge their commitment to form part of the army. The suns' rays illuminated the many faces, and Santos was struck by the diversity that surrounded him.

Tala then turned to his people, and speaking in their clan's dialect, instructed his people to form ranks and add their names to the lists that hung before them adding to the numbers since there were so very many of them. Interestingly, not one from desert tribe was present.

Then from among the nomads Namid stepped forward with grace and poise. Her dark, charcoal-brown hair caught the sunlight, giving her a distinct presence. She approached the wall, she chose not to sign her name under the letter "N." Instead, she inscribed the translation and meaning of her name in her native dialect— *Bliss*, a person of peace. Each stroke of the quill was deliberate, embodying the essence of who she was and what she stood for – a reflection of her desire to foster harmony in a world steeped in conflict.

Santos watched her as she signed her name on the scroll, a puzzled look came across his face. Once her name was inscribed on the scroll, she turned and met Santos, who was now walking towards her and smiled with a gentle, knowing smile. As Namid walked past him to return to her place in the crowd, she patted him on the arm. It seemed to him as though time slowed and stood still just a little. The bustling of the crowd around him faded away, and the warmth of her touch sent shivers down his spine; it was friendly yet electric, ingrained with layers of meaning that stirred just beneath the surface, awakening feelings he had yet to fully understand. The touch seemed more than just a kind gesture; it was a promise, a quiet acknowledgment that their paths were now intertwined, in ways he could only begin to comprehend.

"Say, you gonna carry us, quantums and all? You and your brother are big enough! Ain't ya Big Hammer?" Aryan turned and said jokingly to Hlok as he looked across the few lines of people between them, Hlok, towering over them all holding his hammer in his hand, snuffed and shrugged his shoulders. Several began to laugh as they waited their turn.

"There ya go, boss!" Aryan said aloud, drawing Santos' attention to him, "You can just pick me now, save everybody time!" he said with a big smile.

"Everyone will get their chance at the trials, my friend. Even you will be put to the test," Santos said.

Santos turned once again, looking for Namid but she had disappeared into the crowd, though her presence remained vivid in his mind. The lines, continued to grow, each person adding their name to the scrolls, their pens moving against the parchment like the heartbeat of the realm itself.

With every name inscribed, Santos felt a profound sense of hope surge within him. This was the beginning of a journey towards unity. In that moment, he realized that what started out as a vision, was now evolving into something greater, a tapestry woven from the threads of many lives, a realm coming together, fueled by a shared dream of peace and true justice.

### (Present Day – Epic War)

The cool breeze shifted into a warm arid wind, blowing on the faces of the Iron Horse team. The hot afternoon suns beat down on the mountain valley. General Santos emerged from his hiding position, his face set, determined. With a swift gesture, he signaled his troops into position.

Bliss settled into her perch atop a nearby hill with a few more of her sharpshooter team, her laser rifle ready. "Here we go," she slowly whispered to herself as she looked through the high-powered scope of her longrifle.

The Dark Prince's ship, a fortress of monstrosity, sat vulnerable as it reloaded supplies connected to the recharging tower.

Santos' goal was to reach the recharging tower, connect to the data panel, and upload the code. Thus, allowing The Professor to then control remotely the veloci-pods and turn off the massive engines.

Santos saw their chance and took it. With a fierce battle cry, they launched a full-on assault on the ship. Hammer's heavy blaster roared from the forest's edge revealing his group's position, cutting entire trees down with the power of each pass of the blasters. Bliss' eyes narrowed as she aimed, providing cover for the General's advancing troops.

The Amphibtius guards were caught off guard. They stumbled and staggered as they scrambled to defend the ship, but they were not alone. Back-up came pouring out of the ship's belly down the loading ramp, an endless stream of enemy soldiers from each race.

"Ace, we need all of you down here! Where are you?" Santos called over the intercom.

"Thought you'd never ask boss! Coming down the valley now, who weeee!" Ace screamed back as he and his team of quantum riders came flooding down the valley, shooting their blasters as they rode.

Santos got closer, the tower was just within his reach, only about 100 yards to go. His troops fought valiantly, their blasters and corundum (ray swords) clashed with the enemy in deadly, ear-shattering noise. Bliss' riffle zapped out a steady beat, picking off enemy soldiers with lethal precision.

Despite their bravery, Santos' team was outnumbered in an instant. The Dark Prince's troops seemed to keep coming, wave after wave. Santos' soldiers began to falter, their movements slowing as fatigue and injury took their toll.

"Come on, you scum!" Hammer shouted as he and his line of Clydesdale-clan troops with heavy blasters advanced a few steps at a time, spraying rapidfire as they went.

The air was thick with the smell of smoke and sweat as the battle raged on. As Hammer swung his heavy blaster, he failed to notice the figure emerging from the dusty haze. Out of nowhere, a mighty Bisonteaus warrior leaped over a fallen tree, and with his double-bladed axe, he swung in a wide sweeping arc, slicing through the air with deadly precision. The blade bit deep into the barrel of Hammer's blaster, shearing off the end with a shower of sparks. The force of the blow sent Hammer crashing to the ground, his massive frame tumbling to the ground. With great shock, he looked up and saw it was Kiowa.

Kiowa was dressed, not in his traditional clothes, but in a futuristic style armor, a shaved mohawk on top of his head and a braid-less beard, stood above him axe raised in his hands. With a loud trumpeting sound he shouted into the air, as 50 or more warriors of his realm came running out of the forest, flanking the Clydesdale team, and attacking them with all their might.

Kiowa did not pause to savor his victory. His eyes locked onto a figure in the distance. General Santos, fighting for his life against a horde of enemy soldiers as he pushed closer toward the energy tower. With a fierce scream, Kiowa launched himself towards Santos, his axe ready.

"Santos!" he bellowed, his voice carrying above the commotion of the battle, "I'm coming for you brother!"

As Kiowa charged forward, hurdling fallen trees and debris, the soil seemed to shake beneath his feet. He easily pushed attacking troops off, smashing them with his shoulder. His axe flashed in the sunlight, leaving a trail of destruction in its wake. Many soldiers fell to his right and left as he cut through the chaos on his way towards Santos.

Then in an instant, with a zap, Kiowa fell, tumbling to the ground. Bliss fired precisely, hitting him in the leg and bringing the warrior into a tumbling somersault, knocking the wind out of him. He struggled to catch his breath. Santos from far off, not seeing Bliss, but knowing she was there, nodded with gratitude, saluting her as he blocked a thrusting spear with his corundum and arm shield.

Then, just as all seemed to overwhelm them, a massive explosion rocked out of the ship, sending debris flying in all directions. The blast wave knocked Santos, his troops, and even many of the Dark Prince's army off their feet, sending them tumbling to the ground.

As the dust settled, Santos regained his footing, struggling to his feet, his eyes scanning the chaos for any sign of his team, but before he could assess the situation, a sinister, deep voice cut through the valley.

"General Santos," the voice boomed, "I've been expecting you. You're just in time to witness the beginning of my destruction of your pathetic attempt at an attack."

From the top part of the ship's silhouette of the head, what would be the mouth of a chess knight, opened ever so slightly, revealing a platform and amounted blaster gun greater than any they had seen before this point. Santos' eyes locked onto the speaker, his heart sinking as he took in the sight of the Dark Prince himself, standing on the ship's platform, like a throne over the small valley, a triumphant smile spreading across his face.

Chaos reigned around Santos. His team and his friends were scattered, their fates unknown. Some of his troops lay motionless on the ground, while others fought on and others, stumbled through the wreckage, their eyes vacant and their movements mechanical.

Santos frozen, felt a shiver run down his back as the Dark Prince's gaze locked onto his. He tried to speak, to scream out the questions that burned within his heart, but his voice was caught in his throat. The Dark Lord's eyes held a thousand secrets, a thousand lies and Santos knew he was looking into the face of his greatest enemy.

For a moment, time seemed to slow, and Santos felt a sense of strange clarity come over him. He saw the Dark Prince, really saw him, for the first time with his own eyes. He touched a small button on the side of his rangefinder, zooming in on his view of his enemy's face. He saw the calculating glint in his eye, the cruel curve of his smile, the imposing posture as he stood, smug and confident.

It was in that space of time, that Santos felt a disturbing resolve settle over him. He knew, with a cold, unwavering certainty, that he would have to face the Dark Prince alone. No team, no backup, no help. Just the two of them locked in a struggle that would eventually determine the fate of Terraqueous.

Santos steeled himself, his jaw stiffened in determination. He knew he could not defeat the Dark Lord with brute force alone as he was an expert in manipulation, like a skilled chess player who always thought several moves ahead.

No, he would have to use his wits, his cunning, and his willingness to take risks. He would have to be prepared to face his fears, his own doubts, and weaknesses. He would have to be prepared to give his all, even if it meant his own life.

"Come on, what are you waiting for? Here I am," the Dark Prince spoke aloud to himself with a smile that grew wider, as if he could sense the tension growing in Santos.

They stared at each other from their positions, and Santos knew that the game was on. He would face the Dark Prince, one-on-one, and only one of them would walk away.

**- End of Part 1**

# PRONUNCIATION GUIDE

## World

**Teraqueos:** /tɛrəˈkiːoʊs / Teh-rah-KEE-ohs

- **Equiantus-Realm:** / iːkwiˈæntəs reɪlm/Eh-KWEE-an-tus Rehlm

- **Bisonteaus-Realm:** / baɪˈsɒntiəs-reɪlm/Bee-sohn-TEE-ohs Rehlm

- **Amphibtius-Realm:** /æmˈfɪbtiəsreɪlm/ Am-FIB-tee-us Rehlm

- **Terrartius-Realm:** / tɛˈrɑːrtiəsreɪlm/ Teh-RAHR-tee-us Rehlm

- **Mareviteaus-Realm:** /mærəˈvaɪtiəsreɪlm/ Mah-reh-VEE-tee-ohs Rehlm

- **Aprosmarteaus-Realm:**/æprəˈsmɑːrtiəsreɪlm/
  Ah-prohs-MAR-tee-ohs Rehlm

- **Cornuea Cervieteaus Race:** /ˌkɔːrnjuˈiːə,sɜːrviˈtiəs
  reɪs/ KOR-nu-eh-ahSer-vee-TEE-ohs Rays

## Characters
- **Houlton** /ˈhoʊltən/ HOHL-tuhn

- **Lord Hyram II** /lɔːrdˈhaɪrəm  səˈkənd/  Lord
  HYE-ruhm II

- **Catodus** /ˈkætədəs/ Kah-TOH-duhs

- **Aylo Kuang** /ˈeɪloʊkwɑːŋ/ AY-loh Kwahng

- **Lord Systrico** /lɔːrdˈsɪstrɪkoʊ/ Lord SISS-trih-koh

- **Sir Cysilian** /sɜːrsɪˈsɪliən/ Sir Sih-SILL-yuhn

- **Lord Estracks** /lɔːrdˈɛstræks/ Lord ESS-traks

- **Santos** /ˈsæntoʊs/ SAN-tohs

- **Dantias** /ˈdæntiəs/ DAN-tee-ahs

- **Namid** /ˈnæmēd/ Nah-MEED

- **Kiowa** /ˈkaɪoʊwə/ KYE-oh-wah

- **Hlok** /hlɒk/ Hloh-k

- **Aryan** /ˈɛəriən/ AH-ray-uhn

- **Captain Amin** /ˈkæptənəˈmēn/ Captain AH-meen

Fauna

- **Behemoth** /bɪˈhiːməθ/ bih-HEE-muhth

- **Quantum** /ˈkwɒntəm/ KWAHN-toom

- **Tyrianciacol**/ˌtaɪriˈænsiəkɒl/tye-ree-AN-see-uh-kohl

- **Sombru-Dragon**/ˈsɒmbruˈdrægən/SOHM-broo DRAY-guhn

# ABOUT THE AUTHOR

Nathan L. Cole   is a devoted husband, father, and the author and illustrator of *The Houlton Saga, The Little Nibbin*   , and *Jeffry's Story*  series— tales that explore adventure, wonder, and the enduring questions of courage, hope, and destiny. A lifelong admirer of fantasy and science fiction, his imagination has been shaped by timeless works such as *Star Wars, The Karate Kid, The Lord of the Rings, Narnia,*     and the like.

Raised in Iowa, Nathan began his early years as an artist and writer, where stories of distant worlds and heroic journeys first took root. He holds a degree in theology and has spent much of his life engaged in missions—experiences that continue to influence the depth, themes, and heart of his work.

Now, inspired by his bilingual family life, his creative pursuits, and love for martial arts, Nathan crafts stories that invite readers to imagine boldly, reflect deeply, and look ahead with vision toward the worlds yet to come.

www.ingramcontent.com/pod-product-compliance
Lightning Source LLC
Chambersburg PA
CBHW032135190626
46814CB00005BA/1699